Peak Season
A CW McCoy Novel

JEFF WIDMER

Allusion Books

Published in the United States in 2015 by Allusion Books, Sarasota, Florida.
Allusion Books and the Allusion Books colophon are registered trademarks
of Jeff Widmer.

http://jeffwidmer.com

FIRST U.S. EDITION

ISBN 978-0-9964987-0-8 (print)
ISBN 978-0-9964987-1-5 (e-book)

For Karen, Mike and Katie, with love.

1

I SPOTTED THE GUN as soon as I walked through the door. Nicholas Church aimed a Glock 22 at his wife and daughter, arms straight and locked, his finger touching the trigger. His wife's hands held nothing but air. The daughter gripped the back of her mother's dress. Church's eyes looked hard, the wife's anguished, the little girl's wide with terror.

"Bitch!" he roared and the sound echoed throughout the dead kitchen.

My face burned. After leaning out to call for backup, I stepped fully into the room and identified myself. He knew me. We'd worked together for two years. I held my hands away from my holster where he could see them. Non-threatening. No show of force. Talk him down.

Church filled the kitchen. He stood over six foot six and weighed more than 250 pounds, black hair slicked back, khaki slacks still creased despite the hour, white shirtsleeves rolled to the forearms to reveal a blue Marine Corps tattoo nestled among a thatch of hair. Under the fluorescent lights his silver badge glowed. Two years ago he'd received a citation for rescuing a woman trapped in a car. A year later the department had placed him on leave for beating a suspect during a drug bust. The wounded hero.

At five foot five, Anita Church shrank before her husband. She looked mid-twenties with a sharp nose and wisps of blond hair that floated around dangling earrings. She wore a sundress of pale yellow and blue, belted at her slender waist, and ballet shoes. Her wedding and engagement rings sparkled, as if to mock Church's badge. When I moved closer, she glanced at me as if to say, *you're a woman, you can save me,* and reached behind to clutch her daughter.

The girl was maybe seven, dressed in jeans and a sparkling pink T-shirt that depicted one of the Disney princesses. She wore pink slippers with rabbit ears. Junie, I thought. Nick called her June Bug.

For the third time that night I reminded myself that I didn't belong there. Patrol responded to domestics, not detectives. My luck I was passing the neighborhood when the call came in. I inched forward, using Church's name, reminding him that I was a cop and understood his anger, telling him to lower the weapon, showing him that we could talk. I gestured in slow circles, sliding to the right, watching his face, his fingers.

No one else in the room. Copper-bottom pots hanging from the ceiling. Two openings arching into shadow, one on the left that led to the laundry, one to the right that opened onto a formal dining room. In the silence I could hear him breathe, shallow, nasal. Somewhere in the house a clock chimed.

Where the hell is backup?

Church stood to my left, aiming across a table set with flowers and fruit, feet braced, both hands gripping the gun. With the slightest movement of his head he glanced right and ordered me to leave.

Tension clawed my neck. "Nick." I kept my voice steady, my hands where he could see them. "You don't want to do this. Put the weapon down. We can talk, whatever it is, we can talk."

Behind me I sensed movement. A young male officer drew his weapon and crouched into firing position, his boots chirping on the tile. A radio squawked. Anita Church clutched at Junie and started to wail.

I shoved my hand into the holster and raised my weapon while edging to the right. In a voice deep from the gut I yelled, "Drop the gun!"

He kept the pistol trained on his wife. "Stay out of this!"

I tightened my grip, arms and stomach clenched, breath and blood pounding in my ears. "Drop the gun! Now!"

I watched his face, watched the eyes refocus on his wife, the jaw muscles tightening with the finger of his right hand, his stance shifting as the gun settled on the target. My vision narrowed and at the end of the tunnel Nicholas Church took in a deep breath as his index finger moved backward in slow motion.

Bam! Bam! The shots exploded in the tight space. The first round hit his chest and turned him. The second knocked him into the refrigerator. He slumped, his gun rattling on the tile. Anita screamed. Clinging to her mother's dress, Junie gasped for air.

Ears ringing, the tang of gunpowder biting my nose, I holstered the weapon and put two fingers against Church's neck and rose to call for an ambulance and the coroner. Walking across the kitchen to Anita and Junie, I guided them to chairs in the dining room. The crying crushed their faces.

They'd soon slide from grief to shock. My arms shook and my stomach threatened to crawl out of my mouth.

Another officer entered the kitchen and called for a second ambulance. I looked through the arch. White dinner plates sat empty on a white tablecloth, flanked by fat knives and forks. Pewter, from another time and place. They didn't belong there, either.

Junie had turned as pale as the dishes. She lowered her head onto her arms and shook. Anita Church stared through me. At her temple, a blue vein ticked like a watch hand.

She took in a lungful of air and said, in a distant voice, "You shot him."

"I'm sorry," I said. "I'm so sorry."

I've repeated that over and over, every day of my life.

2

H E WALKED INTO MY office dressed like the Invisible Man. The long-sleeved brown shirt, pants and flap cap covered most of his body. Theatrical makeup, padding and wrap-around sunglasses obscured the rest. Just another lawn-care worker in Southwest Florida. No one would recognize the former banker. As I watched him slide across the room and take a chair, I felt as if I'd seen a ghost.

"CW McCoy." His voice sounded flat, as if my presence had confirmed his worst suspicions.

"Mr. Darby." I didn't bother to get up and shake hands. From across the desk, I could smell the faint scent of spice. Eleven a.m. and his five o'clock shadow looked like midnight. I would have considered him attractive if his head came up higher than my chin, or he hadn't bilked his investors out of millions.

"You recognize me." His smile looked like a slit wrist.

"You're supposed to be dead," I said.

"What did Mark Twain say about the reports of his death?"

"Mark Twain wasn't filmed as he leapt naked from a ferry off the coast of Florida."

From the holder on my desk he took a business card and turned it over and back again. "So you sell real estate now."

"You in the market?"

He didn't answer. As if doing a magic trick, he flicked the card back and forth between pinky and thumb. "I never did know. . . . What do the initials stand for?"

"Candace Ward, not that it's any of your business."

He nodded, as if my answer confirmed another deeply held suspicion, something about women with multiple names. "Do you mind if I call you Candy?"

"Yes."

"Yes, I can?"

"Not unless you have a death wish." My mother had taught me to be polite, but jeez Louise. . . . "And no Hatfield, Real McCoy or 'Hang on Sloopy' jokes."

"My," he smiled, "aren't we sensitive."

"Just setting the ground rules."

He lifted the sunglasses to reveal eyes the color of wet slate. They scanned me, from face to waist and back. Normally when catching up on paperwork I arrived at the office in a T-shirt, cargo shorts and flip-flops. But because I needed to show a house that afternoon, I'd worn my meet-the-client outfit: black slacks, an abstract floral blouse in blues and black and a single-button red blazer in a silk-cotton blend. The cork wedges represented my one departure from formality, which compelled me to paint my nails—in this case, a sparkling garnet red. The blazer hung on the back of the chair, giving Darby an unobstructed view of my breasts. Luckily I hadn't worn a skirt or I'd never get him to leave.

He swung his head around the room. "Not much of an office."

"Spanish Point is a high-rent, low-wage town. Not all of us run portfolios for the one percent."

I'd set up shop in a yellow cinderblock cube jammed between the North Trail Diner and Motel 41. My front yard consisted of a shell-covered parking lot and the busiest highway in the city, Route 41, known to the locals as the Tamiami Trail, for its circuitous route from Tampa to Miami. The office measured twenty-by-twenty and came furnished with a scuffed metal desk and two filing cabinets that doubled as a table. A white fan and mini fridge rattled in the corner next to a dying ficus. The gray carpet looked as thin as lunchmeat and the floor cleaner smelled strong enough to etch concrete.

Darby glanced at the opposite wall where I'd hung a poster of Wendy O. Williams slicing through a guitar with a chainsaw. She wore electrical tape across her nipples and shaving cream on her bush. Darby squinted as if the image hurt his eyes.

"Bad actor," he said.

"I've heard the same about you."

From my cell phone atop the desk Clint Black sang about having no time to kill. Darby should take his course. Reluctantly I tapped the screen to mute the music and walked to the filing cabinet. "Coffee?"

"Yes, please." A fugitive, but a polite one.

I poured two mugs. One depicted an alligator, the other a pink flamingo. When in Southwest Florida. . . . "Cream, sugar?"

He drank his coffee black. At least we had something in common. I handed him the flamingo and we sat in silence. The coffee tasted good. Since I didn't wear a watch, I tapped the smartphone's screen. For a man on the run, he liked to take his time.

"You know who I am."

"I think we've established that." Maybe he'd spent too much time in the sun.

"I know you worked with my wife, Ginny, but unfortunately we never had a chance to meet."

"What a shame." He appeared immune to sarcasm. Some people were.

His eyes continued to roam. "You know I'm wanted in three states for bank fraud. The SEC is after me, too."

"Something about raising millions from investors to start a bank and then disappearing with the cash."

He grimaced. "That's what the media say."

"And the probable cause affidavit."

He kept scanning the room. "Same thing."

"And you stashed the money in the Caymans or a coffee can after you faked a suicide and your wife had you declared dead."

"That's true, except for the part about the money." He slurped coffee and honed in on the girls. If he stared long enough he could name them, like something from *The Vagina Monologues*. I touched the blouse buttons to make sure I'd only left the top one open and felt irritation crawl up my neck. While I hadn't had a date in, say, forever, I'd rather attract a tax audit than this guy.

I folded my arms and, since sarcasm hadn't worked, tried irony. "To what do I owe the pleasure?"

"Ginny said you were a detective on a police force somewhere up North."

"In a previous life. I sell real estate now. It's a respectable job. You should try it."

He looked around the office again and frowned. "Have you ever thought of joining an established real estate firm, one with international connections? You could sell a condo on Spanish Key to a cute Swedish bachelor named Ulf. Two birds with one stone."

My broker would scold me for entertaining such a thought, considering the time he'd invested in coaching a neophyte in the byzantine laws of Florida. I took a deep breath, leaned forward and knitted my fingers. "Mr. Darby, besides thumbing your nose at law enforcement, why are you here?"

For a moment I hoped he might bolt. But he took one last look around the room and, not seeing any law enforcement, got down to business.

"I've been framed."

"That's what they all say."

"I want you to clear my name."

That made me pause. "Why don't you turn yourself in and let the FBI handle it?"

He shifted in his seat, as if he'd padded more than his face. "Because I'd be dead before I left their office."

I leaned back. "Mr. Darby," I began but he cut me off.

"Call me Bobby Lee."

"Mr. Darby, you're a fugitive from justice. You're wanted by the police, the FBI, the IRS, the Postal Service and no doubt the welcome wagon for giving this town a bad name. Helping you would ruin mine and make me an accessory to a crime."

"What would it take to change your mind? Money? Drugs? A house on Spanish Key?"

"What I would like," I said, "is an explanation. If you're innocent, why did you run?"

"Because the FBI was on its way to arrest me."

"How do you know?"

"Because I got a tip," he said.

"So you fled with the money."

"I fled with nothing," he said. "I left with two shirts and a passport I can't use."

At the mention of the word *shirt* I tugged my blouse to obscure his view. "And you continued to deceive people, especially your wife."

7

"Harv said it would keep the feds off my back."

"Harv?"

He shifted in his seat again. "Harvey Shaw, my business manager. Former business manager, before he received immunity, the little prick."

"You were free. Why come back?"

"You think I want to spend the rest of my life dressed like this?" He pointed to the cap.

"You don't think the feds are going to arrest you? You ran the leading investment advisory firm in Florida. You used a dummy corporation to gain control of a bank and fled with the cash."

He shook his head. "I bought that bank so we could invest in real estate. Then the housing market tanked and people bailed out of their homes. We could have scooped up properties in bulk and rented them back."

"Very noble."

"Whether they can pay their mortgage or not, people still need a place to live."

"True." If I didn't sell a house in the next thirty days, I could face the same problem. I clasped my hands over a knee I said, "So what went wrong?"

"We're privately held. We couldn't go to the equity markets. We needed a ready supply of inexpensive capital."

"So you bought a bank and plundered it."

"I invested those funds in private equity."

"Your own?"

"No, no." With a thud he set his coffee cup on the desk and pointed a finger at me. "I invested that money, every penny of it, but the timing was off. The Fed dropped interest rates to zero, so you couldn't buy or sell bonds, and the stock market crashed. We were gasping for cash, so we shorted the market and borrowed more money and put it into real estate. It should have been a ten-bagger."

"And when the market turned, your investments went down tenfold."

He raised his palms. "Who knew?"

"As a wealth manager, shouldn't you have known?" I paused to let that revelation sink in. It didn't. "Then what?"

"The losses were horrific, and they kept coming, and then there were the margin calls. Christ, brokers are like loan sharks. The investors would have panicked and the feds . . . they would have shut us down before I could recoup the losses."

"So you and Harv covered it up."

"I don't know how much Harv knew. It was a separate unit and I kept the books. Ginny didn't know dip. She never wanted to know anything about the business—too busy raising money for the wigs in town."

I sipped coffee. It had cooled, along with my interest. "So you siphoned what was left and funneled it offshore."

"Not true. That's what they want people to believe." He licked his lips, tamping down small flakes of translucent skin.

"Who are *they*?"

"The cops, the feds . . . the people who are trying to frame me." He lurched forward. "OK, I invested the money and lost some of it, a lot of it, but I didn't steal anything, not a frickin' dime."

"The feds just made that up?"

"Somebody falsified the books, the computer files, whatever the feds used to get the indictment."

I sat back and folded my arms. "So, what are you doing here?"

"I want to drive my own car and sleep in my own bed, and I can't do that until someone clears my name."

"I mean, what are you doing in my office?"

"You can move around, go where I can't go. And you know Ginny. You worked with her on that charity thing at the theater."

I remembered. A dozen of us from the real estate association had helped Ginny Alexander raise money for special-needs children. As members of the theater troupe, both she and Darby had performed an original play so awful their daughter Claire had refused to attend. I'd helped with a second fundraiser to rescue the theater itself, a misguided act that would only delay the inevitable. The theater reference would explain Darby's costume.

He leaned forward. "Ginny said you're good at recognizing patterns."

I shook my head. "The only pattern I see here, Mr. Darby, is one of greed. The FBI has cleared everyone they've interviewed. Who's left to frame you?"

"I don't know. Harv, our competitors?"

"Their stories checked out."

"Maybe one of the investors."

I took a deep breath. "Which one? You just said none of them knew you'd lost their money."

"They know now."

"Your wife?"

"Ginny?" He grunted. "She can't even balance a checkbook. Claire has to do it for her." He scratched his chin and made eye contact for the first time that morning. "You're wondering what's in this for you."

"No, I'm not."

"I can pay you as soon as you nail the guys who framed me."

I was about to tell him where he could store his money when my cell phone rang. I make a point of never talking or texting in the presence of a client but Darby wasn't one and the caller ID showed it was my grandfather.

"Excuse me," I said, rising as I scooped up the phone and opened the door. Heat and noise rushed in—more unwelcome visitors. Braced in the doorway, I noticed two objects in the drive—a rusted bicycle with balloon tires and a classic black-and-chrome Kawasaki 500, circa 1971. I owned the motorcycle. I didn't own the bike. Sticking a finger in my free ear I said, "Pap? Everything OK?"

A dozen years ago my grandfather purchased a house in one of Spanish Point's blue-collar neighborhoods. Now in his eighties, he got confused at times and forgot to eat or take his meds, even though I was living with him. I kept telling myself the situation was temporary, just until I could find a place of my own, which shouldn't have been that hard for a real estate agent. What was that saying about the cobbler's children?

"We're fine," he said.

I pictured his wry smile and sparkling eyes under a full head of white hair. After all this time, he still spoke in the editorial "we" he'd used during his years in the newspaper business.

"Pap, I have someone with me at the moment."

"I don't want to interrupt if it's a date."

"You sound like Walter." Suddenly self-conscious, I glanced back and caught Darby checking out my ass. Walter, the former Pennsylvania State Police commander, might tease me but he'd never stare at my butt. "I'll be home to make dinner around six. Maybe we can watch something on the History Channel, find out who won the war."

He chuckled. "OK, sweetheart."

"Take care, Pap."

"Will do. Bye for now."

I disconnect and set the phone on the desk. Its rubberized case made a small *thump*. I remained standing.

Darby's lips twisted into a smile that didn't reach his eyes. "Pap?"

I flushed. "It's short for pappy, although why I'm still talking to you, I haven't a clue."

"I've never heard of that."

"It's a coal-region thing." I walked to the door and opened it again.

Darby rose slowly. "You have kids?"

"No."

"You have parents?"

"My parents are dead." A spot of cold pricked my chest.

"But you have Pap."

The cold spot spread. "I'm sorry, I have to leave . . . and so do you."

He stood in the opening. "You're going to turn me in, aren't you?"

"You knew I would."

"I was afraid of that." He eyes seemed to shrink. "At least you didn't shoot me."

I felt the air go dark and my vision narrow.

"I had hoped for your understanding." He snugged the sunglasses over his eyes and smiled, and the bright and clever banker disappeared.

I leaned against the frame, the door hanging open like an unfinished thought. My throat felt thick. "Mr. Darby, I don't work for criminals."

He laughed as he mounted the bicycle. "We're all criminals, Candy. It's just a matter of degree."

3

I MADE TWO CALLS. The first to my next-door neighbor, Officer Cheryl Finzi of the Spanish Point Police Department, the SPD for short. She wanted to know why Darby had chosen me for his coming-out party, and when I could come over for a drink. That's Cheryl's code for trouble with her ex-husband, Sal Finzi. I said I'd stop by after dinner.

The second call went to Walter Bishop. Walter is the former commander who eats nails and glass for breakfast. He's also a good ear and the person who convinced me to move south. He said he'd meet me on his boat at the Spanish Point marina at noon.

Climbing on my bike, I had visions of roaring along the Tamiami Trail toward the downtown with hair flying behind me like a flag. The Kawasaki will do zero to sixty in less time than it takes to say the name. It's like riding a time machine: I can get to the marina before I leave the office. Except during peak tourist season.

Walter lives on a former cattle ranch east of I-75 but spends a lot of time on a sailboat he named the *Mary Beth*, after his late wife. A forty-one-foot Morgan with a single mast, she looks small next to some of the yachts in the harbor but cuts a fine figure on the Gulf of Mexico. He's got a berth at the marina where the Trail bends like a pretzel around glass-walled condos and office towers.

Donning my helmet—I like the feeling of freedom but I'm not that crazy—I slogged through bay-front traffic as it trickled around the city's iconic sculpture of an American sailor kissing a nurse on V-J Day. A crowd surrounded the replica of the famous photo, including an Asian couple holding hands. *At least someone has a love life*, I thought. *I'm still living with my grandfather. How pathetic is that?*

I spotted Walter before he saw me. Bending toward the deck, he was washing down the deck with a hose, muscles working against a faded red T-shirt and khaki shorts, his eyes shrouded by wrap-around sunglasses and a baseball cap. He'd furled the sails so the craft looked sparse.

I snapped a quick salute. "Permission to come aboard?"

Walter shut off the hose. Louie, his black lab, heard my voice and bounded up from below decks. I stroked the top of his head. It felt warm and smooth and I crooned into his ear, "You're a good boy." He accepted the compliment with grace.

"Dog gets all the press." Walter stood about six-two with a broad chest and slightly bowed legs, as if he'd ridden a horse rather than a patrol car in his early days. The sun had tanned his thick arms and etched his cheeks, but gray had only started to invade his deep brown hair.

He looked at my clothes. "You have a date?"

"Why is everyone always asking me if I have a date?"

"Because you're usually half-naked when you visit."

"You wish."

"At least you didn't wear heels." He coiled the hose into a neat spiral and moved aft. "What are you having?" His voice sounded deep and full of command.

"The usual."

He went below and reappeared with two iced teas in those thermal glasses that aren't supposed to sweat but do. Even in winter things perspired on the Gulf Coast. We stood for a while and sipped and looked at the mooring field, the masts bobbing like Popsicle sticks, the sun sharpening the glass-walled restaurant to a knife edge. In front of the marina, on a manmade spoil island the city turned into a park, four bronze dolphins spit water at the tourists. I knew how the dolphins felt.

I lifted my glass in a toast to Walter's boat and his freewheeling lifestyle. "Very Travis McGee."

"I get around more."

I laughed. Walter had become a virtual hermit since he'd moved from Pennsylvania. Yet there were times when he appeared to miss the job, like he missed crouching in a wet blind on the first day of deer season.

We sat on a cushioned bench in the cockpit and watched the tourists swarm through the entrance to Bayfront Park. They ran in herds, crowding the beaches, the restaurants, the jewelry stores. Welcome to peak season on the Gulf Coast, where the rarest find was a parking place.

The silence grew.

I took a sip of tea and let an ice cube rest against my upper lip. "What do you think of the Rays' chances this year?"

Walter set his glass on the deck and crossed his arms. Even behind sunglasses I knew his eyes never left my face. "Good, if they'd spend a little money."

"The Bucs didn't look too bad near the end."

"Never should have fired Tony Dungy." He tipped his head and grinned, the gap in his top front teeth like a second smile. "I didn't think you liked professional sports."

"I don't."

"Ah." He headed below decks, calling over his shoulder, "Almost noon. How 'bout I make some lunch."

"I'm not very hungry."

"I'll fix a salad."

"I'd rather have a burger and beer." I followed down the steps.

"Fresh out." In the galley he reached into a tiny refrigerator and removed half of the contents. Layering dark lettuce leaves into bowls, he chopped celery, scrubbed carrots and added peppers, almond slices and dried cranberry, topping the salad with sliced pear and balsamic vinaigrette.

I glanced around the cabin. Lots of books, some awards but no photos, no bottles on the shelves, no wine or beer in the fridge.

After he filled Louie's bowls with kibble and water, we went topside and sat in a pair of lawn chairs.

"What do you want for your birthday?"

I laughed. "That's random."

"Let's start again. What do you want for your birthday?"

I pointed a carrot at him. "To be left in peace."

He took a bite of salad and washed it down with tea. "We could have a party on the boat. I know a couple of guys who like girls with cuffs."

Crossing both index fingers, I held them aloft to ward off evil spirits. "Don't you dare."

We chewed in silence. Finally he said, "You didn't come all this way to talk sports."

We watched a shirtless man with curly brown hair take pictures of a pelican. Like many tourists, he had a big camera and a burnished tan. Only the tourists burned. The locals knew enough to stay out of the sun.

"Somebody giving you trouble?"

"I just had a visit from a ghost." I told him about Bobby Lee Darby and his proposition.

He pursed his lips. "You call SPD?"

"I called Cheryl Finzi."

"You call the sheriff's office?"

I shook my head.

"The Florida Highway Patrol? The FBI?"

"I didn't have another dime."

"Candace."

"You know I'm allergic to authority."

He shook his head. "We'll go downtown and you can give a statement."

"I'm showing a house this afternoon."

He frowned.

"Cheryl said she'd take care of it. She'll alert the rest of them and they'll issue a BOLO, but if they haven't caught the guy by now. . . ."

I told Walter about the bicycle and how Darby had darted across North Trail and disappeared behind the college. "No car, no tag, no way to trace him. He could vanish into a parking garage, a mobile home park, the homeless camp."

He nodded and took another drink.

"FHP can issue all of the Be-On-the-Look-Out reports it wants, but the locals would never notice a guy like Darby," I said. "He blends in with the people who mow their lawns. It's the perfect disguise."

Walter wiped his mouth with the back of his hand and went below to refill our glasses. When he returned, Louie followed and curled at Walter's feet. He absently stroked the dog's ear, sliding it through his fingers like fishing line. "What's he look like?"

"Like he squeegees windshields for a living. You'd never know the man wore a suit." I paused to watch the marina's party boat motor into the bay, tourists waving from an upper deck trimmed with mermaids and palm trees. "You think he's living rough?"

"No," Walter said. "It doesn't fit his prior lifestyle."

"He could have holed up in a short-term rental, or knows someone with an empty condo."

"Or he could be on a boat."

I shrugged. "SPD's marine unit would have picked him up."

"Maybe not. They've only got one boat, and you could hide a small yacht in some of the mangrove caves along the intercoastal."

I felt exasperated. "But where is he working? How's he getting food?"

"The same way he got to your office."

"That's going to be harder now." I turned my chair to keep the sun out of my eyes. "I guess that's your point with the BOLO."

He smiled. "You're pretty smart for a broad."

"Glad you noticed."

"That you're smart or that you're a broad?"

I set my glass on the deck with a thunk. "Why is it that every experience I have with a man these days is sexually charged?"

Walter laughed. "Because you are."

I opened and closed my mouth and said, "We've wandered from the topic. What I don't understand is why Darby risked blowing his cover. For what . . . money, reputation?"

Walter took in the boats, the dock and the park in a slow, sweeping motion. "Revenge, maybe. I'll give him this, the guy's got balls."

"Or a death wish."

"Or both, which makes him dangerous."

We sipped tea and watched the charter boats ply the water. They resembled giant insects, their black fishing rods waving like antennae. The wake slapped the concrete dock.

Tipping onto his side, Louie revealed a whitish gray expanse of belly. Walter reached down and rubbed it slowly with his knuckles.

"How did he act?

"Odd," I said.

"Odd?"

"Passive-aggressive, a mix of cocky and contrite. Not like someone who could sweet-talk sophisticated investors out of their money."

Walter tightened his mouth. He must have used that look during interrogations because I suddenly felt an urge to explain.

"He claims he lost most of the money in the market and that someone stole the rest. He says it was poor judgment, not criminal intent."

Walter crossed his arms. "You believe him?"

"No. I believe he enjoys deceiving people, including himself."

Walter shook his head. "Wasn't he with that group of amateur actors at the Little Theatre?"

"He and his wife Ginny."

"What I'd like to know," he said, "is why you?"

"You mean, besides my girlish good looks."

"Besides that."

"That's what Cheryl wants to know."

"So will the detectives."

Ears raised, Louie sat up and stared at the parking lot. Tourists trolled for parking. Cars sat at the traffic light. I didn't see anything unusual.

Walter looked over the dog's head. "He didn't know you were in real estate, yet he knew you'd worked as a cop."

Sensing where this was going, I shifted in my chair and willed Louie closer so I could occupy my hands. "He could have read the reports. Everything's on the Internet these days."

"He knew about the shooting."

I nodded. "And he'd know that internal affairs cleared me."

"They did."

My stomach clenched. "But I haven't, is what you're saying."

Walter crossed his arms. "It'll get better."

I stared at the condos, the sun baking them like bread. "Will it?"

"One day at a time."

With his reddened face and bulging arms, he looked like a photo of a Native American chief, minus the headdress.

"We've wandered off topic again," I said, rattling the fork in the salad bowl. "What's Darby really doing?"

"He thinks he can turn you."

"Guys like Darby think everyone's corrupt."

He frowned. "And now that he's exposed, he's desperate."

I didn't say anything.

Walter removed his cap and scratched his head then snugged the hat over his buzz cut with both hands. "He reminds you of your father."

"My father's dead."

Walter looked away. "Unconfirmed."

"You don't think he did it, my father."

"We find him, we'll ask."

I shook my head. "You mean you think he was framed, like Darby."

"Just running scenarios."

"Here's the only scenario I know," I said, listening to the heat rise in my voice but doing nothing to stop it. "I heard him arguing with my mother downstairs and then someone locked the bedroom doors and set fire to the house. They found my mother curled in the kitchen with her head bashed in. My brother died of smoke inhalation. The county sent me to live with my grandparents. I was five."

An ice cube clanked. Walter said nothing.

Feeling tired and damp, I drained the last of the tea and stood. "You think Darby'll be back."

He must have read something in my expression because he raised a finger and said, "Follow me." Below decks he unlocked a drawer and withdrew two dark velvet bags. "Candace, I know you said you'd never use a weapon again. . . ."

My heart began to race and I could feel sweat sting the back of my neck.

From the bags he slid a Glock 17 and a Beretta subcompact 9mm. In the dim light of the cabin they seemed to glow, as if they were too hot to touch. "They're small but effective at close range, lighter than the Glock 22 you carried, greater stopping power than the Beretta .25 you used as backup."

I shook my head and slowly headed up the stairs. "I've got to get the truck. Can't haul the clients around on the back of the bike. Thanks for lunch."

"Candace," he said, his voice drifting out of the hold. "You had no choice."

As I walked down the narrow concrete strip of the pier, I realized I hadn't said goodbye to Louie.

4

NOTHING ABOUT RICKY HUNT had changed since I'd shown him half of the homes and condos in Palmetto County last week. At five-eight and something like 240 pounds, he dwarfed the white rental. Late forties, with big hands and button eyes. He'd dressed in white slacks, a pleated white guayabera open halfway to his navel and docksiders with no socks. Gray-black hair stood straight up in spots and a shark's tooth dangled from a leather lanyard around his neck. He wore diamond studs in both earlobes and, perched on his forehead, white-framed sunglasses that went out of style with Boy George.

Hunt dropped his cigarette in the lot and crushed it with a two-step twist of his shoe. As the eyes bounced like Ping-Pong balls from breasts to face and back, he yelled in his best imitation of an Alabama auctioneer, "Hello, sugar." *Two dogs in one day*, I thought. *How lucky can a girl get?*

Drawing the red jacket around me I said, in the most cheerful voice I could muster, "Sorry if I kept you waiting, Mr. Hunt."

"No problem. And call me Ricky." He smiled, his lips like fat trimmed from a steak, and drummed his fingers on a jagged scratch in the car's door. "I think I asked you this the last time, but what's the CW stand for?"

"My parents named me Candace but everyone calls me CW."

"Anyone ever call you Candy?"

"Not among the living."

He snorted and bent to kiss my hand. I pulled back quickly and jangled the keys, wishing I still carried cuffs so I could chain him to the marina's bike rack in full sun. Then again, he might like it. I sighed and hoped he didn't notice.

So far I'd shown Ricky Hunt close to fifty homes up and down the Gulf Coast and he hadn't liked a single one. He hadn't received pre-approval from his bank, either, and never brought his wife, although he'd probably need her signature to close. As I looked at Hunt's bulging arms and plastic smile I felt frustrated and uneasy. Even in peak season the only things you hear in some of these big houses are echoes.

With all of the warmth I could muster I smiled and said, "I have several properties to show you in two counties in a wide range of prices." Glancing at the marina, I noticed that Walter's boat stood empty and wondered if he'd driven into town just to see me. Turning to Hunt I asked, "Ready to see some fabulous homes?" If I kept this up, I could work for QVC.

"I'm up for anything."

I bet you are, big boy.

We climbed into my SUV and I had to remind Hunt to buckle his seatbelt. As we headed north on Tamiami Trail, he leaned back and popped his knuckles and stared out the window. "I changed my mind. I want something bigger—two stories, six-thousand square feet or better, big pool, wine room, wet bar on the lanai. We do a lot of entertaining—Matt Damon, Bono, Jay Z, those guys."

I thought, *those guys wouldn't pee in the same Zip Code as you.* What I said was, "I thought you'd retired from the music business."

"They still call me to produce." He stared at a miniature golf course with pink flamingos guarding the holes, his reflection sour. "Jennifer wants palladium windows, granite countertops, appliance upgrades. Terrazzo throughout so it's easy to clean."

I hadn't met his wife but couldn't imagine Jennifer Hunt cleaning her nails let alone the house, and terrazzo, with its pitted surface. . . . "Where is she today?"

"The wife?" He looked out the window. "No idea."

"Does she have a car?"

"She marches to her own drummer—Keith Moon most of the time. He was the drummer for the Who, died of a drug overdose. They all do, except Keith Richards. The fucker's indestructible, excuse my French." He grinned and the lower side of his mouth drooped. "Little before your time."

I changed the subject. "We didn't have much time to talk during our last tour. What brings you to Spanish Point?"

"Money. Nevada was cheaper than California, but Jenn hated the dust, and she didn't want to move back to Texas—bunch of redneck rodeo clowns think they invented freedom. My advisor reminded me that Florida doesn't have an income tax and I figured, why not? Get a house, build a studio, invite Angus and the boys over for drinks. You know Brian Johnson has a house on Spanish Key."

I preferred Willie and Waylon to AC/DC but dissing Ricky Hunt wouldn't sell homes. I forced a smile into lips and voice and said, "I would have thought you'd come for the glorious weather."

Hunt snorted. "Feed that one to the tourists. What's mine is mine, and I want to keep it."

I remembered the last political rally in town. "You should fit in nicely here."

"I have investments in the area." He smiled and his eyes shrank. "Mind if I smoke?"

"Yes."

"Touchy."

"Healthy."

To break the tension, I went into tour-guide mode. "There's a wealth of culture in Spanish Point, including Baywalk, on your left.

He craned his neck to look past me. "Sounds like bad TV.

"It's a mile-long stretch of attractions along Spanish Bay."

Hunt pointed to a silver bivouac anchoring a corner of an open lot. "What's that god-forsaken thing?"

"The Spanish Point Convention and Visitors Bureau—until they can build more modern quarters."

Hunt snorted.

"The building that looks like a seashell is the Vaughan Williams Performing Arts Center—we call it V-PAC." My voice sounded uncomfortably chipper. "It's where the Spanish Point Orchestra and other acts perform. And ahead is the Ringling Museum. It's housed on grounds originally owned by John Ringing, who created Ringling Bros. and Barnum & Bailey Circus, and a good portion of the keys."

Hunt fiddled with a gold lighter and watched the buildings pass. "Not exactly Dudamel and the Getty, are they?"

And I painted my toenails for this.

I corked the travelogue. The further north we drove, the more the neighborhood devolved into liquor stores, bail bond agents and small motels with names like Paradise Cove and the Beachcomber. As we passed my office, I decided not to call attention to the little yellow cube on the left. After all, it wasn't exactly Grauman's Chinese Theatre, or whatever they called it these days.

We hung a right and inched through traffic on University Parkway south of the airport. At this rate, it would take all day to cover eight miles. I could fly to the islands and back in less time. Instead I said, "I thought we'd start with some higher-end homes in the next county and then head over to Braden Ranch. It's a large, master-planned community with its own restaurants and shopping."

As soon as the SUV stopped, Hunt launched himself into the driveway and reached for a cigarette, finishing it before I'd gotten the lockbox off the door. He didn't like the house near the parkway ("too old") or the homes in Braden Ranch ("cookie-cutters"). We looked at one place east of I-75 ("too far from town"), two in the center of Palmetto County ("too much yard") and finally headed west. As we drove toward Tamiami Trail, I checked the dashboard clock. Another day shot in the ass. I felt hungry and tired and wondered, not for the first time, why I'd given up stakeouts without a bathroom for this.

Ricky Hunt caught me staring at the clock. "We've got plenty of time," he said and stretched. "What else can you show me?"

The door, I wanted to say but held my tongue. I wondered where Hunt and his wife were staying, and why she never showed. Maybe he'd locked her in the trunk of his car to keep an eye on the little woman. I kept my voice low and steady, with no uptick at the end of the sentence. "It's getting late and your wife is probably waiting for you. Why don't we pick up tomorrow where we left off?"

"I've got some people to meet."

"Sunday, then. You could bring your wife. I'm sure she'd like to take part in the process."

"Who knows?" Plucking a piece of tobacco from his upper lip, he resembled Bluto, the character Popeye used to fight. Maybe I should keep a can of spinach in the truck along with the emergency kit.

I tried to think of a plan to get him moving but settled for the straight-forward approach. "I'm sorry you didn't like any of communities we saw."

"I've seen potholes bigger than those lakes. I want a place on the water, real water. Lots of space, and a beach. A showcase."

"OK." I let out a slow breath and headed south on the Trail toward the small town of Venice. "I thought you were concerned about storms and being too close to the Gulf. That's why we ruled out Spanish Key."

Hunt looked out the window at a wall of green that separated the mainland from Spanish Bay. "I want a boat dock with a lift and at least an acre. I don't want the neighbors bothering us. Too many people begging for money down here."

"Philanthropy is an important part of life in Southwest Florida."

"You bet. Everybody's got their hand out. They find out you have money and you can't get rid of them. I knew a guy who gave ten million dollars to a college. They put his name in the paper. Next thing you know, somebody kidnapped his wife."

"At least he knew where she was."

He scowled. No sense of humor when it came to his own affairs.

"I apologize," I said. "That was less than sensitive."

He smiled to show teeth bright as quartz. "You're lively, I'll give you that."

I tried to think of a listing nearby that wouldn't dump us into the gridlock traffic of the barrier island. I remembered a place on the bay, a newer listing in a gated community called the Willows, and pointed the car in that direction.

"What's going on?" he asked.

We rolled up to a gatehouse the size of the Capitol Rotunda. The guard, a man in his seventies, wore black pants and a long-sleeved white shirt with a gold security badge. He looked hot, tired and bored. I handed him my business card and he waved us through.

"This is a very exclusive community," I said. "It has two golf courses, two community pools, tennis courts and a clubhouse with three restaurants and a fulltime chef—great for entertaining larger parties. The home just came on the market this week. It's a little smaller than what you're looking for, 3,100 square feet under air, but it has plenty of outdoor space for entertaining, and a great view of the water."

We pulled into a driveway of multi-toned pavers, the colors echoing the paint scheme and barrel-tile roof. A stairway wound up both sides of the front to a double red door, a Spanish version of the house in "Gone with the Wind." Like many of the homes on the water, it offered parking beneath the elevated second story to accommodate a half-dozen cars . . . and a six-foot storm surge. Mature palm and live oak shaded the front yard. No willows, but so much vegetation I could barely see the neighbor's house.

Ricky Hunt looked around the property. "Lot of maintenance."

"Palmetto County has many professionals who can maintain the pool and grounds for you," I said as I slipped a cylinder of pepper spray into my pants pocket. I left my purse and hat in the SUV and locked it.

We climbed the stairs.

Hunt whistled. "How much?"

I fiddled with the lockbox on the front door. It finally gave and we entered a spacious foyer. "The asking price is two-point-two million but I'm sure we can negotiate, especially if you plan on making an all-cash offer."

That didn't seem to faze him. He looked around the living area. "What's the square footage again?"

"Thirty-one hundred."

"That's," he raised his eyes and did the mental calculation, "seven hundred dollars a square foot. I can buy a penthouse in one of those new glass towers at the marina for six hundred."

I could have told him the lower floors might go for six and change but the penthouse would set him back a thousand dollars a square foot, plus condo fees. Instead I bit an already ragged tongue and said, "Wait until you see the view from the pool."

Leading him across the tile, I pulled back one of the sliding glass doors and stepped onto the lanai. Spanish Bay stretched for miles. The only thing blocking the view to the Gulf was Spanish Key, one of the barrier islands preferred by people with more money than sense.

I pointed to the left. "If you look very hard, you can see Stephen King's house."

He grunted. "Never read him."

"I imagine reality's stranger than fiction in LA."

He stuck a finger in his mouth to dislodge something from his gums. "You bet."

He smiled. I smiled. Masters of deception.

Dark clouds had started to build on the horizon and a shadow muted the glimmering pool. Hunt came up behind me and gave a low whistle.

Despite the warmth of the day I felt his body heat and shuddered, my stomach curdling at the smell of tobacco and musk. I touched the pepper spray in my pocket and quickly moved to the kitchen. The new cabinets and appliances glowed. As I talked, I used the languid hand gestures I'd learned from watching Vanna White. Hunt stared at the coffered ceiling and peered inside cabinets and inched closer with each inspection.

From down the hall a clock ticked. It seemed to say, *Get out, get out.*

I cleared my throat. "The kitchen is large enough for a catering crew. I'm sure your wife would love it."

In the dying light his face looked as waxy as Bobby Lee Darby's. He kept clenching and unclenching his hands. Putting the kitchen island between us, I headed for the front door.

"What about the bedrooms?"

"Maybe another time, Mr. Hunt."

He followed me to the door. "You have a pretty good voice, you know? You ever sing?"

"Not on the job."

He pulled on an earlobe. "It's a smoky kind of voice, a lot of throat, and the way you carry yourself. . . ." He cocked his head. "You remind me of Scarlett Johansson, sort of old school, you know?"

"Really?" I felt off balance. Some men think I'm a cross between Sandra Bullock and the U.S. Olympic ice hockey team. Those dates, I'm glad to say, were one-hit wonders. When I came out of my daze I realized Hunt had kept talking.

"Sugar, I could get you a recording contract, no sweat."

That should have surprised me but didn't. "I thought you were retired."

"Ricky still has connections. How about dinner? We can talk house and career at the same time."

"I have a career." I checked my cell phone, "And another appointment in twenty minutes."

He followed me out. "What's the commission on this place? Six percent?"

"Three." I looped the box around the front door handles and locked it. "Buying and selling agents split their fee."

"People in LA spend that much on coke in a week." He flopped into the SUV, slid a cigarette from a gold case, frowned at me and shoved both in a pocket.

"Thanks for the warning," I said as we drove north on the Tamiami Trail. Dark clouds continued to build and, except for a few dozen tourists milling outside the marina restaurant, surprisingly few people walked through the park. Even the threat of rain drove them indoors. As we climbed from the SUV, I left the engine running, door open, purse behind the driver's seat—all the elements for a fast get-away.

In a final attempt to recover my investment of time I said, "We've seen several homes that might meet your needs. Are there any you'd like to revisit?"

He lit a cigarette, inhaled, waited a beat and said on the exhalation, "Too small for the money."

"Then you have my card."

He unlocked the rental and gave me the famous Ricky Hunt grin. "Change your mind about dinner?"

In the angled light, the scratch along the door looked like an open wound, and I wondered if he'd gouged the car himself. "Sorry. Press of business."

"A drink?" He spread two fingers the width of a shot glass and wobbled them.

"Tempting, but I really do have an appointment." My jaw ached from smiling. To keep it from breaking, I watched the boats. Hidden by the clouds, the sun began to set and the marina lights flicked on. The water looked purple. Walter's slip stood empty.

Hunt followed my gaze. "I think your date stood you up."

I felt a chill and drew the jacket around me. "Pardon?"

"Your appointment. The guy you met earlier, on the boat. You looked like a couple, although the guy's a little old for you, if you don't mind me sayin'."

I was about to ask how he knew that when my phone rang. I leaned into the car to check the caller ID on the dash. It was Pap. With the phone running through the SUV's speakers, Ricky Hunt would overhear my business, but I could never dig the phone out of my purse before Pap hung up. And two calls in one day seemed unusual, even for a man in the early stages of Alzheimer's.

Punching a button on the steering wheel, I said, "Pap, I'm just leaving the office. I'll be there in fifteen minutes."

"Take your time." The reply sounded deep and resonant through the speakers. It took a second but I recognized the voice of Bobby Lee Darby.

I flushed hot and cold. "Where's my grandfather?"

"I don't think you took my request seriously today."

I enunciated very clearly. "Where is my grandfather? I want to talk to him. Now."

I heard a shuffling sound and then the familiar voice. "Hi, sweetheart."

"Pap, are you OK?"

"Fine, fine. Sorry about all this."

"Pap, don't apologize. It's my fault. I should have gone to the police right away."

When Darby took the phone, his voice sounded sweet. "You did the right thing."

"So you abducted my grandfather."

"All I want is a little help from someone who can move around."

I started to sweat. "Darby, I will hunt you down. . . ."

"There's no need for threats."

"The hell there isn't." I jumped in the car and slammed the door.

"All I'm asking is that you solve the case."

"Darby, there is no case."

"So you won't mind if I keep Pap a while longer while you think about it, sort of like insurance."

"You son of a. . . ."

"I'll call tomorrow to see how you're doing." And he broke the connection.

Heart pounding, I jammed the car in reverse and burned rubber through the parking lot. In the rearview mirror I caught the smiling face of Ricky Hunt.

5

FLYING PAST BARS AND NAIL salons and auto body shops, I gunned the SUV down a side street and into the driveway. For the past two years I'd called this home but now the place felt deserted. My grandparents had left the snow and culm banks of Eastern Pennsylvania for this working class section on the edge of the city and thought they'd landed in heaven.

Arthur and Alma McCoy had painted their house sunshine yellow and wrapped it with a white porch and enough flowers to rival an arboretum. Like many of the single-story cement block structures in the Gulf Breeze community, it had an Old Florida feel, with a carport anchoring the right side of the house and a forest of bamboo towering over the roof on the left. In the front flowerbed my grandmother's prized bird of paradise still bloomed yellow and blue. Her yard decorations consisted of a terracotta birdbath gray with dirt and a chrome ball on a pedestal. All had outlived my grandmother. I reminded myself to mow the lawn.

Fog threaded the trees like moss. From down the street drifted the muffled sound of a car door slamming. I stood on the steps, key in hand, trying to remember the last time my parents had taken me to see Nana and Pap and couldn't. Instead, I saw an image of Robert Lee Darby's canine smile and Ricky Hunt's smirk and felt a chill. I'd called 911 immediately and given the dispatcher a description of Darby. Then I'd called Cheryl and Walter. Both said they'd meet me at the house. That offered some comfort but I still felt sick.

I shouldn't have been there. I should have hit the road to look for Pap.

Instead, I grabbed a handkerchief from my pocket and tried the door. It yielded and I let it swing open. The air inside felt hot and moist. In the living room, Pap's rocking chair formed a hump-backed shadow. To the right, a light glowed over the stove. Careful not to touch too much, I moved inside and switched on the lamp next to the couch.

On the back of the rocker lay Pap's yellow golf sweater. I picked it up. It smelled faintly of citrus and menthol. He'd get cold, wherever Darby had taken him, and he'd need his medicine for Parkinson's and dementia. I replaced the sweater and checked the bathroom cabinet. Someone had taken the meds. I opened the door to his bedroom closet. His suitcase and some of his shirts and pants were missing. Same with underwear and socks, and the book about World War II Pap kept on his bedside table. Thorough. Either Darby cared about Pap's comfort or he was settling in for a siege. Both scenarios bothered me.

Everything else in the house appeared undisturbed, including the room in which I'd slept for the past two years. I checked the closet and ignored the itch to look at the lockbox under the bed where I kept the Beretta.

The first time I visited Florida I wore jeans and a long-sleeved shirt. As I walked off the plane, I felt as if I'd stepped onto another planet. After months of darkness and snow, the climate felt unreal, the air so thick it clung to my face. When I moved a few years later, most of the clothing went to charity.

I'd come to Florida before the start of my freshman year in college and everything had seemed OK. Spanish Point felt like a steamer on clam night but Nana and Pap didn't seem to mind. I got busy with college and work and thought everything was fine. And it was . . . until three years ago when Nana died. Since then, Pap's health had declined. Sometimes he forgot to eat or take his meds or pay the bills. Socialization became an issue. Spending all his time with Nana, he had no close friends, and no family other than me. When I arrived a year later, I found a bent twig of the man I'd known as a child. I thought we'd always look after each other, and in that, I'd let him down.

I sat at his desk and examined the drawers. Nothing looked out of place. On the back of the desk we'd positioned a few family photos—Pap and Nana on their wedding day, the pair posing during an anniversary party, Pap with his arm around me at graduation. He wore a short-sleeved plaid shirt and white pocket protector filled with pens and a comb. In my robe and mortarboard and heels I towered over him. We both squinted at the sun. In all of the pictures, Pap reminded me of Tony Bennett the year the singer turned seventy, his dark hair and brows scattered with gray, his nose broadened with age, eyes twinkling, dimples surrounding a generous smile. When I was a kid, Pap would bounce me on his knee and sing. Not exactly Tony Bennett but I loved it all the same.

The kitchen counter looked undisturbed, the glasses I'd washed that morning still drying on the counter next to Pap's blue cereal bowl—he started each day with the newspaper and oatmeal topped with cinnamon and bananas. I was turning to leave when I noticed the stain, just a few drops on the beige tile in front of the sink. Pap suffered from nosebleeds. I was always bleaching his handkerchiefs. I told myself that was it, that no one had cut themselves, that Darby wouldn't need a knife to abduct Pap, that he would have gone peacefully, especially if Darby had posed as a home health worker and said I'd sent him to check on Pap, which is what I would have done, if I'd wanted to terrorize an old man and his family.

I took in a chunk of air and let it hiss through my teeth. *Calm down. Breathe.* The bloodstain bothered me, and I wanted to sit in Pap's rocker and cry. Instead I picked up his sweater and leaned against the wall and let the hollow feeling spread. The house felt deserted. Shadows gathered in the corners like dirt. In the distance, sirens mourned. I pictured the gun under the bed and my promise never to use it, a promise Walter called my vow of chastity.

The noise behind startled me.

"Cheryl?"

Still in uniform, her duty belt bulging from slender hips, Cheryl Finzi gave me a hug. With the exception of her nametag, silver badge and the blue SPD patch on the left shoulder, she wore dark blue, shirt, tie and pants, with black shoes glazed to a mirror finish. She stood a few inches shorter, and a few pounds lighter, than me, about five-seven and still slim after having a child seven years ago. Her light green eyes looked clear but the job had etched fine lines around her mouth and streaked her dirty blond hair with charcoal. Mascara clumped by her left eye.

She examined me just as closely. "Are you OK?"

I shook my head and told her about the bloodstain and the missing meds.

She put a hand on my arm and led me to the porch. "You touch anything?"

"I used a handkerchief. One of Pap's."

"You take anything?"

I lifted the sweater, a lightweight nylon cardigan with a small image of a golfer embroidered over the chest. I'd given it to Pap my first Christmas in Florida. "Just this. He'll need it."

The sirens grew louder.

"Where's Tracy?" I asked.

"With a neighbor."

A white car with Spanish Point Police Department painted in blue pulled to the curb. Two officers in dark blue got out of the first car and approached the house. Officer Charles Stover stood about nine foot ten. He had a long, rectangular face the color of nutmeg with short curly hair, broad nose, bony cheeks and arms that could touch the moon. I'd heard Cheryl talk about him and wondered if they were seeing each other. I didn't recognize the second officer, a lean, muscular man with black hair that shot straight up like antennae. His nametag read *Pettinato*.

"Chip, Bernie," Cheryl said. They nodded and stood stiff as nightsticks as an unmarked car pulled to the curb and a dark man in a long-sleeved white shirt and khaki slacks climbed out, gold badge and paddle holster anchoring his belt. He mounted the porch steps without touching the railing. In his mid-thirties, he stood a little less than six feet tall, with broad shoulders and a trim waist. He wore the handsome, confident face of an actor or athlete.

"Det. Antonio Delgado."

"CW McCoy."

He extended a large hand, his grip as firm as his eye contact.

"Ms. McCoy."

"CW," I said and swallowed.

He had close-cropped wavy black hair with a sheen, small ears and a tiny dent in the middle of his forehead. With the exception of a thin white scar that divided his chin, his face appeared flawless, with high cheekbones, full lips and jaw like a vice. His dark eyes looked as if they could melt steel.

Cheryl nodded. They didn't bother to shake hands. To the male officers he said, "Search the grounds and talk to the neighbors." They unhooked heavy black flashlights from their duty belts and disappeared around the side of the house.

Delgado turned to me. "You live here?"

"Yes."

"Have you been inside?"

"Yes."

"Did you touch anything?"

I held out the sweater. "Just this."

He nodded and Cheryl and I followed him into the house.

"Anything missing?"

"His meds, some clothing and a suitcase."

He scanned the room. "Anything else?"

"I haven't had time to look."

Car doors slammed and the criminalistics unit arrived—two men and a woman in black cargo pants and green shirts with *SPD* printed in yellow on the back. They looked tall, young and pale. One of the men carried a camera and bag. The others carried cases. They stood to the side while the photographer worked the room.

Delgado asked if I'd noticed anything unusual or out of place.

"There's blood on the floor," I pointed, "by the sink."

When the photographer had finished in the kitchen, the female tech walked into the sink and bent toward the tile. She removed a camera from the case and took pictures, plotting the distances from the large drop to the spatter marks with string. She photographed, measured, wrote in a notebook and repeated the procedure. It seemed too clinical. I stood between the kitchen and living room and felt helpless.

Cheryl squeezed my hand. I glanced at Delgado. In the harsh light he seemed a jumble of contrasts, the dark eyes, the white shirt, the intense red tie. He reached as if to touch the back of my hand but withdrew quickly and asked, "Would you like to sit?"

I dropped into Pap's rocker. Delgado balanced on the edge of the couch, a small black notebook resting on his knee.

My jaw felt tight, my mouth pasty. "What do you think? Abrasion, knife wound? I didn't see any signs of a struggle."

"No telling at this point."

I tried to swallow. My throat didn't work. "I'd like to see the lab report."

He shook his head. "No can do."

Cheryl came up behind me. "She used to be a detective."

"I know who she is, officer." Looking at the notebook, Delgado asked if Cheryl had seen or heard anything. No, she said, she'd just gotten off shift when I'd called.

He turned to me. "I understand Robert Lee Darby visited you this morning. Tell me about that."

I did.

"And you reported it."

Cheryl put a hand on my shoulder. "She called us right away."

He looked ready to ask another question when I heard feet scraping the welcome mat and looked up to see Walter Bishop. Delgado rose. They shook hands. Walter had a good two inches on the detective. They stepped back and eyed each other, Delgado standing, Walter leaning against the wall with his arms crossed.

The shock had started to wear off and I felt restless. Rising from the chair I said, "Can I get you and your team some coffee?"

"No, thank you. Please don't touch anything until they're finished."

I folded my arms. "Then why don't we just stand here in the dark and twiddle our thumbs." From the corner of my eye I could see Walter slowly shake his head. Something about his expression reminded me of a question I wanted to ask the detective but it wouldn't float to the surface.

Delgado asked about Pap. I gave him a physical description and the photo of the two of us that sat on the back of the desk.

"He looks a bit like Tony Bennett." I rubbed my palms on my pants.

The detective continued to scribble. "We'll issue a Silver Alert." When he finally looked up from his notebook he said, "You said you live here with your grandfather."

"Yes. I look after him."

"You might want to find another place to stay tonight."

For a second I could smell smoke and hear crackling in the walls and the voices of fire fighters deciding where to put the five-year-old. And then, like a fever, the image passed.

Cheryl squeezed my shoulder. "You can stay with us."

Delgado stepped toward the door. "I'd like you to come by the office tomorrow and sit with a sketch artist."

"He's been on the run for a year," I said. "You think you'll have better luck this time?"

I was about to add a couple of other law enforcement agencies to the list of questionable investigators when Walter said, "She'll be there." He pushed off the wall, pecked me on the cheek and left.

Delgado raised an eyebrow. "Your father?"

"Pennsylvania State Police commander," I said as we walked to the porch. "Former head of the commonwealth's Homeland Security Task Force."

Delgado didn't blink. He shook my hand and had covered half the distance to his car when I remembered the question.

"Detective," I said. "Have you interviewed Darby's business associates and family?"

"A year ago."

Arms crossed, standing a few feet to the side, Cheryl shifted her feet, her rubber-soled boots making a scritching sound on the porch.

"His company still in business?" I asked.

"The investment firm, yes. The bank, no."

"Who's running it?"

He flipped through his notebook but the rapid delivery told me he'd memorized the name. "The business manager, Harvey Shaw."

"He check out?"

"The FBI cleared him."

"What about Ginny Alexander?"

He looked puzzled.

"Darby's wife. She goes by her birth name."

Delgado didn't speak for a moment and then said very slowly, "I would proceed with caution with Ms. Alexander." He pronounced Ms. with three z's.

"Why?"

"The bureau cleared her."

"The bureau," I said, "would have cleared Custer."

He tipped his head back slightly, as if stifling a laugh. "She was cited for her outstanding cooperation."

"But you didn't buy it."

"Ms. Alexander expressed a concern about the investigation into her husband's disappearance."

I raised an eyebrow. "She liked the FBI but not the locals?"

"She felt," Cheryl said, "that some of our people may have acted above their station."

My turn to smile. "That person wouldn't have been a certain detective, would it?"

Delgado grinned, his teeth bright against his dark skin. Damn if he didn't look attractive.

Cheryl answered for him. "The wife said if we continued to harass her, she'd go over our heads."

"How far over?" I asked.

"Way over," Cheryl said.

"She is a very influential person," Delgado said. "Many important people seek her counsel."

"He means," Cheryl said, "that a lot of schmucks with money attend her parties."

I looked from Cheryl to Delgado and back. "So?"

"Some of these guys," Cheryl said, "are on a first-name basis with the Secret Service."

"Ah," I said. "Money."

"You'd need one of Darby's yachts to hold it all," Cheryl said.

"I would keep my distance." Delgado dug a wallet from his pants, extracted a business card and scribbled something on the back before handing the card to me. "My private line and cell phone number. "Call me if Darby makes contact again."

"Yes, sir," I said.

Delgado gave a curt nod. "Ms. McCoy, Cheryl."

"Detective," I said.

As the first crack of thunder rolled in from the bay, he slid into his car and disappeared around the corner. I took in a boatload of air. "I don't think Antonio Banderas likes me."

"I think he does," Cheryl said.

"How can you tell?"

"Because he used more than three words in a sentence."

I shook my head. "You think he knows about my situation?"

She laughed. "Everybody in law enforcement knows about your situation."

"That's encouraging."

"You're part of the brotherhood."

"Brotherhood?" I asked.

"You've got street cred."

I felt astonished. "With the guys in blue?"

"The ones who count."

"All done," the female tech called as the pair came through the door. She pulled it shut. Officers Stover and Pettinato returned to seal the space with yellow crime-scene tape.

"Thanks," I said.

"We're on it," Stover said and nodded to Cheryl. "Tomorrow night?"

"Sure." Her voice sounded distant and I wondered how comfortable she was with the relationship, especially around other cops. I also wondered how her ex would take the news. Sal Finzi didn't strike me as an especially open-minded man.

Everyone climbed in their cars and drove away. In their wake, the street fell quiet, the houses empty and dim.

"I guess you know him," I said.

"Chip? Yeah, he's a good guy."

"Got to be better than Delgado," I said.

"He's not so bad."

"Pap's missing, the cops lost Darby and Delgado tells me to stay home and bake cookies. No, I stand corrected. To find some other place to live and bake cookies."

Cheryl sighed. "You were a cop. You know what he's up against."

"They're supposed to be looking for this clown."

"They'll find him," she said, "and Pap."

"Delgado couldn't find his own shoes."

Cheryl look at the sky and spread her hands. "Oh, boy, aren't we in a mood tonight."

I laughed. "My Nana used to tell me I had a mouth. Picked up the habit in kindergarten."

"Putting those little round blocks in square holes will do that."

I nodded and felt my last quart of energy swirl down the gutter.

Cheryl took my arm. "Grab some things and come over. I'll have supper ready in half an hour." And with that she walked next door.

I found myself holding Pap's yellow sweater. It smelled like memories, like home. As I gazed at the empty house, I thought my heart would break.

6

CHERYL'S HOME SAT ON the corner like a gas station, a street sign and concrete driveway consuming most of her front yard. The house looked small by local standards—two bedrooms and a bath in a 1,223 square-foot open floor plan. I'd sold places with pool cabanas that were bigger. To boost the living area, the previous owner had enclosed the garage for storage, so Cheryl now parked her subcompact in the drive. Because her former husband had welched on his alimony and child support payments, the house in Gulf Breeze was all she could afford. I should know. I'd sold it to her.

I had mixed feelings about that. On one hand, she'd found a sturdy home in a good neighborhood next to Pap and me, at a price that allowed her to pay the mortgage during the housing crisis. On the other hand, she and her daughter Tracy deserved something bigger and better, a place with a lawn for Tracy and kitchen bigger than a thumbprint. I'd sold properties on and off the Spanish Key to celebrities who made hundreds of millions by hitting a ball or their girlfriends, and here was this conscientious, single mom, the person protecting those same people, and the only place she could afford was a two-bedroom, single-bath in a neighborhood where people swam at the Y, if they could afford that.

My Nana was right, God rest her soul. I have a mouth.

"Aunt Candace!" Tracy shrieked as she answered the door.

I gave her a hug and stepped back. Tall for her age and impossibly thin, she had brown hair to her waist and green eyes like her mother. Despite the hour, she still wore her school uniform of white blouse and tartan skirt.

I kissed the top of her head and held her at arm's length. "I think you've grown since the last time I saw you."

"You're silly!" she said, running off to tell her mother I'd arrived while calling over her shoulder, "That was yesterday!"

Cheryl had changed into shorts and a T-shirt with an image of Willie Nelson in pigtails. Both looked comfortably worn. The high arches of her bare feet curved gently on the tile. Her voice sounded naturally hoarse with a touch of a New York accent that turned *coffee* into *kwoffe* and added an "r" to anything ending in "w."

"You're just in time," she said and placed salad bowls on the table. "Tracy, can you get the silver?" And then to me, "Is pasta OK? I didn't have time for anything fancy."

"Fine," I said.

She plopped down at a glass-topped table we'd picked up at a consignment shop and looked at me with smudged eyes. "How you doing, kiddo?"

"Lousy."

"Me, too."

I sat across from her and propped my chin in a hand. "How was your day?"

"God, I've always wanted to come home to that."

"I could pitch my voice lower," I said.

"Somehow it wouldn't be the same."

"So," I said, "what's the story with Chip?"

"What do you mean, what's the story with Chip?"

"I mean, how long have you two been dating?"

"Dating? We're not dating. What makes we're dating? We go for a drink once in a while, when I can get a sitter for Trace. We work together, we're friends."

"Nothing more?"

"Not yet," she said.

"Why wait?"

"It's causing a little friction with Sal."

I wanted to follow up but Tracy brought the flatware and joined us. As she set the table, I glanced around the room.

The house looked similar to Pap's. The corridors narrowed into small rooms and a tiny closet. The combination living/dining room sported a single window. In the kitchen a pillar supported the ceiling. The floor was parquet, the countertops and cabinets laminate. Cheryl had done a good job of decorating the place with a limited budget. Almost every surface glowed with pictures Tracy had colored. Through a slider I could see the small patio in back with its uneven pavers and plastic Adirondack chairs. Cheryl referred to it as her office.

We ate our salad and walked the empty bowls the three paces to the kitchen. Cheryl drained spaghetti into a bright red colander that matched her nails and said in a quiet voice, "I have to go to court again."

I slid a pitcher of iced tea from the fridge and poured two tall glasses. "Milk for Tracy?"

"Sure." She pulled a loaf of Italian bread from the oven, kicked the door closed with her heal and began slicing. "He still won't pay."

"What's his excuse this time?"

"He says the job at the marina doesn't pay enough to fund our extravagant lifestyle." She waved the big knife in an arc that took in most of the house.

Something about the pitch of her voice and the way she wielded the blade troubled me. I didn't like Sal Finzi but I didn't want Cheryl doing hard time for manslaughter. He had threatened her before and his behavior grew worse when he drank, wore his uniform or ran short of cash. All three seemed to occur with greater frequently these days. Divorced a year ago, neither had found new mates, so they occupied their time fighting over money.

During dinner, Tracy talked about a book Cheryl had read to her. It was narrated by a cow dog named Hank who was always getting into trouble over misunderstandings. *The story of our lives*, I thought. My eyes must have misted because Cheryl touched my hand. I got up to clear the table.

"You and the ex ever talk about kids?" she asked as we rinsed bowls and loaded the dishwasher.

"He did."

"But you didn't"

"It was kind of a monologue. You know what the job is like."

Cheryl dispatched Tracy to finish her homework and we took our iced tea out back, sitting at the small table and listening to the hum of traffic on Forty-one. Thunder sounded in the distance, a series of muffled booms as a cold front rolled in from the Gulf.

"I know," Cheryl said, picking up the kitchen conversation. "You deal with the bad guys and then you have to deal with the good old boys. Sometimes I don't know which is worse."

I sipped the tea. The cold felt good. "And you try not to bring it home."

A low-watt bulb enclosed in what looked like a Mason jar hung off the back of the house. It cast enough light to show the tension in Cheryl's face. Her mouth had thinned and the cords of her neck tightened when she talked. A small flat mole dotted the left side of her neck. She looked tired and vulnerable.

I must have looked the same because she squeezed my hand and said, "Don't worry about Pap. We've got half the state looking for him."

"I'm more worried about you," I said. "You look like you haven't slept in weeks."

"I wouldn't say you're wrong."

"What's going on?"

"You know how Sal is always complaining that he lost half his pension in the divorce? He showed up last week driving a new motorcycle." She stabbed the plastic tabletop with her nail. "That money could have gone into a college fund for Tracy . . . if she had one."

"And he's still behind in his payments."

"Now I've got to hire a lawyer and take him to court, and he'll give them the same old song and dance he always does and get away with it. I swear women judges are harder on us than men. And get this. Our priest says marriage is sacred and we should try getting back together for Tracy's sake. What does a priest know about marriage and kids?"

"They read a lot," I said, remember my brief experience with the church. "He suggest counseling?"

She waved her hands. "We tried that and Sal bailed after the first session. The counselor—it was a woman, by the way—said a lot of guys with his background have anger issues and he flew into a rage and walked out."

"Background?" I asked.

"Strict Italian. You should have seen him. His eyes bugged out and his face looked like the sauce his mother used to make and he stared pounding his thighs with his fists. For a moment I thought he'd throttle her. Maybe he should have. Then we could have put him in jail where he belongs, the bastard."

I took a deep breath. "I don't know how else to say this, but has he hit you?"

She shook her head. "He wouldn't do that. He's shoved me a couple of times, but that's about it."

I raised an eyebrow. "In front of Tracy?"

"No, not when she's here." Cheryl must have seen something in my face because she touched my arm and said, "He's not a bad man, he just can't get a break. He wants to be a cop and here he is working security and counting grommets on rich people's yachts."

I didn't like the back peddling. I could understand why she'd chosen appeasement over confrontation for Tracy's sake but I'd seen enough domestics to know where that could lead. "Have you thought about filing for a PFA?"

Her laugh sounded like a squeak. "You know as well as I do a piece of paper won't stop anybody from coming through that door."

"Do you want Walter to talk to someone? He knows the state attorney and a few of the judges."

She squeezed my hand. "You've got bigger problems than me."

"Bobby Lee Darby."

"Blast from the past."

I shook my head. "He lays one finger on Pap and I'll kill him."

Cheryl squeezed harder. "Don't say that."

"I can say it to you."

"Don't ever say that to a cop."

I stared past the swing set into the neighbor's yard and the wall of palmetto palm into a darkness that consumed the world. "I hate that man. He's brought nothing but pain and misery to everyone he's touched."

Cheryl withdrew her hand and shifted in the chair and in a soft voice said, "Good thing you don't carry anymore."

I took another sip of tea and watched the sweat from the glass drip onto the table. "Good for some of us."

The ice clinked in our glasses. Traffic swirled on Route 41.

"Listen," Cheryl said. "I can help you track down this Darby character."

"How? He skipped town a year ago and no one's caught him yet."

"Oz can find him."

"Oz?" I asked.

"He can find anyone."

"Who's Oz?"

"He's our contract IT guy," Cheryl said. "The department just got new software and he's installing it."

"Oz?"

"It's short for Osborne."

"Given name?"

"Francis Xavier, but he hates it if you call him Frank."

"Odd but intriguing," I said. "Is he good?"

"He's the best. Just ask him."

"What's he like?"

Cheryl smiled. "Tall, mid-thirties, bald as a cue ball. He lives in a fantasy world of comic books and video games but he can trace anyone. And I think he's sweet on me."

"I thought you were seeing Chip."

"Oz never met a woman he didn't like," Cheryl said. "He's harmless . . . as long as you're fully clothed."

I raised both eyebrows.

"I'm just running my mouth." She pulled her smartphone from a back pocket—I'd always wondered how people sat without cracking the screen—tapped the device and handed it to me. "That's his cell number. Tell him if he helps, I won't turn him in for watching porn at work."

I laughed and jotted the number in a notebook I carried in a back pocket without fear of breakage. "You think Oz—that's going to take a while to get used to—you think he would meet me tonight?"

Cheryl looked me over. "Honey, Oz would meet with you any time, day or night."

"He's not another dog, is he?"

She shook her head. "He's a geek's geek—loves his work and ignores everything else, except women. You think I don't get any sleep. . . ."

"So he's a workaholic with no social skills and you still like him."

She pulled her ragged hair into a ponytail and let it fall. "It's been a long time, you know?"

"I know." I tried mopping the condensation with a fistful of napkins but gave up. "Sounds like a dream date."

"Don't knock it until you've seen him. If I didn't have Tracy to consider. . . ."

I raised my eyebrows. "That good looking?"

"He has big thumbs."

I laughed. "It *has* been a long time. You mind if I call him now?"

"Be my guest. I'll give you some privacy."

I rose to protest but she scooted into the house with a grin and slid the door shut. I placed the call. Francis Xavier Osborne picked up after one ring.

"CW." The voice sounded low and husky.

"How'd you know who I was? I've never called you."

"Cheryl gave me your number." Like some cartoon version of mist turning into a hand, his voice wrapped itself around my ear and tickled it.

"Creepy," I said.

"I am the all-knowing Oz."

Not another one, I thought but tried to stay on topic. "So you've heard about the situation with my grandfather."

"Not yet. Cheryl said you'd have details."

I felt a little uneasy confiding in a stranger but Oz might have more resources than Delgado, and a warmer personality. We agreed to meet later at the bar beneath the central parking deck downtown.

"How will I know you?" he asked.

"Tall, late twenties, dark chestnut hair with a luxurious sheen. How's your hair?"

"Non-existent," he said.

"How will I recognize you?"

"Not so tall, mid-thirties with a Van Dyke, no moustache. Black head to foot."

"Very grunge," I said.

"Grunge is dead."

"Very Goth, then."

"Goth is deader than dead."

"Jeez," I said, "I'd hate to hear what you think of disco."

In the background something beeped. "Sorry, gotta fly," he said and disconnected.

The sky rumbled like an upset stomach. I walked inside. Cheryl stood at the kitchen sink, mopping the counter.

"Nothing seems to dry in this climate," I said.

"Including ink on the divorce papers. So how is the great and powerful Oz?"

"Full of himself," I said. "And abrupt."

Cheryl nodded. "Patience isn't his strong suit."

"At least we have that in common. We're meeting at Parker's."

"You're staying here tonight, right?" she asked.

"I thought I'd sleep in my own bed," I said and heard the echo of Darby's voice when he'd given precisely that reason for returning to Spanish Point.

Cheryl swiveled her head and gave me the eye.

I put up a hand. "I know. The detective won't like it."

"Stay here. Tracy can sleep in my room and I'll take the couch."

I had a vision of her ex roaring up on his cycle in the middle of the night and wondered if she did, too. "You think Sal might drop by for a visit?"

She twisted the dishcloth as if wringing a chicken neck.

I put a hand on her arm. "Cheryl, tell me what's going on."

She took a deep breath. "I'm worried."

"About?"

"About him, about money, about Tracy, about what all this fighting is doing to her."

Her eyes grew larger, her breath more shallow. I led her to the kitchen table, grabbed a glass of water and sat.

"It's OK to be scared," I said, "as long as you do something with the fear."

Ignoring the water, Cheryl bowed her head, staring into folded hands, her voice small and distant. "It's not OK. I'm a cop. I should be able to handle this."

"Nobody can handle this, at least not very well."

"You did."

My palms started to sweat. "That's not a solution."

She looked up. "It was for his wife and kid."

I shook my head. "Cheryl," I started but she held up a hand.

"That could have been Tracy and me, you know that."

I studied my hands.

"I've never told you this, never told anyone, but I admire you for what you did."

A bolt like an icepick hit my stomach. "Cheryl. . . ."

"I know you only did what you had to do, but he was a monster. He would have killed her sooner or later, killed them both."

"Cheryl," I began again, "you're not thinking of. . . ."

"Somebody should."

I swallowed. "I know people at the resource center. They can help."

The harsh kitchen lights carved deep shadows under her eyes. She shook her head as if dismissing an idea and looked up. "Would you listen to me?" Her voice rose and wavered. "Here I am complaining to someone whose grandfather's been kidnapped."

With two quick taps she patted my hand and walked to the sink, where she emptied the glass of water and placed it in the dishwasher. "Stay here tonight. We can paint our nails and read about the Kardashians."

I laughed. "Thanks. I've got to see Oz and collect some things."

"I'll be up."

I looked at the smeared mascara and the red blotches on her face and said, "It's going to be OK," and knew that it wouldn't.

7

RAIN SPATTERED THE DRIVEWAY, kicking up the smell of dust and motor oil. For once I felt justified in leaving the motorcycle in the parking garage near my office. I drove the SUV the eight miles north on Tamiami Trail to downtown Spanish Point. By the time I passed the hospital I could feel the car behind me. As the rain hardened into a downpour, the mirrors produced little more than a blur of headlights. I tried changing lanes without causing a wreck and thought I spotted a tail but lost it when I ran a red light north of the marina. Swinging onto Palm Avenue, I drove past one of the theaters that had declined to produce Darby's play. Smart choice. At the parking deck I gunned the truck up the ramp and pulled into a slot near the stairs.

The more I thought about the situation, the angrier I became—at Darby, at Delgado, at the clown who might have followed me. Then I got angry at myself for getting angry. I needed direction and hoped that Francis Xavier Osborne could provide it.

A damp darkness overflowed the parking deck. The sound of the slamming car door bounced off the walls. The engine ticked.

I flinched when my phone rang and scrambled to dig it out of my pocket.

Jackie Stevens wanted to know if I was bringing anyone over to see their house on Saturday because she and Kurt wanted to be there during the showing—a bad idea in any market. Ignoring my advice, they'd set their price far above what comparable houses in their neighborhood would fetch and then complained about the lack of traffic. Jackie, who'd quit her secretarial job to study for the real estate exam, wondered if she should find another agent. Even a wild guess at the balance in my checking account told me that was an even worse idea.

I didn't want to get into it and said, "Why don't we meet early next week and revisit our strategy," and disconnected.

No one followed me downstairs. Lucky for them.

It's amazing what architects can create with concrete. The city had combined a parking garage with a bus depot and tried to soften the façade by painting the walls with silhouettes of antique cars—a Model T, a Packard, a Rolls Royce. Between the exhaust fumes, planners had sandwiched a grocery store, a restaurant called the Deck and Parker's tavern and grill. They should have just named it Rebar. The whole place consisted of concrete, steel and glass and clashed with the Spanish Revival architecture that dominated Spanish Point. It felt very post-industrial, a big-city statement to make an aging town feel hip.

Judging from the crowd, the hip thing had worked. Walking downstairs, I ran into a wall of people and noise. The bar consisted of a great curve of gray concrete and blue acrylic glass crowned with a thatch of corrugated tin. All it needed were tiki torches made from mercury vapor lamps.

The man formerly known as Frank stood at the bar in a black shirt, vest, pants and a tweed driving cap. An inch or two shorter than me, he looked close to forty with enough tattoos to fill a museum. For some reason that made me feel better. We introduced ourselves, shook hands, ordered beer and found a table away from the drafty stairs.

On his left forearm, a snake entwined the arms of a German Cross. On the right, a pair of skeleton keys crossed beneath a skull. "Nice tats," I said as we sat under a neon cowboy with an orange hat. "You're wearing more ink than a printer at the *New York Times*."

He raised the beer bottle to his lips. "What's print?"

"It dates back to the days of cuneiform tablets."

He took a drink. "Along with your computer skills?"

"Along with the attitude that girls can't handle science or math."

"Ouch." He smiled and dipped his head.

"If that's an apology, you're forgiven . . . on a provisional basis."

He had thick brows, large gray eyes and long lashes, with a broad nose that veered to the left. Pointed beard, full lips, hollow cheeks and a fan-like pattern of scars at his left temple completed the picture. Attractive, in a rough way.

I pointed to the tattoos. "I can't believe SPD lets you in the building."

"I'm just another thug, only better looking."

"At least you're not wearing a gold chain."

"The Wizard needs no enhancements."

I felt tempted to agree but didn't want to appear too eager so instead I asked, "What do I call you?"

"Oz is good."

"Why not Frank?"

"Why?" he said.

"Because your parents named you that?"

"Why CW?"

"Because I want to punch people who call me Candy."

"Good to know."

"So," I said, "how did you get into this line of work?"

"Legalized spying?" he said. "I illustrated comic books."

I laughed. "And that qualifies you to run the IT department for the police?"

"I also did voice-over work for commercials." He sat back, took a deep breath and sang "Racewayyyyyyyyyyy Park!" in a helium-fueled voice. "Only my real voice is lower."

I thought the beer would squirt from my nose. "I noticed," I said when I could finally breathe. "I grew up on the PA-Jersey border and my grandparents used to listen to those radio spots. Did you live near the raceway?"

"About forty minutes west, near Princeton. My father taught shop at the local high school and my mother worked in the cafeteria. What about your parents?"

"They're dead," I said.

"Sorry."

"So you went to Princeton," I said.

"Full parental scholarship."

"When did you graduate?"

He leaned forward on his elbows. "Dropped out. Figured if it worked for Bill Gates. . . ."

"Right idea, wrong school."

"Yeah." He tipped the bottle back and sipped.

"So you were interested in programming?"

"I was the geek to end all geeks—glasses, pocket protector, receding hairline." He removed the driving cap and stroked the top of his polished head. "I spent all my time coding, and selling dope. Pulled a one-nine in my last year and said, 'who needs this?'"

"And?"

"And my free-market parents agreed and ended the free ride."

I nodded. "Then what?"

"I took a job with a Big Pharma, the legal dope dealers. Those guys don't have a sense of humor. Their idea of time off is the commute."

"How did you get to Florida?" I asked.

"Spring break. We stayed on Spanish Key. 'When I make some money,' I said, 'I'm gonna buy me a piece of paradise.'"

"And did you?"

"Yup."

"With beach access?" I asked.

"Yup."

"And that was. . . ."

"Ten years ago," he said. "I've had offers from people who want to tear it down and build a mansion."

"Which you continue to resist because you are pure of heart."

"Or until someone makes a stupefying offer."

"Someone will," I said. "You like living on the Gulf?"

"I rent to a retired exec from Newark who pretends he's Thoreau with a sand bucket. Just him and a hundred thousand of his closest friends."

"Somehow," I said, "I don't see you as a landlord."

"The property manager handles that." He pulled at the beer, the foam glistening from his bare upper lip. "You think you could sell it?"

I watched his dark eyes prowl my face.

"In a heartbeat."

"But," he let out a huge sigh, "I don't think you asked me here to unload property, or drink." He pointed to my beer, which I had barely touched.

"OK," I said. "Down to business." I told him about Pap and Darby and how I needed to trace them, and everyone associated with Darby's company. "You know about him?"

"Head of IAG, the Intercoastal Advisory Group," Oz said. "It's one of the biggest financial firms in Florida. The bank went belly-up when Darby disappeared but no one's found the assets."

"The business manager was cleared," I said. "So was Darby's wife, Ginny Alexander."

"The gadabout philanthropist."

"That's the one. The cops haven't been able to trace Darby so far."

"Not much new to go on," he said.

"Someone's giving him food and shelter. I think the family or the investors are the key to finding him. I can surveil the family but I need help on the financial side."

He emptied the bottle and pointed to my beer. "You want that?

"Help yourself."

Through a thick pool of condensation he slid the bottle across the concrete tabletop. "So," he said, "you want me to use the resources of the Spanish Point Police Department to aid a private citizen in the illegal surveillance of another citizen, without the knowledge of that person or my employer."

"That's it."

He raised his hands, palms up. "And for this I get. . . ."

"The knowledge that you've rescued another human being?"

He folded his hands and bowed his head.

"My undying gratitude?"

"Better," he said and looked up. "What do you need?"

"Everything you can tell me about Darby and his business manager, Harvey Shaw."

"What about his wife?"

"Check her out, too, and any investors in the bank. Someone might bear a grudge and want to find him faster than the police."

He nodded.

"Oh, and a client of mine, a guy named Ricky Hunt. He claims he's a retired music producer from LA."

"Why him?"

"He creeps me out."

Oz smiled. "Works for me."

"How will you trace Darby?"

"The department just licensed new software," he said. "We'll do an analysis through Accurint, TLOxp and LInX."

"English, please."

"They're databases the police use to trace suspects. A search will show Darby's legal records, financial history, property and vehicle ownership, associates, police reports if they're filed with a case number, credit card usage, neighbor complaints. It'll even search the country for vehicle sightings within the last thirty days."

"Good reason to obey the law," I said. "You need anything else to get started? I'm staying with a friend and her daughter and they get up early, even on weekends."

"No," he said, rising to reach for the back of my chair.

I felt touched by the chivalry but waved him away. He started backing out the front door.

"One more thing," I said. "I think somebody's following me."

"Did you get a tag?"

"No. It was raining. Light-colored compact, maybe."

"Make? Model?"

"Toyota, Hyundai, Kia. They all look alike."

He nodded.

"I'll try to pay more attention next time."

"Always helps."

We locked eyes and I felt slightly off balance.

He took my elbow. "You OK to drive?"

"Yes," I said and flushed. "I'm worried about my grandfather."

"You ride your bike?"

"No," I said and glared at him. "How did you know I had a bike?"

"DMV," he said.

I felt a tug of caution and desire. "You really did check me out."

Oz dug a hand into the pocket of his black jeans and came up with keys. "Hard not to."

8

LOUIE!" I SAID AND threw my arms around his neck. He hung halfway out of the passenger window, tail whapping the seat, his bright eyes and goofy smile saying, "Ain't it great to be a dog?"

Who was I to argue?

Walter shooed him into the back and pushed up the armrest and I popped the door and climbed in. The seat radiated Louie's warmth and smell. Walter eased the Merc into traffic—not an easy feat during peak season, since the car resembled the space shuttle, minus the fuel tanks.

Last night's heavy rain had rinsed the air until it shone a brilliant blue. We avoided the Trail and zigzagged north on Orange Avenue.

"You know this is a waste of time," I said as we crawled through an intersection.

"Haven't had your coffee yet?"

"Who works this early on Saturday?"

"Cops," he said and parallel parked with the ease of a person breathing.

From the outside, the headquarters of the Spanish Point Police Department looked more like an office condo than a home for law enforcement. The aluminum-and-glass structure rose six stories to peak at a canopied roof with a wall of windows overlooking a park. I was admiring the digs when my phone rang. I recognized the caller ID and grimaced.

"Hello, Mrs. T.," I said as cheerfully as a person can sound on an early Saturday morning. "What can I do for you?"

Cupping a hand over the phone I whispered to Walter, "Marion

52

Taggert. I sold her a house last year."

"I am so sorry to disturb you," she said, "but there is no one else I can call."

Mrs. T. was a small woman with a voice that sounded as if someone had stuffed it into a can. From the slight shake, I could tell she'd encountered another problem with the property. As the buyer's agent, I'd sold her an older home with a pool in a deed-restricted community with more rules than the floor of the U.S. Senate. Ever since then she'd called whenever something went wrong—sticky doors, leaking pipes, sporadic cable TV service. I sighed, reminded myself that she was Pap's age, in her eighties, and living alone.

I sweetened my tone. "Is everything all right with the house?"

"We have ants."

"Ants?"

"Little ones. They're crawling all over the kitchen counters and the bathroom sinks and I've even seen them on the lanai. Of course we had them back home, bigger ones, black ones that came in the house in trails through the woodwork and under the back door of the porch, you know the one I told you about, the screened-in porch that George built when we first moved to Pittsburgh, and he always set out traps and that took care of them. But these little ants, they just swarm all over everything, and I'm afraid they'll get into the food."

"You don't think they'll carry away the refrigerator, do you?" I asked.

"Oh, dear."

"I'm sorry," I said. "I don't mean to make light of the situation." I took a deep breath. "They're called ghost ants because they're so small. It's a common problem in Southwest Florida. Did you call the exterminator I recommended?" I'd given her a name and number and suggested she set up a schedule of quarterly treatments to prevent further problems.

"Oh, yes, I remember, you gave me a card. Now where is it?"

I could tell from the clank of metal and swish of paper that she'd empty all of her drawers before finding the card.

"Mrs. T.? I have the number. Why don't I call the exterminator and have them contact you?"

"Oh, would you, dear? That would be wonderful."

"Great. I'll do that now."

"Oh, and one more thing," she said.

Louie nosed the armrest down and stuck his head between the seats and panted. I knew how he felt.

"Yes?"

"I hate to bother you, but we have lizards," she said.

"Lizards?"

"Small ones, all over the place, in the sink, in the bathtub, on the windowsills. The cats chase them all over the house and I'm afraid someone will get hurt."

"They're called anole," I said. "I'll take care of it." I disconnected and called the exterminator. Jim and I had worked together on dozens of homes. He laughed when I told him about Mrs. T.'s reaction and said he'd call her that morning.

Walter rolled down the windows for Louie and we climbed out of the car. "A woman's work is never done," he said.

"Roger that."

Inside the SPD lobby the design changed dramatically. The architect had replaced windows with doors and daylight with banks of fluorescent lights. A cement-block bunker squatted in the center. Except for the color, a deep police blue, the booth reminded me of a bomb shelter, or my office. I leaned toward a silver metal disc planted high on the window and as if ordering tickets to a movie told the receptionist we had an appointment to see Det. Delgado. The officer, a long-faced Latina, smiled through the bullet-resistant glass and buzzed Officer Finzi. I felt grateful Cheryl had arranged that with reception. Delgado and I hadn't exactly hit it off, and after my time on the force I'd vowed never to set foot in a police station again.

Cheryl appeared at the door to the patrol section looking like a ninja with a tie. She acknowledged Walter and me with a nod and a rigid smile. We took the elevator to the third floor and walked down a long corridor lined with photos, awards and offices on the right. On the left, floor-to-ceiling windows overlooked the lush green of a park. Fountains sprayed, children rode the merry-go-round and a runner traced a footpath around the perimeter. From here, at least, the world looked at peace.

Cheryl led us past the communications center, its banks of computer screens glowing blue and white through an interior window. Three people, two women and a man, stared at the monitors. Oz's bald head rose above the equipment. I considered waving but didn't want to feel more awkward than I already felt.

Walter never appeared self-conscious. He walked as if he commanded the place. Cheryl didn't. Her face looked pinched, her eyes squeezed as if she had a headache.

"You OK?" I asked as we rounded the corner by the evidence room.

She glanced at Walter, who politely avoided looking at us. In a low voice she said, "He called this morning, just as I got into work."

"Sal?"

She nodded.

"What did he want?"

"He said the only way he'll pay is if he gets more visitation. He wants me to agree before we go to court."

"And you're concerned about Tracy," I said.

"I don't know," she said as we passed internal affairs. "It just doesn't feel right."

"And you're in a bind."

"He knows I need the money to keep the house," she said. "I can't take a second job and look after Tracy. It's like he's punishing me."

We stopped in front of the detective division. Unlike the squad rooms in which I'd worked, there was no open-floor plan here, no desks or bodies jammed together. In fact, there was so little noise I could hear the low hum of the air conditioning system. Closed doors lined the hallway—offices on one side, interrogation and conference rooms on the other.

Cheryl turned, her face like a plowed field. "I can't stay," she said. "He doesn't like 'help' with his investigations." She curled her fingers into quotation marks. Knocking on the first door to the right, she announced her visitors and left.

We entered an office lit only by a banker's lamp on the desk. Antonio Delgado of the Spanish Point detective division hunched over a sheet of paper, a pencil clamped between his teeth, his dark hair spiking at odd angles. He rose, seemed momentarily surprised to see us and shook hands.

"You remember Walter Bishop," I said as we sat.

"I do," he said, face impassive.

"He's an interested party."

Delgado shrugged as if he could do nothing about the situation. He wore a long-sleeved white shirt with gold cufflinks and a burgundy tie with small figures of polo players. In the dim light he looked dark and chiseled, the shirt tight across his chest. Disconcerting, as Pap would say.

The office walls held framed diplomas and photos of award ceremonies and SWAT teams in body armor. I assumed Delgado featured prominently in all of them. The desk looked spare, with a phone, an in-box and three framed photographs. I couldn't tell if the people in the photos were parents, children or wives, although the detective didn't wear a wedding ring.

Delgado walked around the desk and sat in his chair and asked if we wanted anything to drink. We said no, thanks.

He pulled up a blank incident report on his computer and I started talking. When we were done, he printed the paperwork and asked me to review it. I handed it back and said it looked accurate and we stared at each other.

He spoke first. "We've notified the U.S. Marshal's Fugitive Task Force. We've also issued a Silver Alert and released the photo of your grandfather to Crime Stoppers. It should be on the evening news."

I nodded.

"Before I turn you over to the sketch artist," he said, "I want to clarify a procedural matter."

I looked at Walter. He, too, wore the police mask.

"We'll need to monitor your communications in case Darby calls again."

"OK," I said.

"You should report any contact the moment it happens."

"I can do that."

He leaned forward and folded his hands. "We'll do everything we can to locate your grandfather."

"Good," I said. "He's going to run out of meds."

"That said, Darby's dangerous."

"I know."

He looked at his hands and then at me, his eyes deep pools of brown. "Please don't take this the wrong way. We'd appreciate it if you'd let us handle the situation."

I felt something hot bubble up from my stomach. "How should I take it? Law enforcement doesn't exactly have the best track record when it comes to finding this guy."

His eyes never left mine. "You remember what it's like."

All too well. I stood to leave. Walter followed.

"You know where you're going?" he asked and picked up the phone. "Down the hall, elevator to the second floor. It's on the left."

As we filed out I heard him tell the sketch artist to watch for us.

Beware the aggrieved relative. She is worse than a woman scorned.

As we moved into the corridor my phone rang. I checked the screen for an ID. Jackie Stevens. I let the call go to voicemail.

"Trouble?" Walter said.

"Sellers are underwater, one's unemployed. Lots of pressure on the family."

"Lot of that going around," Walter said.

We passed the glass wall that overlooked the park and watched the children play on seesaws and swings. They never seemed to age.

"You didn't say much in there," I said.

"Not my place." He looked straight ahead.

"What do you think of Delgado?"

"Hard to tell."

"You've met him twice."

When we reached the elevator, he pushed the button and folded his arms, a gesture that indicated thought rather than belligerence. "He knows as well as you they have little to go on."

The elevator car arrived. We stepped in and I punched the button for the second floor. "So?"

"So why press him?"

"So he'll get off his ass and find Pap."

As the doors opened, Walter grinned.

"I saw that," I said. "You think I'm a pain in the butt."

We started down a windowless corridor lined with cubicles, reading the names of officers posted on the fabric walls.

"I would channel my energy in another direction."

"And what direction is that?"

He pointed to a nameplate that read *Shannon Yost.* "Here."

A petite brunette in a dark blue uniform rose to greet us. She looked a hard forty, with a lot of teeth and eye liner. Age lines serrated her upper lip. She smiled broadly, shook our hands and offered us seats in a cramped, gray cubicle I've heard people call a *coffice.* Two large computer monitors dominated the wrap-around desk, flanked by those multi-tray printers that resemble small ovens. Pictures of children lined the back of the desk. A designer purse emblazoned with interlocking letters hung from a hook on the side of the cubicle—probably the most expensive thing in her wardrobe.

"The detective filled me in on the details." Her voice sounded soft and reassuring. I thought she'd work well with nervous sources, or suspects during hostage negotiations.

She explained the procedure. Unlike the old days, when an officer would sketch individual body parts—hair, eyes, nose, lips—the computer presented a more holistic view. She'd ask questions, I'd answer and together we'd create a composite. When she jogged the computer, a stylized version of Robert Lee Darby filled the screen.

"I've started with the images we had on file," she said.

As I stared at the photo, my stomach clenched. *Surprising, but not unexpected.* I glanced at Walter. He nodded and crossed his arms and I felt glad he hadn't reached out to reassure me, especially in front of the officer.

Clearing my throat, I ran through a description of the new Darby, closing my eyes to recall the details. When I'd finished, I took a deep cleansing breath and stared at the result.

Shannon Yost worked the drop-down menus of the application to alter the size and tone of each feature. "Is this right?" she said and pointed and adjusted until she turned and asked, "Is this accurate?"

"Yes," I said. "You've nailed it."

She said she'd deliver the before-and-after images to Delgado by noon and that he'd circulate both, along with the picture of Pap. We stood and shook hands, walked the long corridor to the elevator and slid down to the first floor and through the bomb-proof lobby and into the sunshine. Just another day in paradise.

"Delgado," I said as we climbed into Walter's car. "That man is completely disengaged." I reached into the back seat to pet Louie. He licked my hand.

"Unless you challenge him."

"How hard do you think he'll look if we don't?"

Walter headed north to avoid the farmer's market that barricaded parts of the downtown every Saturday morning. In case his master needed a navigator, Louie stuck his head between the seats and panted.

"Sometimes," Walter said, "you have to turn it over."

"Is there a twelve-step program for cops who shoot cops?"

"No." He kept his eyes on the road.

We drove past the market and headed toward the Tamiami Trail.

"We have a plan? Walter asked.

"No."

"Drop you at the office?" he asked.

"Might as well. I need to check the MLS listings to see what's rented in the past two weeks. Darby might have used an alias we'll recognize. And I want to call his wife and find out if she'll see me."

Walter stopped the car at a light and signaled to turn right on North Trail. "And what are you going to ask the grieving widow?"

"What did she tell the FBI when her husband disappeared? What did he take when he fled that didn't make it into the reports? How much money did he have? Has he contacted her or their daughter Claire? Do they have relatives in the area? What are his habits? Does he gamble, avoid crowds, frequent prostitutes?"

Walter headed north on the Trail. "She'll like that."

I turned in my seat to watch as he smoothly shifted lanes. When he grinned I could picture him as a boy, running through fields with a buzz cut and freckled face and a gap between his teeth that braces would never touch.

He crossed the highway at the light, did a U turn, pulled into the parking lot of my office and parked next to the SUV.

"You're kind of cute when you're sarcastic," I said.

"Lots of practice."

We crunched over shells to the front door.

"You know what we should do?" I dug through my pocket for the key. "Check out Ricky Hunt."

"Your real estate client?"

"He keeps dropping names, people with money, celebrities, agents, rock stars. He wants to come across as a player. And he keeps asking me out." The key slid into the lock but didn't turn. "And I think someone's following me. Maybe it's him."

"Better have Cheryl run a background check."

I turned the key the other way and back. Had I forgotten to lock up? Walter edged to the side and pushed the door with his shoe.

I was about to say I'd make coffee when I saw the destruction.

9

ONCE WE GOT INSIDE, the damage didn't look so bad. The furniture stood where I'd left it, the computer rested on the desk and the white coffeemaker sat unbroken on the file cabinet. But the file drawers pitched open and spewed papers across the carpet. Everything else looked untouched.

Walter moved quickly, glancing behind the door and inside the bathroom and confirming the single window in front remained secure.

I stood in the middle and surveyed the walls. "At least nobody defaced my poster of Wendy O. Williams."

"That's a relief."

I blew out some air. "Thanks."

"For what?"

"For going first."

"Chivalry lives."

"And for not drawing your weapon."

"Glad I made your day." He looked around. "Start cleaning. I'll call Delgado."

"No," I said sharply and then dropped the shrillness a notch. "What's the point? We just obliterated the fingerprints on the door handle and he probably used gloves anyway."

"He?"

"It's got to be Darby, or the guy who's following me. Nobody else has a reason to do this."

Walter surveyed the room. "Guy's good with locks. And he works fast." He picked up a piece of paper and set it on the desk. "Can you tell if anything missing?"

"Who knows?" I sighed. "It's going to take days to put all this paperwork in order."

"Business records?"

I nodded.

"You keep valuables here? Anything personal?"

"Just things I might need to grab in a hurry—the hazard insurance policy, mortgage documents, my PI license."

He raised his eyebrows.

"Joking," I said. "Maybe that's why Delgado doesn't like me. He thinks I'm a wannabe."

"He might," Walter said. "But he likes you."

My turn to raise a brow. "And you know this how?"

"When you push him, he doesn't push back."

"Selfless devotion to the job." I held up a hand before Walter could comment. "Or he could be a closet chauvinist."

I picked up an empty file folder and winged it into the wall.

"You should go through everything."

"It'll take days." I fell into the desk chair and opened drawers and tried to compare what I saw with a mental inventory and gave up. The ceiling in the corner dripped. From her perch on the wall, Wendy O. gave me a stare full of circus menace. Did Delgado see me that way? God forbid, did Walter?

He moved toward the door. "I know better than to ask if you want help."

Taking a deep breath, I let the air hiss slowly through my teeth. "Yes, you do."

"Call me if you want to do a drive-by on the rentals."

I spun the chair and looked up at the poster. With my back to the door, hand raised above my head in a half-hearted wave, I felt more than saw Walter leave as a shadow flickered through the opening.

"Wendy," I said into the empty space. "It's all an act, isn't it?"

"What's an act?" came a small voice from a tall girl who stood in the doorway.

She looked sixteen, with bony hands and dangling arms and shoulder-length brown hair dyed white at the bangs. Fishhook lines bracketed a cupid mouth. She wore a flannel shirt over a blue T-shirt with a photo of Ringo Starr holding up two fingers in a peace sign. Purple eye shadow darkened her lids and a pink plastic band encased her left wrist. The right one bore a tattoo of a rose. Her fingernails looked dipped in tar.

She closed the door and stared at the mess on the floor and asked, "Do you need some help?"

"Story of my life." I motioned to the chair in front of the desk. "Why don't you have a seat? Coffee?"

"Never touch the stuff."

Damn.

Her large chocolate eye darted around the room and settled on the poster of Wendy O.

"I like it."

"It's the chainsaw," I said. "It gives her that kick-ass look."

"I think it's the tape and the shaving cream," she said. "She has no limits."

I smiled. "Almost."

We stared at each other. She spoke first.

"You know who I am."

"You father sat in that chair yesterday and said the same thing."

"He was framed, you know."

"Did he send you here to tell me that?"

She chewed the inside of her cheek. "He needs your help."

"Claire," I said, "you're a little late. He abducted my grandfather, a man who is no doubt scared out of his wits by now. I can tell you this: the only help your father's going to get is when I put him in jail."

"He said you'd say that."

"You're in contact with him?"

She chewed some more. "He called and said we'd see his picture on the news tonight and that he's trying to turn himself in but can't. Not unless you help."

"So now he's dragged you into this."

"He's not a bad man." She picked at the pink wristband. "I know you're thinking, that's what the daughter is supposed to say because she's naïve and he's manipulating her, but I think in his own weird way he really cares about the family."

Hands folded across my stomach, I tried twisting my wedding band when I realized I no longer wore it. "I know this hasn't been easy for you, or your brother, but you still have your mother."

She gave a humorless laugh. "Mom cares about mom. My brother's the lucky one. He got out."

"What's your brother doing?" I asked.

"Bagging groceries for a company that will only give him thirty hours a week. That's what college buys you these days."

"And you?"

"I can't wait to get out," she said.

"What does you mom think of that?"

"She complains that all I want to do is play basketball. She says it'll make me more awkward than I already am. I told her I didn't see how."

Despite the circumstances, I could sympathize with Claire. "Your mother doesn't consider that ladylike behavior?"

"She doesn't like sweat, unless her trainer approves it."

"And she won't help you find your father."

"She wouldn't even cook him dinner, unless it involved getting her picture in the paper for donating a hospital wing."

"What about your brother? Does he know where your father is?"

She snorted. "He thinks it's all the Jews' fault and blames dad for being taken in."

I felt something cold slide down my neck. "Claire, you don't believe that, do you?"

"He's really not a bad guy, my brother," she said. "He fell in with a bunch of guys who need to blame someone for their screwed-up lives. Anybody who makes more money than him is the enemy, and that's just about everyone."

I thought about how losing a brother can damage a child but scrubbed the idea of sharing it. Leaning back in the chair, I stared at Wendy O and wondered at the ways anger can twist a body. "So you came here thinking I could help."

"Mom said you raised a lot of money for special-needs kids."

"Your mom had the contacts."

"And Dad said you used to be a police officer."

"In another life."

"He said you know people who can do things the cops can't."

"Claire, I'm sorry to repeat myself but, no. He's wanted for bank fraud, he's kidnapped my grandfather and if you or your brother know where he is, you need to tell me now, before someone gets hurt."

She chewed her lip.

"Would you tell me if you knew?"

"Not really."

"At least you're loyal."

She examined her split ends, as if looking for clues. "You really think he's guilty?"

"It doesn't matter what I think. He's abducted my grandfather and I want him back."

"He says he was framed."

"Why?" I asked. "Who would frame him?"

"He says that's why he wants to hire you."

She rolled up on one haunch and from a back pocket extracted a wallet, setting it on the desk. Someone had stickered the billfold with pictures of Teenage Mutant Ninja Turtles. "I can give you money."

"Claire. . . ."

"It's not much but it's all I have."

"How often does your father call you?"

"Just the once."

"Did he say he'd call again?"

She examined another split end. The turtles smiled at me. "I don't know."

I felt my heart go soft. "Claire, how did you get here?"

"I rode my bike."

"All the way from Spanish Key?"

"We're in season. It's faster than driving."

"Come on." I grabbed my keys. "It's time we had a talk with your mom."

10

WHEN DID YOUR FAMILY move to Spanish Key?" I asked as we crossed the bridge and drove the narrow road that sliced the barrier island in two.

"A couple of years ago." Claire rested her head against the window and didn't look up.

She looked forlorn, orphaned. I wished I'd brought Louie along to keep her company.

"What made your parents want to buy out here?" I asked.

"Mom heard it was cool."

For tourists, the southern end of Spanish Key Beach held the most appeal. The city had built tennis courts, picnic tables and gazebos that sold sandwiches, ice cream and beer. Wooden bridges led through thickets of sea grape toward a line of lifeguard stations. The porcelain sand reflected so much light I'd often check to make sure I was wearing sunglasses. The northern end of the beach compensated for its lack the amenities with a highway maintenance shed.

"You know last year this was voted America's number-one beach," I said. "Do you ever come here?"

"I can live without skin cancer."

Even though it was still early, we had to stop to let a line of people with bikes and strollers cross from the condos to the beach. I gripped the steering wheel and prayed that since I'd called ahead, Ginny Alexander would meet me at the door with a steaming cup of coffee.

"Crowded," was all I could manage to say.

Claire glanced at me. "Don't you sell property here?"

"Yes," I said, feeling the tension ripple up my neck.

"You know what they say."

"What's that?" I asked.

"If you not part of the solution . . . ."

Near the pass that separated Spanish Key from Largo Key to the north, the condos thinned and vegetation screened the beach. It created the ideal spot to house maintenance buildings. And bulldozers. To install a new drainage system, construction crews had torn up the western edge of the street, including the side road to the sheds. Mountains of concrete pipe and sand lined ditches big enough to swallow a car, or walkers, if they weren't careful.

"Good planning," Claire said. "You always want to do major construction during peak season." She glanced at me. "I didn't mean to bust you earlier. I know you have to make a living."

"If you can call it that."

Across the road I spotted a tall man in a blue Oxford shirt and white hardhat holding blueprints and talking with two workers.

"Hang on," I said and pulled into the sandy lot in front of the construction trailer labeled Fox Construction—New York, Philadelphia, Tampa. I rolled down the window. The man waved back and headed our way.

"You know him?" Claire asked and then smacked her forehead with her palm. "Duh. Of course you know him."

"CW," he said, offering a hand.

"Has anyone ever mentioned you look like James Caan?"

He straightened and laughed. "Only the women. The men have other names for me."

"Dean, this is Claire Darby. Claire, this is Dean Caldwell, the construction manager at Fox. He's a friend of a friend."

Dean removed his sunglasses and leaned a hand on the doorframe. "I'm sorry to hear about your grandfather."

"Word travels fast," I said. "I didn't think the police had released the news yet?"

"Walter called. He wanted to know if we had any employees who met Darby's description. I told him we hired the crew months ago."

"Anything out of the ordinary?"

"Just the usual vandalism on a construction site," he said. "Minor stuff. Kids gets bored hanging with their parents on vacation so they try to bust up the equipment—sugar in the fuel lines, that kind of stuff."

"Do you post guards?"

He laughed. "This is a municipal project, lowest bid gets the job. The boss couldn't afford guards. If it was Philly, we'd put up chain-link, but this place is pretty laid back." He glanced over his shoulder as a backhoe bit into the sand. "Did you need something?"

I smiled. "Claire had a question about construction."

Claire flushed.

"She wanted to know why the city would schedule a construction project in the middle of peak season."

He held his hands. "It's like roadwork. You gotta do it sometime. We get another storm like we had three years ago and they'll be laying on this sand in Cuba."

Clouds skirted the horizon, grumbling in protest as the wind urged them inland.

"Dean," I said, "I know it's unlikely that either Darby or my grandfather would turn up at a beach, but could you keep an eye out?"

"Sure." He glanced over his shoulder to watch one of the two men wave. "What are they wearing?"

I described Darby's lawn-care outfit and said Pap always wore faded blue stretch jeans, Velcro shoes and a golf sweater—probably green, since I had the yellow one.

"Will do. Tell Walter it's his turn to buy coffee."

"That was fun," Claire said as I nosed the SUV into the nearly unbroken line of cars.

"It's always good to check in." I pointed two fingers at my forehead and toward the floor. "Eyes on the ground, you know."

"That is so Jason Bourne."

"Like the spy who came in from the cold."

She shook her head. "You need to watch more TV."

"The only TV I watch is with Pap, and I'm not doing a lot of that lately."

We drove in silence. Once clear of the beach, traffic thinned and we passed a row of showcase homes rimming the northern tip of the key. The views, as my colleagues in the real estate trade would say, were dramatic.

From their pools and decks, residents could view thousands of curious tourists on excursion boats. They could listen to the constant thrum of motorboats and be the first on their block to watch the hurricanes roll in. See and be seen. The urge was universal, and expensive.

"You're worried about your grandfather," Claire said.

"And I imagine you're worried about your father."

We cornered and glimpsed the top of the house.

"Mom isn't," she said. "She's been through this before."

I let that one slide.

The Darby estate sat on a spit of land so thin it could only accommodate the road and a single row of homes on either side of the key, but the location offered a nearly endless view of water that took in the Gulf, the pass and Spanish Bay. I turned into the driveway and Virginia Alexander buzzed us through the wrought iron gate. We rolled to a stop between a white Jaguar and a black Jeep with roll bars and no top.

"Why didn't your parents buy a home in a gated community?" I asked. "They'd have more privacy and better security."

The second the SUV stopped Claire opened the door. "You don't know my mom. She spends her whole life impressing people."

I popped the hatch, unloaded Claire's bicycle and took in the surroundings. Standing on a slab of marble, I felt as if I'd stepped into another world. The house belonged in St. Maarten or Curacao rather than on a barrier island in Florida. The architect had designed the home in the Dutch West Indies style, with blazing white walls, warm wood and blue tile accents. Under a gabled roof, narrow doors and windows nested deep in stucco while a white security wall surrounding most of the building tapered toward the beach. It would sell for millions.

I leaned Claire's bicycle against a curling pillar and even though she stood next to me, rang the bell as a courtesy. From deep within the house, a gong sounded low and long as if beckoning us into a cathedral.

Claire opened the door just as her mother gained the entryway.

Ginny Alexander had changed in the past year. Once amply proportioned, she looked as if she'd gained thirty pounds. On the downhill side of forty, she stood a little taller than her husband but a few inches shorter than me. Broad shoulders and hard muscle definition in arms and legs showed a devotion to the gym. Her tan skin hinted at wrinkles about the mouth and eyes, and a spangle of freckles banded her cheekbones and nose. While her hair appeared black, on closer inspection it looked dark brown with hints of red, expertly layered in bangs that swept above her ears. She wore silver hoops as large as hubcaps in each lobe and a silver ball at the top of her left ear.

Put an apple in her hand and she'd resemble Disney's Snow White.

The clothing looked too refined for her figure. A pink-and-white-striped leotard descended into black shorts, ending with flip-flops in sparking silver. A silver band ringed her right big toe and a silver chain surrounded her left ankle.

She puckered blood red lips and held out a big hand roped with veins. "Ginny Alexander." Her grip felt tight and for a moment she looked more like the wicked stepmother than a princess.

"CW McCoy. We worked together on the benefit last year."

"Yes, I remember. You helped set up the decorations at that gala for the handicapped kids."

Actually, I'd taken twenty students with disabilities through a ropes course while she posed for the media. I thought I'd gotten the better deal. What I said was, "Yes, you did a great job of organizing the event." I could out-smarm the best of them when I needed information.

She leveled gray eyes at me. "Thank you for retrieving Claire. I still don't understand what she was doing at your office."

"Mom," Claire said and scooted past, just as a man materialized from the interior of the house and crossed the marble foyer. He wore tight blue nylon shorts and a red tank top. Each bicep looked as if a boa had swallowed a goat.

He walked backward through the open door and twirled his fingers. "Tuesday, my dear?" he said with a faint German accent.

"Yes, Sascha," Ginny Alexander said. "Try not to be late."

As he disappeared into the Jeep, she turned to me. "My personal trainer. He's big on muscle tone but hasn't learned to tell time."

The sound of a mezzo-soprano and the smell of lacquer drifted from the interior. I wondered if did she her exercise routine and nails at the same time.

Claire had disappeared. Ginny led me through the foyer into the living room. Almost every surface gleamed, from the white walls and ceiling to the Henry Moore-like pieces on the coffee table and mantel. The neutral tones contrasted nicely with the dark wood accents of exposed ceiling beams and walnut floor. Glass tables reflected a wall of windows that faced the pool and the Gulf of Mexico.

"Can I get you something to drink? Iced tea? Water? I have sparkling or still."

No coffee? I thought but managed to croak, "No, thank you."

I sank into the couch. Ginny oozed into a chair a few feet away and watched me examine the room. White space dominated, with no sign of pets, books or electronic devices. I bet she banned red wine when she entertained guests.

"Before I married I was an interior designer." She swept about an acre of space with her hand. "In here I created a group of matching sofas in linen. The throw pillows have a West Indies pattern. The carpet's Persian."

"Did you and Mr. Darby build this?"

"About five years ago. We bought at the height of the housing boom. You saw the shacks on the way in?" She pointed toward a south-facing wall.

"Yes."

"They're blocking our view. They were single-story homes when we moved—two if you count the flood-zone elevation. I don't understand people who tear down a perfectly good house so they can build a McMansion."

"Teardowns have become the trend in Spanish Point."

"It's changed the neighborhood. We had two break-ins in the last month and I've had to install a new security system. They're expensive, and the salesman tried to frighten the hell out of me with all that talk about armed intruders. Bunch of savages. They're worse than theater critics."

"Was anything taken?"

"No, that's the strange part. The first time, someone ransacked my bedroom." She paused. "I'm usually the one who does that." Her smile revealed a full set of teeth and gums, like a lizard with a good orthodontist. "I got home from shopping and must have surprised the thief because he left without taking the jewelry."

"And the second?" I asked.

"That was strange, too. The burglar rifled my office . . . our office, Darby used it, too. There were papers everywhere."

I pictured the mess at my place and felt the hair on my arms lift. "Was anything missing?"

She laid her hands in her lap. "Nothing that I could see."

"Are you putting the house on the market?" I itched to drop the bombshell about Darby's reappearance, but if I could get the listing, and an excuse to search the house. . . .

Ginny Alexander sighed. "The court-appointed receiver seized and sold most of Darby's real estate holdings to repay his investors. They allowed me to keep the house, but that's about it."

"So you're staying."

She exhaled enough air to fill the *Hindenburg* and stared at a spot on the ceiling. "It's far too big for the two of us, and between the taxes, insurance and maintenance. . . . I can't even afford a pool cleaning company. Harvey Shaw, he was Darby's business manager, he offered to hire someone to maintain the place—the pool, the lawn and the boats—but I don't see the point. There's no turf grass, it's all ornamental. The creditors took the yacht. And the powerboats just sit there. I don't think anyone uses them except Claire, and she's hardly here these days."

She met my eyes and waited, a silent demand, perhaps, to explain how her daughter had landed in my office. That conversation could wait.

Her calves bulged when she re-crossed her legs. "Darby kept the keys in the boats, under the seat cushion, if you can believe that."

"With all the burglaries, aren't you afraid someone will steal them?"

She wrinkled her nose. "Do you have any idea how much it costs to maintain a boat, let alone two of them? They're like horses with barnacles. I *wish* someone would steal them. I think Darby did, too. He got bored so quickly."

I smiled to show that I sympathized. Just a couple of girls bonding over the burden of luxury goods. "If you ever decide to sell," I said, "I'd be happy to take the listing."

"Well, then." Rising from the chair, she pushed a bang out of her eyes. "Let's give you the nickel tour."

The kitchen looked magnificent, long and spacious with a fully plumbed cooking island, appliances built into cabinets, a professional chef's gas range and miles of granite countertop in a warm honey color that contrasted nicely with the woodwork. I didn't see any sign that she cooked. Not even a bowl of apples.

She sighed. "I'm so tired of white. It's like living with Mr. Clean."

The rest of the house looked equally impressive. As we toured the rooms, Ginny called out the highlights: high ceilings, wine room and a heated salt-water pool with dock and a hundred yards of private beach on either side of the key. Perfect for relaxing or entertaining or cruising to the mainland.

We stopped at a long corridor between the main house and a guest wing with a private entrance. "I can sell it furnished or unfurnished," she said. "I'll keep the artwork, of course, but that's all."

"And these?" I asked, pointing to a wall of eight-by-ten black-and-whites in silver metal frames.

"Memories."

Judging from the number of images, Ginny Alexander had collected photos from every play she'd ever done in community theater. There were pictures of her and Darby on stage in *Oklahoma* and *Show Boat* and others showing the pair with actors long past their prime. In every image her expression looked more like a grimace, with unnaturally large eyes, jutting upper and lower teeth and lips stretched to the breaking point. She'd greased them with dark lip gloss.

Retracing our steps to the living room, Alexander opened the sliding-glass doors and we stepped onto a lanai the size of a small airfield, the covered patio complete with rattan furniture, a full kitchen and wine storage. The space offered a panoramic view of the Gulf of Mexico, Spanish Bay and, in the distance, the marina. Watercraft sailed just off shore, navigating the pass between the house and Largo Key to the north. In the midday sun, the pool glittered a sapphire blue. Apparently Harvey the business manager did a good job of maintaining it.

The one drawback to the house, aside from its susceptibility to hurricane damage and a narrow escape route, was the yard. It looked as if an army of gophers had invaded the turf. The same hillocks littered the beach.

"That," Ginny Alexander said, "is a travesty."

"It looks as if someone's been digging for buried treasure."

"When Darby disappeared, the police dug up every square inch of our property, and they keep coming back. Someone was here just last week."

That didn't sound right. "Looking for the missing money?" I asked.

"They said they'd restore it to its original condition. You can see what they consider original."

"I guess you don't like the police department."

She sighed. "They have no sense of propriety."

"Your husband . . . did he leave you with anything?"

"Not even the proverbial pot," she said.

"I noticed on the photos inside that you use your birth name instead of Darby."

She shaded her eyes and watched a schooner drift beyond the gentle breakers. "Would you take that as your name? I was a fool to marry him. I can't say I'm disappointed he's dead."

Something powerful well up inside me. To find Pap, I needed to find Darby. Whether she'd help, I couldn't say, but telling her the truth seemed the only way to find out.

I took a deep breath. "He's not."

Her hand came down quickly and her face contorted. "What did you say?"

"Your husband has reappeared."

"When? Where?"

"Yesterday, before noon, in my office."

She moved closer and I felt a power like water behind a dam, the kind that would scare the crap out of a young woman like Claire. "What did he want?"

"He claims he was framed and wants me to clear his name."

"And you're helping him?" She cocked her head, her hair falling away from a reddened face.

"No."

"So you're helping the police find him."

"Not exactly," I said. "He asked me to clear his name. When I refused, he kidnapped my grandfather."

"Is that why Claire came to you this morning?"

"Yes. I'm sorry if I appear disingenuous but I had to see you. I don't really care what the police do to your husband. . . ."

"Former husband. The marriage died long before I had him declared dead."

". . . .but I want my grandfather back healthy and whole, and I need your help to do it."

"Claire's been in contact with her father?"

"I think so, but she's not saying."

She turned to look over the water toward the city. "She never does."

"Ms. Alexander . . . Ginny . . . do you know where your husband would hide?"

"The police and the FBI asked me that and I'll tell you what I told them—I have no idea."

"Does he have relatives in the area?"

"They disowned him or died," she said.

"What about friends from high school or college?"

"They're all up north."

"What about his associates?"

She crossed her arms. "I never involved myself with the business."

"Did he leave any records here?"

"As I said, we shared an office . . . a den, really."

"The one you said was burglarized."

Alexander turned toward the house. I followed her into the office. It consisted of white walls and white bookshelves, credenza and a pair of swivel rockers, all done in rattan. A desk with curved cutouts on either side sat in the middle. The desk stood bare except for a pair of photographs in gold frames. As in the living room, a glass wall opened onto the pool. The opposite wall sagged with autographed photos of actors.

From the bottom desk drawer Alexander grabbed a group of file folders and thrust them at me. "This is all that's left. The FBI took the rest, and his computer."

I leafed through the folders. One contained instructions and warrantees for appliances, another receipts for household repairs. As I rifled through the stack, the sound of a very agitated tenor drifted in from the living room.

Alexander stood in front of the window, her face in shadow. "I love opera. I always wanted to play the Met."

"Every time I hear a soprano I want to call 911."

She turned, gave a mirthless chuckle and touched her fingers to her throat. Very demure. "Why, may I ask?"

"All of that screeching. I always think they're in pain."

"Darby hated it. He wouldn't know Pavarotti from a pierogi. If I wanted to see a local production, I had to go with Harv."

"Did he mind, your former husband, I mean?"

"He was too preoccupied with business."

She crossed to the desk and palmed one of the pictures. "I came to marriage late. Bobby Lee was a bit of a desperation move."

"Sorry to hear," I said. "I've taken up enough of your time. Will you be home tomorrow?"

"Most of the day," she said.

"Is it all right if I stop by with the contract and a camera?"

She nodded.

"I'll do comps, but have you thought about a price?"

"We paid $1.7 million for the lot. I don't know what the house cost but we did a lot of upgrades. How does $7.2 million sound?"

"The high-end market has recovered, especially on the Keys. I think you might get it."

She led me through the living room to the foyer and opened the door. "I notice you keep asking questions about Darby and the house but avoid answering mine about Claire."

"Sorry," I said. "I wasn't sure you'd understand."

She crossed her arms. "I'm not the addle-brained socialite many people think I am."

"I would never assume that."

"Good." She gave me a plastic smile.

I felt as if she'd asked me to take a bite of the apple.

11

I LEFT WITH THE feeling that Ginny Alexander's financial problems included more than the house. I could identify. Punching up the smartphone app for my bank, I checked the account balance and winced. I had to sell something or I'd be out of business by summer, so I drove back to the office with the intention of straightening the place and making some calls. I'd contact Jackie and Kurt Stevens and drop by their house for the Meet Jesus talk. Even if their home sold for less than the asking price, I'd still clear enough to last until we found Pap. But before that, I'd stick to my Saturday routine and stop by the farmer's market to refuel. I'd get my coffee if I had to fly to Hawaii and pick the beans myself.

Taking the bridge to the mainland, I headed north on Tamiami Trail, passing the major landmarks in the city, the marina and the Ringling Bridge and the Spanish Point office tower. Traffic crawled through condo canyon by Baywalk and the performing arts center but thinned the further north I drove. I had just merged left into the turning lane for my office when I spotted the tentacles of the TV news vans, hulking white trucks bristling with satellite dishes and booms, emblazoned with familiar logos and slogans—Action News, Gulf Coast News Network, ABC, Fox, even CNN. Not twenty-four hours had passed since Robert Lee Darby spread his venom and the media had made the connection.

To the angry blare of car horns, I raced through the light, pulled into a service station and called Delgado.

"I need your help," I said when he picked up.

"What's wrong?" His voice reminded me of boots on gravel, the sound of a cop displeased with an uncooperative witness.

"Someone broke into my office and the media are camped out there. I need to work. Can you get rid of them?"

I thought I heard him snort. "No."

"Why not?"

"You ever hear of a free press?"

"I thought you were here to serve and protect?"

This time he did snort. "So now you want me to protect you."

"Never mind. I'll tell the vultures what I really think of the investigation."

"Wait," he said. "Don't hang up. We should meet."

"I'm tired," I said. "Can we make this quick? The farmer's market closes at one and I haven't had my coffee yet." I heard the whine in my voice and mentally smacked my forehead.

"OK," he said. "I'll meet you at Java Jive in fifteen."

The first to arrive, I took up a position at the big red truck parked near Main Street. As I stood in line and smelled the beans and brew, I thought I'd faint.

Two minutes later, Det. Tony Delgado sidled up and said, "I've got it. What do you want?"

"Colombian, Grande, black." I pointed toward the empanada stand behind us. "You want one?"

He nodded. "Spicy beef."

I ordered two, the pastry edges crimped and golden, and tossed napkins and packets of hot sauce in the bag. Delgado walked over with the coffee and we sat at a table outside a Spanish-looking restaurant done in yellow adobe, with iron bannisters on the second floor and flowers spilling through the grillwork. We sipped and ate and listened to a group of junior-high kids play rock on instruments they'd made from cereal boxes, plastic toys and garbage cans. They looked tall and scraggly, as if their chins had just considered the idea of sprouting hair, but did a passable job on a Beatles tune.

Delgado blotted his lips, folded the napkin in half and tucked it under his cup. He wore khakis with badge and holster in plain view and a white polo shirt that fit tightly in the arms and chest. Law enforcement chic. A bit distracting.

I sipped coffee. After the hot sauce, the liquid burned my lips but I didn't care. Between the sunshine and the caffeine, I felt myself revive. I also felt determined to keep my personal issues personal.

"So," I said over the rim, "what's so urgent?"

"You paid a visit to Ms. Alexander this morning."

"How do you know that?"

"You gave us permission to track your phone."

"I didn't make any calls from there."

"You don't need to," he said. "We can trace the signal to within three meters."

I sipped some more coffee. "That's reassuring."

"What did you discuss, if I may ask?"

"Well, detective. . . ."

"Tony."

I nodded, although I didn't feel completely comfortable using his given name. "She's putting her house on the market and has asked me to list it."

He pursed his lips, which made his cheekbones pop. Very distracting.

"Did she say anything about her husband and where he might be hiding?"

"No. She claims she doesn't have a clue, or care."

"Is she telling the truth?"

"Hard to tell," I said.

I told him about Claire's visit and the girl's insistence she didn't know her father's location, either. He nodded.

"That's all I have," I said. "How about you?"

"Darby hasn't used his credit cards or passport. We reviewed the footage from the ferry where he allegedly committed suicide. You can see him place the note on a pile of clothes and jump but that's all. He's not showing up at motels or airports or car rental agencies—only your office."

The band had stopped playing. I gave Delgado a look that could wither an acre of wheat and rose to drop a few dollars in the tip jar. "He's using a bike."

"Right," he said. "You did tell us that."

My phone rang. I dug it out of a pocket and hesitated when I didn't recognize the caller. "If someone had given the media my cellphone number. . . ."

Glancing at the screen, Delgado motioned for me to sit. "Put it on speaker." When he moved his chair next to mine, I smelled the faint scent of soap.

"CW McCoy," I said.

"BL Darby," he said. "I know you've got a trace on this so I'll make it brief. What kind of progress are you making?"

My stomach flipped. "After I talk with my grandfather."

"He's not here."

I listened to the tinny voice and stared at the screen clicking off the seconds and felt a giant hand squeeze my chest. "Where is he?"

"Now, Candy," Darby said. "You know I can't tell you that. All you need to know is that he's somewhere safe."

His voice sounded smooth and casual, as if we were two buddies setting a tee time.

"You still there?"

The possibilities were infinite, and none of them good. I swallowed. "Yes."

"So what progress have you made?"

A vision of the man in my office flooded my head, his face too broad for his body, cheeks puffy, eyes hard as agate. Delgado twirled his index finger in a circle, stepped away from the table and pulled out his phone.

"I talked to your former wife this morning," I said, watching the detective's shoulders as he barked into the phone and returned to the table. "She doesn't like you very much."

"You told her I'm back?"

"I've told everyone you're back."

"Why?" He sounded puzzled.

"More people to track you down."

"Ganging up on me?"

"Your daughter's on your side."

"Claire?" he said.

"She stopped by this morning to plead your case."

Delgado put a hand over his phone and mouthed, "Keep him talking."

"What's that noise in the background?" Darby asked, an edge to his voice.

"The farmer's market. Where are you?"

He chuckled.

"Does Claire know where you are?"

79

"Nice try."

"You're putting her in danger."

"She's a knucklehead but she means well, and you know I do, too. I'm sorry but this was the only way to get your attention."

"Where's my grandfather?"

"You have a one-track mind." He sighed. "He's in a safe place. I didn't think you'd exactly jump at the opportunity to help, so I took out a little insurance."

"How astute," I said. "My grandfather is in his eighties. He has a nasty combination of Alzheimer's and Parkinson's disease. He wanders and falls a lot. Can you handle that responsibility?"

"I've got it covered."

I looked for Delgado but he'd disappeared. "You going to add manslaughter to the list of charges?"

When he spoke, his voiced sounded hard. "You need to stop talking and find out who framed me. Then you get to see your precious pappy."

"How do I know he's alive?"

"I'll send you an ear, and keep one as a souvenir."

"You are such a scumbag."

"Sticks and stones," he said. "Just so we're clear, I've given you a job. It's up to you to determine the execution . . . no pun intended." And he disconnected.

All the anger I'd suppressed came raging back. I stared at the phone as if it had refused to find Pap. Then I called Oz.

"Darby just called. Did you trace him?"

"Delgado's on it."

"Where's Darby?"

I heard keystrokes. "On the water off Spanish Key."

"Can you dispatch somebody?"

"SPD Marine's on the way," he said, "although Darby'll toss the phone before they get there."

"Delgado just left. He's not telling me squat. I need more information."

"You want to meet me at the marina?"

"Where?" I asked.

"The dolphin fountains by the restaurant."

"When?"

"An hour."

I called Walter and Cheryl and left messages and headed to Pap's. Ripping the crime-scene tape from the door, I stormed into my room. From under the bed I slid the metal box onto my lap, popped the lock with the key I kept around my neck and withdrew the Beretta .25. Unlike police-issued weapons, it had a single-action trigger—you pulled once and it fired, no stops in between. Eight rounds in the magazine, one in the chamber, no safety lock. I set the gun on the floor with the rag and went to work, the tang of oil filling my nose, the image of Darby's canine smile polluting my thoughts. I rammed the magazine home and chambered a round. Strapping the holster to my ankle, I stood and practiced dropping to a knee and drawing the weapon, aiming at his imaginary heart. If he had one.

Even gripped in both hands, the gun shook. Is this what my father had done? Had he smashed mom's head with the butt of a pistol and then torched his own house? I felt the blood rise up my neck to scorch my face, old blood, bad blood, the sins of the father visited on the daughter, the fire of anger and frustration coursing through my veins. I gulped air. Unbuckling the holster, I put the works back in the lockbox and shoved it under the bed, praying that Delgado would find the bastard first.

12

FIRING UP THE KAWASAKI, I made it to the marina in twelve minutes. With the helmet tucked under my arm, I walked past sculptures of giant wrenches and heads and waved at the tourists on the Barge, the biggest floating house party in Palmetto County. A filigreed metal archway led to Island Park, a peninsula that hooked around the mooring field like a bent thumb. Only a thread of water separated the fountains from the marina restaurant, which floated on a concrete pier, its glass walls decanting the afternoon sun.

Oz sat at the tip of the park in front of four bronze dolphins squirting water into a pool. Feet dangling in the water, eyes shadowed by a driving cap, his thumbs flew over the surface of a tablet computer. I couldn't imagine reading the screen in the blazing sun but he seemed to manage. Beyond the fountain, channel markers warned boaters to slow to idle speed, yet some raced dangerously close to the restaurant and the outdoor diners, the wake threatening to breach the seawall.

I sat beside him. "This is a weird harbor. The park sticks out into the bay and all the boats have to sail around it to get to the marina. What if you brought a speedboat in here?" I pointed to the restaurant and the dozens of diners perched under umbrellas on the deck. "The wash would drown half the tourists in Spanish Point."

"Designed by the same genius who did the performing arts hall."

"That fire trap without aisles? You're kidding."

He looked up from his tablet and smiled.

"You are kidding," I said.

Oz held up a hand to shade his eyes. They looked pale gray today with long lashes under thick brows, part of a handsome if preoccupied face. "Hello to you, too."

"Sorry, I'm stressed."

"Understandable."

"You want lunch?"

"Nah," he said, "I had a Pop Tart at the office."

I took a deep breath. "OK, enough of the fun and games. Where's Darby when he isn't on the water?"

"I've traced him through a cousin with a record for shoplifting. Cross-referenced that to the last-known sighting of Darby's vehicle and the report of a teller who says a man matching Darby's description cashed a check from a local firm last week."

"Don't tell me," I said. "It's a lawn-care company."

"Close," Oz said. "Irrigation."

"What's the name?"

""Spanish Point Irrigation Services, Inc."

"That's original. Who owns it?"

"Roger Hernandez."

"Roger?"

"Short for Rogelio."

"Where's he located?"

"Nine miles south." He read the address. "You'd better move. The cops'll be there any minute."

I stood. "How'd you get here?"

"Walked."

I handed the helmet to him. "You like speed?"

He smiled and tucked the tablet in a backpack. "Drive on."

* * *

The house sat just north of the city of Venice in an ungated community protected only by palm trees and flowers. It had survived the onslaught of retirees fairly well. We sailed through a pillared entrance and hung a right at the junction of the Legacy Trail, slowing so we wouldn't startle the bicyclists and walkers on the old railroad bed.

The Hernandez house looked like most of the homes in Palmetto

County, a single-story Mediterranean Revival, but with an unusually tall garage and a bright red pickup truck in the drive. The garage door stood open to reveal stacks of pipe and two kayaks bolted to the wall. We walked the pavers to the house and rang the bell.

Roger Hernandez answered the door. Somewhere in his thirties, he looked short and dark and dressed in work clothes of long-sleeved khaki shirt and pants. As Oz and I introduced ourselves, he bowed slightly and opened the door.

"Mr. Hernandez," I began.

"Yes, boss." He smiled to show a row of teeth slanted like a picket fence.

"We're sorry to bother you, but we'd like to know if you've seen either of these men." I handed him the picture of Pap and both the photo and composite of Bobby Lee Darby.

The house extended in shotgun fashion through a living room with brown leather couches to a lanai and pool, a gray bed skirt in a room to the left, a bulky table of carved black wood on the right. The air felt cool and smelled of ground beef and spice.

Hernandez shook his head and returned the photos but stared at the composite.

"He could have changed his appearance since that sketch was made," I said.

"You recognize him?" Oz asked.

"Yes, Mr. Oz. Two weeks ago, I hired a new man, but he quit."

"When?" I asked, resisting the temptation to smile at Mr. Hernandez's deference.

"Yesterday. He didn't show up for work for three days. You don't call in, you quit, capiche?"

"Capiche?" I said.

"Si." He grinned.

"Do you know where he was living?"

Hernandez pointed toward the side of the house. "He rented a room, above the garage."

"May we see it?" I asked.

Fishing a key from his pocket, he led us around the back of the garage and up a flight of stairs. The room looked unoccupied, the curtains open, the bed made. I saw no books, no clothes, no suitcase . . . and no bicycle.

Darby must have cleared out days ago.

"Mr. Hernandez," I said, "what can you tell us about him?"

"He was good with his hands. He was quiet. Sometimes he talk about boats. He knew a lot about them."

"He talked to you?" Oz asked.

"He talk to the men." Hernandez smiled and shook his head. "His Spanish . . . it's terrible."

"So's his acting," I said. "Any idea where he'd go?"

"No, no idea."

We thanked him and were heading toward the bike when Oz turned back.

"Mr. Hernandez, did Darby pick up his last paycheck?"

"No, Mr. Oz, he didn't want one. I only paid him once by check and he said cash only from then on."

"And he paid his rent in cash."

"Yes."

"You didn't think that was strange?" I said.

"It's hard to work in this country." Hernandez waved his hands past his ears. "I don't mean to put flowers in my hair, but I take care of the men. If they need money or a place to stay, I give them. Not a lot of questions, capiche?"

We rode the Tamiami Trail north to police headquarters, sliding into the same spot Walter had used earlier that morning. It felt like a lifetime ago.

I climbed off the bike. "This is the tail wagging the dog."

"A dead dog."

"We're chasing Darby based on where he's been," I said. "We need to focus on the people who have something to lose."

"Hunt the hunter."

"So where does that leave us?"

Oz handed the helmet to me. "Without a date."

"That's random."

"It's opening night at the film festival."

"You have tickets?"

"I have contacts," he said.

"Thanks, but I've got to clean up my office this afternoon."

"I hear one of the Kennedy clan will be there."

I hesitated. I didn't mind a little celebrity sighting as long as nobody expected me to beg for autographs. I'd always gone for jocks in high school and college but I could make an exception for Oz. Bright, energetic, quick . . . he had a smart sense of humor and an unwavering confidence that I admired.

"The dress code," I said. "It's cocktail, isn't it? I'll need to change."

"Pick me up at six," he said. "And wear your leathers."

13

B EFORE I COULD GO anywhere, I had to tackle the office. On hands and knees, I scooped papers into file folders and was sliding them into the cabinet when the front door opened and Jackie Stevens blew in like a tropical storm. She threw her keys on the desk and glared at me. I shut the drawer and watched the coffeepot threaten to topple.

"Mind the drip." Climbing to my feet, I pointed to a ceiling tile that threatened to collapse near her head. "How can I help you?"

Stevens looked more like a forward for the Pittsburgh Penguins than the former admin for an insurance company. Five foot six with flaming red hair, broad shoulders and hips made wider by a too-short skirt, she had small breasts pushed up by one of those so-called miracle bras—although the only astonishing thing about the garment was the amount of money people made on the insecurity of women.

With fists on hips she said, "I want to know what you're doing to sell our house."

I got to my feet. "Everything I can." The coffeemaker had stopped wobbling and I pointed to the pot. "Would you like some?"

"No," she said. Flexing blood-red fingernails, she picked up her keys and dropped them on the desk again. "I want to know why we haven't had any traffic in three months."

The woman bullied her kids and her husband but she wasn't going to get away with it here. I blew out some air and stared up at Wendy O. for inspiration. She had none.

"Jackie," I said in my best Aunt Candice voice, "until you talk to me like an adult, we're not going to have this conversation."

"I want to know. . . ."

I held up a hand and pushed into her space, towering over her, shading her eyes, my nose so close to her forehead I could see the black roots where the ribbon of white scalp parted her hair like the Red Sea. She backed up quickly.

"Why don't we take a moment to put this in perspective," I said. "I know you and your husband are underwater and need a fair price for your house, and I am in complete agreement that it will make a lovely home for a deserving family." I looked into her eyes to see if any of this registered.

She crossed her arms. With Jackie, that signaled a maybe at best.

"I'd like to discuss this when your husband is present so we can all agree on a course of action. Do you and Kurt have any free time later today?"

She reached into a bag with a shiny pull and the designer's initials stamped across the fabric and extracted a phone, scrolling through the calendar and shaking her head to show me she was not only efficient but important. "I have to take Shayla to cheerleading and Ash has a wrestling match tonight but we're free for the next hour." With that she clicked off the phone, shoved it into her bag and, at the last minute, remembered to smile. Grabbing her keys, she pivoted on a pair of wedges and slammed the door on the way out.

"Goodbye to you, too," I said and gave the door a small wave.

She hadn't commented the floor littered with files. She hadn't even noticed.

I took in a breath. Jackie may have acted like her pre-teen children but I sympathized with her. Like millions of homeowners, the Stevens family had miscalculated. They assumed the economic system was stable and run by people who played by the rules. They didn't know about collateralized debt obligations or credit rating services that lied about the pedigree of those debt instruments.

When the pump-and-dump schemes the investment bankers ran eventually collapsed, the Stevens family hadn't calculated that the world's financial system would follow suit, and that they'd wind up paying for other people's greed. So they bought as much home as they could afford on two salaries and got a big mortgage with little down. They didn't realize they'd purchased at the height of the housing bubble, or that prices would backtrack ten years and they'd get stuck with a mortgage that cost more than their house was worth. Or that the resulting recession would force both of them out of work or into inferior jobs.

But bad luck would not derail Jackie Stevens. She and Kurt wanted to move to a larger home in their community so the kids wouldn't have to change schools. Despite my advice, Jackie had priced the house to cover the remainder of the mortgage. For the first three months of our six-month seller's agreement, she and Kurt hadn't budged. I couldn't blame them for wanting to dig out from a mountain of debt, but I couldn't remember the last time we'd shown the home. Now we had to have the dreaded conversation about lowering the price, which would go down about as well as my confrontation with Bobby Lee Darby.

I thought about misplaced trust and injustice on the drive to their gated community in the center of Palmetto County. I'd calculated the time needed to meet, drive home, eat, change and pick up Oz and decided the schedule was tight but doable.

The community of Palmetto Ranch glowed like a jewel, with clean sidewalks, freshly painted streetlamps and lush vegetation surrounding homes and common areas. Builders had created most houses in the Mediterranean Revival style, with the three-bedroom, three-car-garage variety dominating the stock. Most featured landscaped yards, barrel-tile roofs and pavers on driveways and walks.

The Stevens house looked a little more downscale, a two-bed, one-and-a-half bath with a two-car garage. I stepped onto a cracked concrete driveway and looked up at a shingled roof and cement block wall whose mortar showed through the paint. The flowerbeds hadn't seen mulch in years. Not exactly curb appeal. I took a deep breath and rang the doorbell.

Shayla met me at the door. She looked twelve going on twenty with pink hot pants and a T-shirt that showed a roll of belly. She wore a pound of eye makeup and purple nail extensions. I wanted to ask Jackie and Kurt why they'd named their daughter after a porn star but Jackie's manner of dress said it all. The sound of the couple arguing in one of the back rooms mixed with the pop and stutter of a video game as the younger sibling, Ashton, wriggled in front of the TV as if he had to pee. Shayla disappeared. A door slammed. The argument continued.

I looked around the house. Wires and consoles spilled from the TV. Pants and socks hung from the back of the couch. Dishes and pans choked counters and sink. Beer cans in neat rows lined the shelves. At least they had their priorities straight.

Two cats twined through my legs and from the direction of the garage, a dog barked. I smelled the lightly rotted scent of tuna. The house provided a decent amount of space, about 2,100 square feet under air, but the clutter proved they'd outgrown the place. In addition to lowering the price, they'd have to hire a cleaning service.

I heard Jackie say, "Kurt, you are so full of shit," before she walked to the door and led me to a table off the kitchen. Kurt joined us. With his curly blond hair, he looked like an older version of Ken. Too bad he'd married the Barbie from Hell.

Ever the hostess, Jackie didn't offer anything to drink. Spreading a pile of papers on the table, she picked up a pen and furiously clicked the top, her nails glistening like wet paint. Kurt assumed a self-effacing grin and stared through the kitchen window onto the lanai where a pool should have been.

I scanned the countertops for coffee but settled for writing tools. "May I borrow your tablet?" I asked and, as Jackie slid the legal pad across the table, punched up the calculator app on my smartphone. "Now these are just rough numbers—I'm using simple interest while the bank will use compound interest—but they illustrate the situation."

Jackie gave me the killer stare. Kurt looked into the lanai of the neighbor in back.

"You bought the house for $675,000 and put ten percent down, money you received from both sets of parents, I believe, and took out a thirty-year note. That left you with a mortgage of $607,500, or $1,688 per month. With interest, hazard insurance and taxes, your monthly payment comes to about $2,500. Is that correct?"

Jackie gave a nearly imperceptible nod. Kurt continued to stare into the neighbor's yard.

"When the recession took hold, Kurt was forced to take a lower-paying job and Jackie, you left the insurance agency to study for the real estate exam."

"I was forced out."

"I'm sorry," I said. "So you haven't been able to pay any additional principle?"

The sound of screaming cars and gunfire burst from the living room.

Light from the television flickered across Jackie's eyes. I could read nothing beside controlled hostility.

"No," she said.

"OK." I quickly jotted the numbers from my calculator on the pad. "Over the past five years, you've paid about $102,000 in principle, reducing the note to $505,000. That's excellent, by the way. The CMA—the comparable market analysis—I did for you three months ago showed homes of similar size and condition selling in the mid-four hundreds, which is why I suggested a starting price of $465,000."

"I am not going to take a loss on this house," Jackie said and stabbed the table with the pen. "We either get five-twenty-five-nine or we pull it off the market."

"We all have emotional attachments to our homes," I said, "but the house is competing with much larger ones with more amenities in the same community."

From my tote I pulled a thick binder of comps that examined pending, active, sold and expired listings. I showed them prices on comparable homes, all in the four-hundred-thousand-dollar band but most clustered around $449,900. I displayed listings for larger models in their neighborhood, the ones with water views whose asking price ranged from $500,000 to $650,000.

"Homebuyers will pay more for a house that has more space and amenities. If you price in this range," I said, pointing to the larger structures fronting the lake, "you're placing yourself at a competitive disadvantage."

Jackie straightened. "We put a lot into this house with paint and wallpaper and shelves and digging out those stupid fruit trees, and we're entitled to a profit. I'm not going to give the place away."

"And we're going to make sure you don't," I said. "But there are several aspects that handicap the home against some of the larger ones in the community."

Kurt finally spoke, swinging his head to look at my forehead, nose, breasts—everywhere but my eyes. "Like what?"

"The smaller rooms, the shingle roof, the lack of a pool and water view."

"The house across the road just sold for the same price we're asking," Jackie said, giving the paperwork another stab for good measure, "and it's not half as nice."

It doesn't have the extensive collection of beer cans, unwashed laundry and video games, I wanted to say but checked the notepad instead. "I know it's an unfair comparison, but we're competing with 3,200-square-foot homes with four beds, three baths, three-car garages, tiled roofs and pools. Some of them have lake access or water views. That alone can add $50,000 to the price of the home."

"So what are you saying?" Jackie asked.

"I know you need $500,000 to clear the mortgage, and I'd love to be able to honestly tell you that we can get that, but unfortunately the market will give you only what buyers are willing to pay."

"Maybe," Kurt said, looking out the window again, "we should just lower the price."

"I am *not* lowering the price!" Jackie said, banging out every word on the tabletop. "Is that what you're asking me to do? Give up all we've worked for just so someone can make a fast buck on us?"

She gave me the eye and I felt my insides curl.

"What about a short sale?" Kurt asked.

"Kurt, no," Jackie said.

"So we bought more house than we could afford."

"I said no."

"Let's just admit it and move on."

"Kurt, shut up," Jackie yelled, jamming the tabletop with the plastic pen until it snapped. "Just shut the fuck up."

I stood. "How about I leave you to discuss this in private?"

On the way out, I spotted Shayla in the bedroom window. She stood absolutely still, arms crossed, staring at nothing. She looked morose.

I knew how she felt.

14

O
N THE WAY HOME, I dropped by the Spanish Point Fish Camp to
pick up a takeout of blackened grouper sandwich and fries and
brightened when I spotted Rae Donovan behind the bar. Rae
stood about five foot ten and weighed in at close to 190. In winter she
sported a red-and-black plaid shirt. In summer she wore almost nothing at
all, which miraculously tripled her tips. To patrons, she presented the image
of a pleasant woman with a good ear and an easy laugh, a barkeep who
celebrated every moment as if it were St. Patrick's Day. To friends, she was
the woman who'd survived a bitter divorce, built the Camp into a popular
tourist attraction and served as the unofficial leader of the city's Old Girl
Network.

The Camp sat on one of the most desirable parcels in Spanish Point,
sandwiched between the Ringling Bridge and Baywalk with a view of Largo
Key, one of the richest pieces of real estate in Palmetto County. Rae had
taken an old fishing shack and built a tiki hut for the bar and a low lean-to
for the restaurant. The dock served as the dining area, with plastic tables
and chairs lounging under yellow umbrellas emblazoned with the names of
imported beer. In the corner a Wurlitzer stood ready to take coins and, in
the back, two pinball machines beckoned to wizards who lived to see them
tilt.

Visitors drove their Land Rovers into the lot and admired the sunset.
The regulars motored to the dock, tied up, drank up and ignored nature
until it called them to empty their bladders. Lately the Camp had attracted a
mix of bikers, cops, politicians and tourists, all of whom got along fine.

Today was no different. A party of a dozen young women whooped it up at a picnic table on the far side of the dock, encouraged by one of the regulars, a muscular boatman in a ripped T-shirt known as Drunk Eddie, who believed he was God's gift to women and that Bud was the king of beers. O for two. He was at least twice as old and three times as drunk as the women. No one seemed to notice.

I slung a hip onto a barstool and waved to Rae. Standing at the end of the bar, she poured a beer for a fat guy in madras shorts and orange fishing shirt with a flap yoke to let out the steam. In the light reflecting off the water, Rae's face looked rugged with big pores, broad nose and blue-gray eyes under a thatch of brow. She had a broadcaster's voice that could peel beer labels at twenty feet and the courage let her hair go gray. Today she wore hiking boots with socks, cargo shorts in camo green and a pink Oxford unbuttoned halfway to the South Pole. Most of the women and all of the men watched her move. Rumor had it she kept a married boyfriend in town who kept the city from condemning the property for high-rise condos.

Seize the day.

She came down the bar and squeezed my wrist. "I'm sorry to hear about Pap."

"Word travels fast."

"You hear anything from this Darby character?"

I shook my head. "Just another threatening call . . . help clear the bastard's name or something bad will happen."

"This is the finance guy who's supposed to be dead."

"He will be if I get to him first."

Rae released her grip and smoothed my wrist. "Easy girl. Lotta cops and lawyers around, and they don't have my maternal instincts."

I stared at the clutch of women who were falling all over themselves. "Who are those guys?"

"Bridal party, celebrating before the big event."

Raising red plastic cups over their heads, the women teased the bride-to-be and toasted each other. They wore short tops and shorter skirts and fell easily into each other's arms. Holding his own cup in front as if it were a compass, Eddie moved closer. *The better to see you, my dear.*

"They're not driving, are they?"

"They'll stay off the roads for a while," Rae said and brought me an ice water while we waited for the food.

"Their sunglasses are bigger than their clothes."

"Eddie doesn't have a problem with that," she said.

"Eddie never has a problem . . . or a job."

We watched as the woman stumbled down the dock and tipped themselves into a boat, skirts hiked up around their butts and Eddie cheering them on with tips on how to steer clear of the pier. They didn't listen because the bride-to-be backed into one of the pilings and bounced off another before the craft lurched into the bay.

"Drunk already?" I asked.

"Wedding night jitters," Rae said.

"You rent them the boat?"

"Just doing my bit to promote the local economy."

Eddie walked toward us, gave me the once-over and leaned an elbow on the bar. He held his cup in his right hand and used it and his index finger to point at the departing boat. "They're going to need a ton of aspirin tomorrow."

"They're going to need life preservers tonight," I said.

He waved away the comment as if swatting a fly, asked for a refill and wandered into the parking lot to talk to the bikers.

The curly-haired cook came out the side door with a slop bucket and began tossing fish pieces to a brown pelican perched on a piling.

"I see Gus is still your unofficial mascot," I said.

"Hey!" Rae yelled at the cook. "I told you not to feed him. He bothers the customers."

The tourists yelled back and within seconds they were taking selfies with the bird. Rae shook her head and smiled.

"You encourage them," I said.

"They're like city council," Rae said. "Tell 'em what not to do and they'll do it every time."

"Good for business."

"God bless Facebook."

She walked to the end of the bar to pull a couple of beers and when she returned said, "How are you holding up?"

"We've all had better days. Have you seen anybody you don't recognize?"

Condensation streamed off the glasses on the bar. Rae lifted them carefully and mopped the water with a clean dishrag. "I did notice a young woman I haven't seen in here before." The description she gave fit Claire.

"When was this?"

"Today, around one. She had a boat, a small runabout with twin Mercs. She handled it pretty well."

"What did she order?"

"Takeout. Burgers, fries, coleslaw, chips, couple cans of soda and a veggie burger and salad. Skinny girl, looked as if was eating for ten. No booze—she's underage. Left the way she came."

"Which way?" I asked.

Rae pointed down the channel. "South."

A bell rang and she ducked into the kitchen. On the bay, the boatload of women stalled and several leaned over the motors, their halter tops overflowing, causing the craft to list and the guys to line the dock. The women took each other's pictures, the pelican flew a recon mission and, from the parking lot, Eddie waved at the boat, beer spilling down his forearm, his tongue lapping up the foam.

As Rae handed me the paper bag I said, "Too many tourists, Rae. They're going to ruin your image."

"Bitch, bitch," she said. "How are you going to land a guy with an attitude like that?"

I grabbed the bag and hefted my keys and watched the wedding party motor into the bay. "Maybe I'll learn to sail."

15

COCKTAIL ATTIRE MEANS DIFFERENT things to different people. To the crowd milling outside V-PAC, it meant big heels and breasts.

Opening night of the Spanish Point International Film Festival also meant lines. Oz and I arrived at the hall in time to anchor the back of the longest one. On the plus side, our position provided a clear view of the red carpet, with its news crews and photo backdrop infested with corporate logos . . . and a better view of the express lane for VIPs. Despite the heat, they all wore black with slit skirts and necklines that converged near the equator. Around their necks hung badges the size of dinner plates. The albatross of privilege.

Oz and I had interpreted *cocktail* in a more informal way. He wore pressed jeans and a black leather vest over a white muslin shirt with the tails out. I chose one of my meet-the-client outfits of blazer, slacks and blouse in black and teal. I'd accessorized with a small black packet purse on a thin cord. Oz made his concession to fashion with a smartphone, into which he'd buried his head like a duck in a pond.

"Police business?" I said as sweetly as possible.

He didn't look up.

"Something vital to national security, like FarmVille or Words with Friends?"

"Poker."

When he did look up, he seemed surprised to see me.

"Hey," he said, taking in my outfit. "You match the building."

"Color or size?" I said.

"Bad move?"

"Not if you want to remain celibate for the rest of your life."

He trousered the phone.

"Let's try that again," I said. "What's the film tonight?"

"A documentary about Southeast Asia."

"Is it any good?"

"It's an indie film," he said.

"And that means. . . ."

"It means your feet won't stick to the floor."

People-watching proved more entertaining than our conversation. As we inched forward, a woman arrived in a black SUV, dismounted and handed the keys to a valet in a blue vest. Leslie Walker had a pile of blonde hair and more cleavage than the Grand Canyon. An anchor for the Gulf Coast News Network, she wore a silver lamé dress and matching stiletto heels that looked tall enough to cause a nosebleed. With the directors and stars lining up for interviews, she joined her crew before the backdrop. Lights flashed, the sound technician dropped the boom mike into range and Leslie Walker switched her low-beam smile to high.

"Maybe we should have given the bike to the valet," Oz said.

"I'd sooner wear pantyhose."

He glanced at my legs to make sure he hadn't missed anything.

"By the way," I said, "how'd you score the tickets?"

"The detective." He pointed toward the sidewalk, where a well-tailored Tony Delgado walked toward the hall. "Said it was punishment for helping you with the case."

"He did?" I stared at Delgado. "I'm outraged. Simply outraged."

Oz smiled as an Amazon lurch by on platform shoes. I tracked the detective as Walker guided him by the elbow into the shot. We'd reached the entrance to the hall but I pulled Oz aside so we could overhear the interview. Walker asked the detective about the hunt for the infamous Bobby Lee Darby and the oodles of loot he'd squirreled away. The setup took longer than Delgado's answer. To his credit, he stuck to what we knew and declined to speculate. When he saw us, he held up a hand and walked over.

"Nice interview," I said.

"Oodles of fun."

"Thanks for keeping them off my back," I said.

"All part of the service."

He wore dark brown slacks, black blazer and a white shirt with a collar secured with a single cloth-covered button.

"You're looking sharp," I said.

"Clothes make the man," he said.

"You know Oz," I said. "He's my date."

Delgado nodded to him and said, "My condolences," then gave me the once-over before settling on my face.

I flushed and hunted for something to say. "I didn't know you liked indie films."

"I like a challenge." His grin threatened to break into a smile.

"Speaking of a challenge," I said. "I see you've tangled with the bottle blonde. What's she like in person?"

"Aggressive and outspoken. You'd like her."

"Thanks for the endorsement. Anything more on the investigation you didn't share with Miss Action News?"

"Miss Action News has a bachelor's in engineering from Purdue and an MBA from Wharton. In a few years she'll own the station."

I glanced at Walker, noted the way she filled out the dress and wanted to snipe that she'd probably sleep her way to the top. But I squelched the complaint, reminding myself that attacking other women over stupid things would only bring us all down.

Delgado noted the introspection and changed his tone. "In answer to your question, I told them to be on the lookout for your grandfather."

"Thank you."

"And that you said he looks like Tony Bennett."

"Wiseass."

We moved inside, into a wall of people. In addition to building a venue without center aisles in a retirement community full of citizens with leg and balance issues, the architect had located the restrooms and bar near the entrance to the auditorium, making movement nearly impossible.

"What have you come up with on Darby?"

Delgado gave me the cop stare. "I gave you everything we have this morning."

"If anything happens to Pap. . . ."

Our eyes locked.

He spoke first. "You'll do what."

A cold sweat broke out on my arms and neck. "You think I'll shoot him."

Imperceptibly he moved his head. "At this point, I don't think anything."

We edged toward the seats.

I took a deep breath. "Tell me about Harvey Shaw. What do you know about him?"

"What I told you. He was Darby's business manager, and we have no proof of wrongdoing."

"But you think he's involved."

The line stopped moving. Delgado crossed his arms, shoulders straining his sports coat. "He's not a suspect at this time."

"I'd like a crack at him."

"I thought we agreed that you would limit your involvement," he said.

"I got involved the minute Darby kidnapped my grandfather."

"We have the resources to handle it."

The press of people had triggered a mild but irritating version of claustrophobia. "I'll tell you what you need to handle—Sal Finzi. He's welched on alimony and child support and threatened his wife and child." The minute the charge left my mouth I regretted saying it.

Delgado started hard. "Has Officer Finzi reported the threat?"

"No."

"Has she filed a PFA?"

"You know that's next to worthless."

"I know we have to work within the law," he said. "I suggest you do the same." He waved to someone and walked away.

"That was productive," Oz said.

"Whose side are you on?"

"Mine," he said. "Besides, I think you like him."

"He annoys the hell out of me."

"If I wasn't so manly," Oz said, "I'd be jealous."

From the corner of my eye I caught a glimpse of a black-haired woman in a yellow knife-pleat skirt and navy bodice with puff sleeves. She and a large man wearing a hound's-tooth sports coat breezed through the VIP line. As they entered the hall, the man placed his hand in the small of her back and let it trail over her butt.

I pointed with my chin. "Ginny Alexander."

"She looks like Snow White."

"Do you recognize the guy?" I asked.

"Harvey Shaw."

"Ah," I said, trying to get a good look at him and failing. "Let's go."

My phone rang, and as I raced to silence it, recognized the caller ID and fought my way through the lobby. Outside, the wind had picked up and thunder sounded faintly in the distance. I plugged a finger into my ear and took the call.

"Hello, Mrs. T. Is everything all right?"

"I'm just so mad I could spit."

I waved Oz toward me. "What is it? Are you all right?"

"It's the homebuyers' association."

"Do you mean homeowners' association?" I asked, wincing at her mangled English and my misguided effort to correct her.

"Yes, they're fining me a hundred dollars a day for violating some cockamamie rule about painting the house."

"A day?" I asked and mentally told myself to shut up and listen. "What happened?"

"You know how much I like purple. It reminds me of our house in Pittsburgh and the flowerbeds we used to have, and the hat that George gave me for Easter that I wore to church, the one with sprigs of lavender. Well, I decided to follow your suggestion about doing some of the work around the house myself, you know, to keep me occupied since I'm here alone with the cats since George passed away. So last week I bought a can of paint and a brush at the home something and decorated the front doors. They're made from palmeroosa pine and that will take any kind of paint."

"Ponderosa?" I said to no one in particular.

"And now the homeowners have sent me a cease and detest order and told me to put it back the way it was or they're going to throw me out on the street with the trash. They can't do that, can they?"

I thought I heard a sniffle. "Mrs. T., I'm sorry the house isn't working out as well as we'd hoped but this really is job for your son, the attorney."

"I know, but he's so busy, and you've always been so nice."

OK, I thought. *Deep breath.* "Mrs. T., could you call your neighbor, Mrs. Townsend? Maybe she could help."

"Oh, I couldn't bother her. She leads such an active life. Do you know she's still driving at ninety-one? What a godsend, since the doctor made me give up my license. We go to St. Thomas for a case of beer once a week."

Beer? I thought. *Fort Meyers, maybe?* "That's wonderful," I said. "Do you have Mrs. Townsend's number?"

"Oh yes. My son put her on speed dial."

I needed to put my life on speed dial. Oz crinkled his forehead. He had a lot of forehead.

I told Mrs. T. that sounded like a plan and disconnected just as the first drops of rain spattered the lot. *Great*, I thought. I hadn't brought an umbrella. Or the SUV.

We hurried through the lobby and into the hall. It had filled quickly. We bumped knees, excused ourselves a dozen times and finally took our seats in the middle, about five rows behind the Kennedys.

"Crank call?" Oz asked.

"You could say that." I explained that ever since I'd sold Marion Taggert her home, I'd become her go-to person when anything breaks.

"She sounds batty," he said.

"She's eighty-four and in full possession of her facilities," I said, smacking my head at my own confusion. "Faculties. She's in full possession of her faculties, except those involving speech and judgment."

"Sounds like a geek."

"Yes," I said. "The two of you could use your secret decoder rings to communicate."

We settled back and listened to a dozen presenters express gratitude for the weather, their sponsors and the Lumière brothers. Oz yawned three times.

I leaned over and whispered, "How close are to you tracking down the investors?"

"Couple of hours. Come by after this."

"That a proposition?"

He grinned. "No need."

"Women admire overconfidence."

He wrinkled his brow.

"Listen," I said, "I can't stay long. I've got to list the Alexander house tomorrow, and Darby's still loose."

"You could leave that to the pros."

"I could leave my body to science," I said as the auditorium went black.

"Why don't you leave it to me?"

As the film began, a picture of Pap in his yellow golf sweater and putty-colored Velcro shoes flooded my mind. He'd served during World War II, survived the fighting in the Pacific Theater and returned home to create a safe and comfortable life . . . until his granddaughter moved in. It was a wrong I needed to right.

16

THE DARK HEAT STUCK like boiled molasses to my face and arms as we rode to Oz's apartment, an anomaly in the semi-tropical climate with its yellow clapboard siding and external stairwells. The back lot had filled so I parked the bike at the restaurant next door and walked over a fence choked with vines to follow his broad back up the narrow stairs.

The apartment's interior looked as if Goodwill had discarded it. Oz had little furniture, a couch, chair, ottoman, end table and bookshelf. One of each. Nothing matched. Every surface supported a computer or the guts of one. Half were running, their screensavers glowing like lava. Wires hung from monitors, tables and chairs. They curled on the scarred hardwood floor like cats. The Stevens kids would love the place.

"Want anything?" Oz said as he disappeared into the kitchen, a slit between two-by-fours missing the plasterboard cap.

"A place to sit would be nice."

He came back with a long-necked beer, lifted a notebook computer from the couch and waved a hand over the cushion.

"Wait." I pointed to a tablet computer on the floor. "Can I borrow that? I want to see what Leslie Walker did at ten."

The back-from-the-dead story about the fugitive financier topped the news. The anchor mentioned the kidnapping, showed photos of Darby and Pap and a clip from her interview with Delgado. I sat up when the yellow block of my office flashed on the screen and Walker mentioned my name as the sole contact with the vanishing thief. When she launched into the "if you have any information" spiel, I dumped the browser and blacked out the machine.

"That should shake him up," Oz said.

I felt slightly sick, as if the publicity would have the exact opposite effect we'd intended. "I'm afraid of that."

"I've got something." He opened the notebook computer, called up a login screen and entered his credentials. "You said you're listing Ginny Alexander's house."

"If I ever get around to filing the paperwork."

"You know why she's selling?"

The city property records website filled the screen. He tapped a few more keys and I saw the names Robert L. Darby and Virginia Alexander populate the field.

"Because she can't collect the insurance money now that he's alive?" I asked.

"She can't make good on two bank loans, plus the loans she and Darby took out on the other homes."

"She may not have to worry about those," I said. "A court-appointed receiver is selling Darby's assets. The money's going to the victims, not Ginny Alexander."

He jumped to another site and pointed to a column of figures. "Look at this. She's underwater on the house. She has no income and negative cash flow."

"Lovely," I said. "Three percent of nothing is nothing."

Oz flipped to another tab in the browser and punched in more passwords.

I leaned over and pointed to the screen. "What's this?"

"Accurint."

"A database?"

"Right," he said.

"How does this help us find Darby and Pap?"

"You put in as much information as you can and it will cross-reference the data." His voice sounded low and smooth as the darkness outside.

"Show me."

He tapped the screen and started to type. "You key as many variables as you have: first name, last name, street address, vehicle tags. Then you do a relative query. If anyone's hiding him, it'll be a relative."

"Could he pay someone?" I asked.

"You mean like Hernandez the irrigation guy?"

"Yes."

"Then we follow the money."

"How does that work?" I asked.

"We track his assets." He swigged the beer. "I thought you used this up North."

"We used something similar, XP something."

"TLOxp. That lets you search for bankruptcies, foreclosures, liens, judgments. It's pretty good at locating assets."

He switched to another screen. "It also tracks vehicle sightings."

He pulled up a map. "The vehicle search shows a sighting on I-95, but it's more than a year old. Nothing recent, which doesn't mean much. He could have rented or stolen a car."

"You always this chipper?"

"Only when tracking down the bad guys."

I rubbed my neck, trying to work out a crick.

"You look stressed," he said.

"That's a big ten-four."

"You want some wine?"

I shook my head.

"Medicinal pot?"

I laughed.

"Hot oil massage?" His gray eyes traveled my face.

"Are you hitting on a co-worker?"

His face looked relaxed and sympathetic, his smile broad and inviting. "How about lunch tomorrow? I know a place only the locals go. Ribs and beer."

"Sounds tempting."

"They make their own coleslaw."

"You sexy devil."

He dipped his chin and his voice dropped. "Geeks can be sexy, you know."

I took in the nest of circuit boards and wires littering the place. "How's that?"

"We watch a lot of instructional video."

I smiled. "That's what Cheryl says."

"So, no dates when you're on a job?"

Sitting close on the couch, I felt a charge crackle between us, like the air before a lightning strike. He seemed strong and smart and had gone out of his way to help. I didn't want to leave but didn't feel ready to stay.

"Truth is, I'm a little preoccupied."

"So am I."

"OK," I said. "Back to business. What do we know?"

He sighed and turned to the computer. "About what we knew a year ago. Darby's closest relatives are his wife and daughter. The police have questioned them and he hasn't shown up at their door . . . only yours."

"Credit cards?"

"Hasn't used them."

"Bank accounts?" I asked.

"Dormant."

"Former employers?"

Oz tapped the screen. "Nobody's seen him in a year."

"Rental properties where he could hide?"

"None that we can find or haven't been searched," he said.

"What about the other homes he owns?"

"Police checked. All vacant."

"There's got to be something we can trace," I said. "What about Darby's company?"

Oz scrolled through more data. "It's called Intercoastal Advisory Group, but you already know that. Darby offered portfolio management and investment services. Then a couple of high rollers approached him about starting a bank so they could fund their projects. He ran with it, took their money and, well, you know that, too."

"Who are the high rollers?"

"Don't know yet," Oz said.

"What about partners?"

"He doesn't have any. His closest associate is Harvey Shaw and Darby hasn't made contact, as far as we know."

I took a deep breath. The amount of information flashing across the screen blurred my eyes. We had to simplify.

"What do we know?" I asked. "The feds say Darby took the money and ran. Darby claims he lost the money and is running for his life. If that's true, who's after him?"

"You asked me to research the investors." Oz turned the computer so

I could see more of the screen. "Our boy was busy. Three individuals and thirty-nine companies gave Darby money to start the bank."

"Jeez, it's going to take us forever to interview that many people."

"Maybe not," Oz said. "The investors who lost the most have the greatest need to find him."

"And the resources."

"Most of the investors were institutional—hedge funds, venture capital. They look like shell corporations. I've traced them back to their lawyers but don't have any names."

I massaged my forehead. "How did Darby manage to stay under the radar?"

"Dark pools."

I leaned back. "Dark pool? Is that like dark matter?"

"Close," he said. "If you have an hour I can explain it."

"Just tell me how we're going to trace a bunch of faceless corporations and law firms."

He smiled. "Some of them have faces."

"Say on."

"We know the names of the three individuals."

"Yes?" I leaned toward him and caught the faint scent of shaving cream and wondered how often he had to scrape his scalp to keep that polished look. "Who?"

He pointed to the top of the screen. "Charles Palmer, local attorney and financial advisor, and Casey Laine. She owns the biggest real estate company on the coast."

"Married to the mayor. I've heard of her."

"Half of Florida has heard of her," Oz said. "The third investor died shortly before Darby disappeared. I'd hit Palmer first. He might have names."

"Maybe a silent partner," I said.

"Or a partner who wants to silence Darby."

"I'd let him if Pap were safe," I said. "Tell me about Palmer."

"He's touchy about his losses, and his privacy. His son's cool, though. Mitchell."

"What's he like?"

"Tall, athletic, young. Not as smart or good-looking as yours truly."

"Who is?" I said.

Oz grinned. "If his old man won't help, he might."

"And Casey Laine? I should know, she's no stranger to the media."

"Rich, fifties. Built Laine & Co. from nothing into the most successful real estate firm in Florida—five hundred agents, three billion a year in sales, more offices than radio had shacks."

You would shop there, I thought but said, "Sounds like a factory."

"More like a steady paycheck. You might ask if she has any openings . . . if the independent thing doesn't work out."

I drew back. "The 'independent thing' is working out just fine."

His expression told me something else.

I stood and pointed to the computer. "What. You ran my financials?"

When he dipped his head, I knew. Anger flashed and quickly disappeared as I watched the confidence wash out of his face. He hadn't done it on his own, I'd make book on that.

"Delgado," I said.

He nodded.

"He thinks I'm complicit? That I staged my own grandfather's kidnapping?" I paced. "What's he looking for? A payoff?"

"He's trying to get a handle on the situation."

I grabbed my helmet and stormed to the door. "Next time you see him, tell him where he can shove his handle."

17

FROM A SMALL BOOM box propped on the deck, the voice of Dierks Bentley drifted across the *Mary Beth* like foam from a beer glass.

Walter leaned over the edge of the boat and unhooked a line from the dock cleats. Sitting at his master's feet, Louie leaped up when he heard me come aboard, spreading good cheer and slobber over my hands.

I identified the song title and gave it to Walter. "'What Was I Thinking.'"

He cast off the last of the lines. "That your new motto?"

I handed him a sack of bagels. "Just steer the ship."

"Take the helm." He disappeared into crew quarters below decks with the bag and reappeared wearing weight-lifter gloves with the fingertips cut off. "Which I need you to do."

He stood amidships in front of a big silver wheel with metal spokes and started the engine and the GPS device. "Take the helm and steer in the direction you want the boat to head—just like a car."

"This tub doesn't have brakes."

"You never use them anyway."

I crossed my arms in defiance. "We're sailing the Gulf in this? You could fit four of these in one of Darby's yachts."

"At least I own it," he said.

We passed the marina with its glass-walled restaurant and dolphin fountain and cruised through the anchor field.

"That's the mainsail," Walter said, pointing straight up. "And that," he hooked a thumb over his shoulder, "is the line that controls the mainsail.

When we need to turn, I'll yell 'tacking!' and you crank the winch with the black line."

I snapped a sharp salute. "Aye, aye, El Capitán."

Walter and Louie stared at me with pity, although I suspected Louie was still looking for the bagels.

"And when I unfurl the second sail—it's called a headsail or Genoa, in case you're taking notes—you winch the white line." He vaulted out of the cockpit onto the deck and straddled the bow.

As the boat slipped between the red and green channel markings of the bay, Walter ran up the mainsail and unfurled the other one and told me when he wanted me to crank the lines. The wind caught the sails with a *huff* and the boat headed toward the barrier islands.

"A little to port!" Walter yelled.

I eased the helm to the left and we sailed down the intercoastal waterway. He jumped back into the cockpit, shut down the engine and disappeared below decks, returning with the bagels and two bottles of water. We sat in the cockpit on the bench with Louie curled between us and watched the coastline slide by.

I checked the sack and realized I'd forgotten butter and cream cheese. "You didn't think I could handle the ship by myself?" I fed Louie a bite.

"One person can sail from here," Walter said. "It only takes two to dock or undock."

"But you could go it alone."

He chewed. "If I had to."

"Dean says hi."

"You stop to ask if he'd seen Darby?"

"He said you had it covered."

Now that the action had died down, I yawned mightily and stretched until the vertebrae cracked. Louie grabbed the last of my bagel.

"Out late?" he asked.

"With Oz, the IT guy. We're trying to track the investors."

"And?" He waggled his eyebrows in a possible imitation of Groucho Marx.

"And nothing." I looked at the water as it rolled by in small humps.

"*Nothing?*" The gap in his upper teeth seemed to grow wider with his smile.

Despite the breeze, I felt my face flush. "I'm not ready."

"It's been two years."

I snatched another bagel. "You have any coffee on this tub?"

"Nary a drop."

"I thought that's all you guys drank at meetings."

"Iced tea. We're all sons of the South now." He leaned back and folded his arms, keeping a foot on the helm. "So what's going on?"

I filled him in on Rae's sighting of Claire and the other gossip I'd heard—that the city wanted Rae and the mom-and-pop businesses south of Baywalk to sell so they could build a hotel and convention center. I told him about the visit to Roger Hernandez and how Darby had talked about boats; about Charles Palmer and Casey Laine and the short list of investors; and about how I worried all of those leads would turn into dead ends. I saved the worst for last. "Darby called again. He's taunting me. I swear I'm going to crush that son of a bitch."

Louie raised his head and examined us with soft brown eyes, as if to say he'd prefer ladies who didn't use foul language.

Walter patted his head and stood to take the helm and we headed down the intercoastal. As we neared the bay side of Spanish Key, the wind picked up, bringing with it the scent of seaweed and clams. Most residents and visitors stuck to the western shore, with its sunsets, condos and sand. Despite the water view, the eastern shore remained less populated, the trees edging out homes along several stretches. More than a million tourists came through Palmetto County each year, crowding roads and beaches, and yet a few areas remained untouched. I wondered for how long.

"Palmer's legit," Walter said. "His clients say he's honest, a stickler for detail. Very formal."

"A bit uptight?"

Walter grinned. "You could say that. He may not talk."

"Embarrassed because he lost money with Darby?"

"Worse. He lost client money."

"He *is* a straight-shooter," I said.

"His son's interesting. Mitch. Young, bright, knows the Internet better than most pros. Set up the firm's website and social media accounts."

"How did Palmer react?"

"He's convinced no one with money uses a computer."

"Does SEO, SEM?"

Walter raised his brows.

"Search engine optimization?"

He shook his head. "Don't get smart. I'm pushing the boundaries with a flip phone."

"And the real estate mogul?"

"Casey Laine? She did well during the boom years and then the market collapsed. Agencies folded right and left and she went shopping."

"How'd she manage that?"

"Kept her powder dry." He steered the boat toward the shore.

"The only powder I have is for baking."

"You don't bake."

"Spoil sport." The bayside houses drifted by like clouds. Expensive ones. "To quote a wise friend of mine, do we have a plan?"

"I got a tip that might mesh with yours from the tiki bar," he said. "Three boats have disappeared in three days. It lines up with the information Hernandez gave you."

I wondered why Oz hadn't mentioned it. "Where did you hear that?"

"Former marine division cop."

"I thought you never went out. Where do you meet these guys?"

"They're like me, retired. Moved here to get away from the cold and the bureaucracy . . . or their wives. Guy down the street is former Secret Service. An FBI agent moved in next door. Neighbor on the other side ran the SWAT team in northern Virginia. We have coffee once a week."

"That's the most social you've been in years."

Walter grew quiet, so I let it go and kept my eyes on the water. Tacking close to shore, we peered into caves formed when mangroves overran channels cut by the Army Corps of Engineers for mosquito control. We searched dozens of sandbars and spoil islands, mile-long lumps of dirt dredged from the waterway now overgrown with sea grape and oak. We looked for anything out of place—boats without numbers, camouflaged encampments, tents in wildlife preserves. Nothing but miles and miles of water. And disappointment.

"You know," I said, "she would have wanted you to meet other people. Take on some work. Maybe, God forbid, go on a date."

With both hands on the helm he stared into the distance.

"Sometimes I think you're like a battleship that's been decommissioned. You want a princess to spank a bottle of champagne across your bow."

He grinned. "You've been reading again."

"It's Pap's fault. He believes in the education of women."

"Good thing."

"Good thing," I said.

We sailed to the southern tip of Spanish Key and looked across the bay to the mainland at a point where development tapered into an impassible tangle of scrub, a place once dominated by sugar mills and orange groves.

"We sailing to Venice?" I said, regretting the note of futility that deadened my voice.

"Save it for another day." He ordered me to the bow with instructions on how to swing the boom without getting clocked. "Coming around," he yelled, and for a moment the wind died and the boat seemed to hang on the water. Then the sails caught with a *whuff* and we did a tight one-eighty and headed back to the marina.

As he slotted the boat between the channel markings, Walter walked me thorough the process of dropping the sails. With the boat slowing, he reached behind and turned on the motor. We cruised between the red and green markers, the smell of burned diesel fuel drifting into the cockpit. Louie sat on the bench with his face into the wind. Powerboats and fishing charters breezed by as if we were standing still, their wake slapping the sides of the boat. Two shirtless guys on personal watercraft that looked like snowmobiles roared past, shouting and waving in a frantic burst of testosterone.

"Makes you humble," I said as I regained my seat in the cockpit.

The riders lapped the trawlers and banked in front of the restaurant, sending a spray over the seawall close to the first row of diners.

Walter shook his head. "Somebody's going to get hurt."

Threading the boat through the mooring field, Walter eased the *Mary Beth* into the slip, shut down the engine and tossed a line over the deck cleat. He hitched Louie to a leash and we walked the finger pier through the gate and into a tree-lined strip between the parking lot and the boats.

"We have a plan?" he asked as Louie irrigated a bush.

"Dinner at Cheryl's tonight."

"What about the case?" he said.

"I might need some help with Harvey Shaw, and maybe a few of the investors."

"That's Delgado's job, isn't it?"

"It's my grandfather," I said, feeling frustration and hostility rise with my voice. "They took me in when I was five. They raised me. I think I owe them."

Walter held up a palm. "It could be dangerous."

"It is for Pap, if I don't find him."

"You change your mind about carrying a weapon?" he asked.

"You change your mind about dating?"

He pursed his lips. "I guess we're at an impasse."

"I guess we are," I said and walked away.

18

I SPENT THE AFTERNOON at the office, inhaling coffee and reviewing the MLS listings and the other databases I could still afford. If Hernandez got his timeline right, Darby fled the apartment at the irrigation company a week ago for a more out-of-the-way place. I was looking for short-term rentals that had disappeared during that time. Darby could have hijacked a boat or pitched a tent in the homeless camp behind the college, but Cheryl said the department had searched the camp and come up empty, and Walter and I had scoured the intercoastal and found nothing. That left short-term rentals. It was a long shot but, as my frustration and impatience boiled over, I had to do something other than waiting for the good guys to ride to the rescue. And the argument with Walter still stung. Going it alone seemed the only option.

Paging through the listings, I ruled out the most obvious choices: his properties, his condos in town and the rentals on the keys. The FBI had scrubbed Darby's homes and boats and the police would keep them under surveillance. A place in the city would enable him to blend with thousands of others but with the publicity and his disguise, and Pap in tow, he'd stick out too much. Same thing on the tony barrier islands. Even without the makeup, Darby didn't look like a tourist or a retiree, and ever since a group of thugs had started robbing tourists, Spanish Point Police had stepped up patrols on Sara Key and its neighbor to the north.

No, Darby had to stash Pap where trees outnumbered people, where a handyman or lawn-care worker would go unnoticed, and that narrowed the search to three areas. He could have ducked into one of the walled compounds north of University Parkway, in a sketchy part of the city called North Point. He could have picked a trailer south and east of the city in a zone that jumbled homes with cement plants and trucking companies. Or he could have holed up on one of the former cattle ranches east of Interstate 75. Developers scrambled to buy them for the buildable space they offered but I'd shown several of the more run-down buildings and knew how isolated it felt out there. That solitude was one of the reasons Walter chose to live east of seventy-five and not on the water—the anti-Travis McGee. I knew I should call Walter for backup but I couldn't wait. Neither could Pap.

I printed the specs on three of the most promising places and folded copies of Pap and Darby's photos into a pocket. Grabbing the helmet from the clothes tree by the door, I made sure I locked the office, climbed on the bike and headed north on the Trail, veering right at the Ringling Museum onto University Parkway. Sliding past the airport, I bumped the bike over a set of railroad tracks and angled onto a narrow road that ran between storm drain ditches as deep as ponds and walls of slash pine and oak. Slowing by a broken wooden sign with the development's name in faded black, I skimmed a cement-block wall of peeling whitewash and halted in the driveway before a wire gate.

The gate bore a shiny padlock. Pulling the bike around the corner, I crossed the ditch and followed the wall until I found a break where a pine had tumbled onto the block. Luckily there was no barbed wire. I walked the makeshift ramp and landed in the compound and looked around. The house was a single-story stucco with faded blue paint and no cars in the yard. No dogs barked. Nobody passed by the windows.

I touched the pocket with the pepper spray, moved a business card to my shirt pocket and looked for the doorbell. Someone had painted over the button so many times it wouldn't budge. I knocked. A man in his mid-thirties with a hard face and wiry black hair yanked open the door. He looked as if he could pass for Sal Finzi's younger brother. From the back of the house a dog started to bark.

"What do you want." Eyes and voice flat, he kept one hand on the door and leaned against the frame with the right. A tattoo of an owl covered his forearm.

My first instinct was to tell him to show me both hands but instead I said, "I'm a real estate agent. I understand this house is for rent."

He looked past me. "How'd you get in."

The barking grew louder. I glanced at the interior, a dark jumble of boxes and furniture, and knew I'd never get past the door. I also knew this wasn't the place. "The gate was unlocked."

"The hell it was. What do you want."

A German shepherd rounded the corner, barked twice and showed its teeth.

"I have a client who'd like to see the house. Mind if I look around?"

The dog stopped. The guy stiffened. "This is private property. Get the hell out."

I did.

Vaulting the wall, I climbed on the bike and headed south, past the municipal golf course and over another set of railroad tracks and down a road that wound between warehouses and auto-body shops. The mobile home stood behind a worn picket fence on the left. A new looking gray compact with a dented rear bumper sat in the carport and large plastic sunflowers spun over the thinning grass. A gravel path led to the front door and around the back of the trailer.

A woman in her fifties with hair the color of rust and a face that folded in on itself answered the door. She cradled her left wrist in her right hand as if it were a bird that had fallen from its nest. When I introduced myself she let her arm drop and put her hand to her throat and touched a scar that ran down her neck. I decided to drop the pretense of selling real estate and unfolded the photo of Pap and handed it to her.

"My grandfather went missing in the neighborhood," I said. "Have you seen him by any chance?"

She took the photo with both hands and shook her head.

I swapped the photo for the before-and-after pictures of Darby. "What about his man? He would have moved in last week."

"No. I haven't seen him." She handed me the photos and held her arm.

"What happened to your wrist, if I might ask?"

"I fell on the path when I went out this morning."

I checked her face. She had a fresh scratch on the left cheek, as if a piece of gravel had cut her . . . or somebody's ring. "Your wrist looks swollen. Do you need a doctor?"

"No, it'll be fine."

I looked at the joint and didn't think it would. "Do you want a ride to the emergency room?"

"It can wait." She looked away, and I wondered who else was at home, or if that person had left this morning.

"We should put something on that," I said and stepped up to the lip of the door. "Do you have ice?"

"Yes," she said and backed away to let me into a single room with a dining table on the right, a sink and refrigerator straight ahead and the living room on the left. A hallway led from there into what I assumed was the bedroom. I saw and heard nothing.

"Do you have a wash cloth or dishtowel?"

Sliding open a drawer by the sink, she pulled out a towel and gestured toward the refrigerator. I grabbed some cubes and wrapped her wrist and asked if she had any surgical tape. She shook her head.

"Masking tape?" I asked.

She kept that in the bottom drawer, along with a jumble of screwdrivers, batteries, bottle openers and twist ties. I bound her wrist and sat her in a wooden chair with spindly legs. The injury looked like a sprain and would heal on its own. If she'd fallen on the gravel because of a medical problem, she'd probably do it again. If someone had hit her, he'd probably do it again. Realizing I couldn't do anything about either situation, I asked if I could get her some water. She said no and thanked me and I left, grinding my teeth on the way out.

When people say the third time's a charm, they weren't referring to the scrublands east of I-75. The property sat on a back road halfway between Florida and the Ozarks. I bumped off pavement with no shoulder and onto a long sandy drive with grass growing between the ruts and pulled up to a house with a two-story porch, a metal pole barn, a freestanding three-bay garage and an outhouse. When I took off the helmet, the sun beat down hard enough to kill grass. From behind the barn two dogs charged, came to a halt five feet away and kept barking until three guys climbed off the porch and told them to shut up.

"Nice security," I said.

The men looked like the Three Stooges but from their expressions, I doubted they were funny. All were their early twenties, and all went shirtless. Two were white, one darker skinned. The first white guy and the one who could pass for a Latino were about the same height, under five-eight, with pinched faces and enough body art to fill a museum. The white guy had light curly hair, a backwards baseball cap and a bull ring through his nose. The Latino had dark hair swept back so that the sides formed two points on either side of his head. Both wore dirty sneakers without socks. Neither held anything in their hands and, although I couldn't see the back of their cargo shorts, neither looked armed.

The third guy stepped forward and nodded. He stood a little taller, maybe five-nine, and looked thinner, his biceps and ankles banded with tattoos that resembled the manacles prisoners wore in eighteenth-century France. A pair of midnight blue wolves snarled from his wrists. Bare-chested and barefoot, he'd shaved his head to match the rest of his hairless body and wore a single silver hoop in his left ear—Curly playing the pirate. His hands were empty and I saw no sign of a gun.

"Hi, guys," I said and slung the helmet over the handlebars.

Curly's face looked pasty, his eyes a dishwater gray. He crossed his arms and spread his feet. "What's going on?"

"I'm looking for my grandfather."

His expression was the hard challenge of someone with a secret who wanted to keep it that way. "What'd he do, run away from home?"

"He was kidnapped."

Curly turned slightly to glance at his backup singers and out of the side of his mouth said, "You a cop?"

"No," I said. "My grandfather's not well. He needs his meds."

Moe said, "Don't we all." Larry snickered.

I introduced myself and asked who they were and met with a wall of silence.

"What's that got to do with us?" Curly asked.

"He went missing not far from here. Can I show you a photo?"

"You can show us anything you like," Moe said and grinned.

Cute, I thought. He'd look cuter in cuffs.

I handed Curly the photo of Pap. He shook his head.

"How about you guys?" I said.

Curly handed the photo back to me. His eyes gleamed and he smelled of chemicals, like the solution darkroom techs used to use to develop film. It was a scent I hadn't encountered since Pap led me on tours through the newspaper plant.

I unfolded the two photos of Darby and exchanged them for Pap's.

"How about him?"

Curly looked at the two prints, flipped them over and back and turned to show them to his backup band. They looked at the photos, then at him, then me, then over my shoulder as if expecting someone. Or checking to see if the coast was clear.

The dogs growled. I shifted toward the bike and the helmet. The hard plastic made for an effective weapon.

Curly handed the photos to me. "Who is he?"

"Robert Lee Darby, the fugitive financier," I said.

"I thought he was dead."

He gave me the hard stare. I gave it back.

"So did I."

"You said you were looking for your grandfather."

"I am," I said. "He's with this man. Have you seen him?"

Curly stepped back and crossed his arms again. "We haven't."

"And you guys?" I said over his shoulder.

"They haven't, either."

The backup band moved closer. When I got home I'd tell Cheryl about the ranch and the narcotics unit would find out what the boys were cooking, but at the moment all I could do was mount the bike.

"Thanks for your time." I snapped a small salute and roared toward town.

19

THE OFFICES OF THE Intercoastal Advisory Group sat atop an Italianate building of stucco, wrought iron and tile in the heart of downtown Spanish Point. On the outside, the building reflected the non-stop traffic crawling across Main Street. On the inside, its corridors reflected money, from the subdued lighting and original artwork to the hushed tones of wheatgrass wallpaper, dark woodwork and carpet. The impression ended when I opened a heavy wooden door and entered a lobby decorated in dull shades of gray.

The receptionist sat at a small secretary with spindles and a phone. She looked in her mid-twenties. She had platinum hair, a sleek black dress and legs to match. I, on the other hand, felt dusty and parched and would have traded my bike for a bottle of water. Handing her my card, I watched through floor-to-ceiling windows as drivers tried to negotiate the traffic circles the city had just installed. *Good luck with that.*

Sensing a presence behind, I turned to face a large man with rubber lips and ears straight from the vegetable patch. With a dimpled chin the size of a potato, he resembled a cartoon version of Chevy Chase.

"CW McCoy," I said and shook his hand. It felt spongy and moist.

"Paul Harvey Shaw." He had slush-gray eyes and a deep bellow that Pap would describe as *basso profondo.*

"How are you?" I asked in my best let-me-show-you-a-house voice.

"If I was any better, I'd be you."

"Let's hope not."

Blue stubble smeared heavy jowls. His black hair glistened, the dye job betrayed by white fuzz blurring each temple. He looked mid-fifties, with thick belly and thighs. A large class ring perched on the finger of his right hand with nothing on his left.

"You caught me at a good time," he said, leading me to a corner office. "I've been out of town all week." He gestured to a hard-looking plastic chair and said, "Have a seat."

Industrial-grade furnishings graced the office, with desk, carpet and walls in various shades of gray. As in the lobby, a wall of palladium windows overlooked the traffic circle. File cabinets covered a second wall, artwork a third. The paintings consisted of gray abstracts with slashes of silver and gold. The decorator had gone for the look of money and fallen a few dollars short.

Behind Shaw's head, a glass shelf burst with golfing trophies and a collection of photos of Tiger Woods and other players I didn't recognize. On the desk he'd sandwiched glass figurines of female golfers between mounds of accordion-style folders, the kind with flaps and string ties on the front. Except for a corded telephone, there were no computers, tablets or other electronics in sight.

He watched me absorb the surroundings. "Like it? I did the design myself." His wave took in the glittering prints on the wall. "I got all of the artwork at an estate sale for a dollar apiece. The dentist went belly up and died. He had good taste but a lousy relationship with his kids. I got some nice furniture, too—pretty cheap."

Shaw wore a white polo shirt with a small image of a golfer in mid-swing and glen plaid slacks. A green sports coat that resembled the Masters jacket hung on a clothes tree to the left. He leaned back in a gray ergonomic chair, clasped his big hands behind his head and smiled. "So, what can I do you for?"

Overweight and overconfident, I thought. Time to warm up the bench.

"Did you play professionally?" I asked, pointing to the trophies.

"In college. Now I only do it to drum up business. You wouldn't believe the deals you can make at the nineteenth hole."

"Mr. Shaw. . . ."

"Harv. And it's Ms. McCoy, right?" His eyes darted to my ring finger, his smile stretching like a rubber band.

"CW's fine."

"CW. You said this had something to do with Bobby Lee?" Still smiling, he nodded for me to continue.

"Harvey, when was the last time you saw your former boss?"

He tilted his head to his left and peered at the ceiling and said, "A little more than a year ago, just before he disappeared."

"Can you tell me about that?"

"I could," he said, his eyes returning to me.

I waited. He said nothing. "Would you?"

"He came into the office on a Saturday morning and said he needed money."

"Was that unusual?"

"Was what unusual?"

I cleared my throat. "The Saturday visit or the need for money?"

Harvey chuckled. "Both. We played golf most Saturday mornings with the investors, and he and Ginny were always flush. I was here because he said he was going out of town and needed cash." He frowned on the last word.

"Did he take a lot of money?"

"Yeah, a pretty good chunk."

"Then what happened?"

Shaw chuckled. "Then he disappeared. Ginny had him declared legally dead and everybody moved on."

"What if I told you Bobby Lee Darby was alive and back in town?"

Shaw sat up, a momentary look of panic breaking through the mask before he stuffed it back inside. "I wouldn't put much stock in rumor. The police say he committed suicide. They have it on tape."

"They have a pile of his clothes on tape."

"Who told you he's back?"

"He did."

Under heavy brows, Shaw's eyes did the limbo. Speechless. I liked him that way.

"He appeared in my office Friday morning."

Shaw slowly leaned back. "What did he want?"

"He said he didn't take the investors' money."

Shaw's shook his jowls. "That's impossible."

"He said someone else did and framed him."

Crossing his arms, Harvey gave me the dead-fish stare. "He's full of crap. What did he really want?"

"Someone to clear his name."

"And he came to you?" He fumbled on the cluttered desk, looked at the business card his receptionist had handed to him and back at me.

"Yes he did," I said. "Either he finds the people who set him up or he's going to turn himself in and sing to the FBI."

His face took on the color of the room. "I thought you said you were a real estate agent."

"I am."

"Are you working with the police?"

"No, I'm not."

He leaned his elbows on the desk. "Then I don't see where this concerns you."

"It concerned me the moment Darby kidnapped my grandfather to ensure my cooperation. If I can trace one, I can find the other."

When he pouted, his lips resembled the game of Origami triangles we used to call fortune teller.

"You don't know where he's hiding," I said.

"I didn't even know he was alive."

"If he *was* framed, who do you think might have done it?"

Shaw sighed. "The only people who had access to our financial records were Bobby Lee and me, and the FBI cleared me and his family of all wrongdoing. Anyone who says otherwise is making libelous statements."

A warning shot across the bow.

"Hypothetically speaking."

"Me, I suppose, but why would I? Ginny owns the company but I run it. And where's the money?" He swept the office with the hand that wore the class ring. "Look around you. Does it look like I drink at the Ritz every night?"

"What about Ms. Alexander?"

"She didn't have access to the books."

"How about someone who stumbled on his scheme?"

"I know what you're driving at. You think some of the investors got involved."

"Did they?"

"Could it have happened? Sure, but the SEC considers these people sophisticated. They don't have to frame anyone. If you don't do what they want, they'll just rob you in court."

"The police have a list of investors but it's long. Would you mind comparing it to yours?"

"I don't have that information at my fingertips."

I took a deep breath. "It would only take a few taps on your computer."

"I don't use a computer."

"Could you at least identify the people most likely to go after Darby?"

Rocking back in his chair, Harvey folded his arms and stared at the ceiling. "Well now, that would violate client confidentiality, wouldn't it?"

I tilted my head and smiled. "How much money do you run?"

He gave me a figure well north of North.

"And the minimum portfolio you handle?"

"At least a million in investible assets, more like ten to fifteen." He leaned forward and smiled. It was like watching a shark eye a school of minnows. "Why? Would you like to speak to an advisor?"

I felt my face redden and hoped it didn't show. "Not just yet."

He laughed. "Any more questions before you leave?"

"None worth asking," I said and headed for the door.

20

D O YOU KNOW WHAT that son-of-a-bitch did?" Cheryl exploded as I walked in the door. I didn't see Tracy but knew Cheryl wouldn't yell if her daughter could hear.

"He sent me the bill for couples counseling . . . you know, the counseling our priest suggested? We went once and Sal bailed out. Well, guess who he wound up going with? His new girlfriend. Do you believe it? He says she helps him overcome his anger issues. I know how she does it—a hand job in the parking lot."

She lifted a fistful of envelopes. "And look at these. More bills he refuses to pay—child support, alimony, power, cable. I'll tell you who has anger issues—me. He's contagious. He's like poison. He's poisoning my life."

"Hi, honey, how was your day?"

She shook her head. "I can't take this shit much longer."

"Mine was fine. We couldn't find Darby anywhere and his business manager stonewalled me like a three-term politician."

Her face looked about to collapse.

"OK," I said. "We need reinforcements."

I led her by the arm to the dining room table, poured two hefty glasses of wine and pushed one into her hands. Cheryl gulped. I sipped and felt the alcohol burn my sinuses. After he'd paid the alimony, Sal Finzi needed to buy his ex-wife something better to drink.

We knocked back the wine. Cheryl grabbed the bottle, refilled our glasses and lifted hers in a toast.

"To women."

"Hear me roar," I said.

As we clinked glasses, I felt the wine start to lift my spirits. Cheryl drained her glass, refilled it and topped mine. As she set the bottle on the table, her face seemed to drop.

"I'm a sad sack."

"No, you're not," I said, grabbing her hand. "You're a single mom who could use some help."

"I'm a single mom who could use some cash." She reached for the bottle and replenished our drinks.

"Maybe," I said, "we could knock off a bank."

"Maybe we could knock some sense into Sally's head." She ran the words together in a sibilant stream.

"Where's Tracy?"

Cheryl waved over her head. "Neighbors, on the other side."

"Where's Sal?

"At the marina, giving his girlfriend a shot of spumoni."

I rose from the table and drained my glass. "Let's go."

Cheryl emptied hers. "Where?" Her eyes looked bright and bleary.

"The marina. Let's see if we can squeeze your former squeeze."

She giggled and held onto the table as she rose.

"I'll drive." I grabbed her purse from the counter and guided her out the door.

"You sure?" she said as we crossed the lawn to Pap's carport. "He can get real mean."

I got in and fired up the SUV. "So can I."

* * *

The Spanish Point Marina felt different at dusk. During the day, sunlight and tourists flooded the docks, people ate fish sandwiches under umbrellas on the outdoor deck and yachts and sailboats rocked in the anchor field. The harbormaster ran charters out of his office and boat owners washed clothes and swapped stories in the laundry. Once the sun dropped, the streetlamps glared, the water turned black and the tourists retreated to the bar.

Compared to the elegant glass and stucco restaurant, the

harbormaster's office resembled a shack, its wooden siding faded, the metal roof dully reflecting the lights.

"What a dump," Cheryl said as we climbed out of the SUV.

"At least we found a parking space."

Masts loomed in the harbor. Yachts looked abandoned, their cabins dark. We walked to the harbormaster's office and stopped. All of the parking slots were empty, except one. In it sat a motorcycle as black as night.

"That's it!" Cheryl pointed. "That's the damned bike he just bought."

It looked like a hardtail chopper from the '60s, with bullet-hole aluminum wheels and an over/under shotgun exhaust with dual mufflers. No windscreen, saddlebags or sissy bar. Just 700 pounds of muscle.

I whistled. "That's a lot of bike."

"Personally I'd paint it cherry red," Cheryl said.

"I want that bike."

"It's just the kind of thing Sal would buy to impress the new chick."

"I stand corrected," I said, running my fingers over the chrome. "We want that bike."

"We?"

"It'll kick start Tracy's college fund."

"It'll kick our asses into jail," Cheryl said.

"Why don't you stay in the truck, in case you have to call the police?"

"I do *not* know you," she said but took the keys.

Salvatore Finzi sat in a wooden chair at a wooden desk in an office the size of a closet. He had black hair and a black Zapata moustache, both streaked with gray, and raccoon circles rimming his eyes. Odd-shaped freckles spotted his deeply tanned face. He wore black pants and a short-sleeved white shirt with a gold anchor embroidered on one pocket and a gold badge on the other. Too cheap to buy a real shield. Large colorful playing cards glowed on the computer screen. On the desk sat a ring with about a dozen keys. It looked like a dead bird.

Finzi scowled over the top of a can of what could have passed for soda or beer. "Well, well," he said, setting the can on the desk. "If it isn't the nosy neighbor." His voice resonated with a pack-a-day rasp.

"Hello, Sally." I forced a boldness into my voice I didn't feel.

He stood, and in a second his expression went from sour to grim. "What do you want?"

He wasn't wearing a gun tonight. I took a breath and willed my heart to slow.

"Cheryl says you owe alimony and child support for the last six months."

He gave a mirthless laugh. "So what. You her lesbian lover?"

I gave thanks I no longer carried a weapon. I'd shoot him, he'd file charges and I'd be the one to land in jail. No justice there.

"Think of me as a guardian angel."

"Well, angel," he said, moving closer, "you better guard your ass out of here or I'll arrest you for trespassing."

I inhaled the foul roar of booze, tobacco and hate.

"You like pushing women around, don't you, Sally?"

He pointed a thick finger at me. "I never touched her and if she says so, I'll sue her ass. I'll sue you both. Now get the hell out of here."

"Not until you pay up."

He laughed. "Who's gonna make me? You and your pussy-licking friends?"

"If we can't, the courts will, I'll make sure of it. I'll even hire the lawyer."

I fought to keep from stepping back as he got into my face.

"She's a greedy cunt. She took everything I have, half my retirement, half my pay. I'm staying in a shithole and she's living the life of Reilly, in my house, in my bed, and I bet she's fucking every scumbag on the force."

"You are such a gentleman."

He started punching the air with his finger. "She's a cop and she can't do shit, and neither can you. She's not getting another dime, not another dime, and you won't get shit, either. I don't have anything left, so why don't you go home and bake cookies."

"Why don't you man-up and pay."

He closed the gap, the light sharpening every blade of hair on his chin.

"I never hit a woman before, but with you, I'll make an exception."

I felt for the pepper spray. It made a reassuring bulge in my back pocket. "That's not what Cheryl says."

He popped my sternum with a fat palm and rocked me into the wall. "You think you're hot shit because you killed a cop. You know what I think? I think you're a coward. You're a coward who can't do nothing without a gun."

He lunged for my throat. Hands braced against the wall, I kicked his gut with both feet. He went *ooof* and sailed backwards and smacked the desk. I grabbed the pepper spray and, when he charged, blasted his eyes. He clutched his face and doubled over and started to yell.

I felt like screaming. Did everyone in the universe know about Nicholas Church? Did every guy have to punch and bully his way through every woman in his life? I wanted to kick the living crap out of him so badly my legs shook, but I didn't know if I could stop. Cheryl would have to arrest me and then the bad blood and rage would turn me into the brawling savage my father had become.

I sucked in air. Grabbing his keys, I pried off the one for the motorcycle and tossed the rest onto the desk. "I'm taking the bike as collateral. Pay up and you get it back . . . in one piece."

The last thing I heard as I shut the door was the growl of a wounded animal.

"My God," Cheryl said when she saw my face. "What happened?"

As I straddled the bike, I gave her the short version.

"Holy shit!" she said. "I'm going to have to arrest my best friend."

"Consider it collateral," I said, "a down payment on his debts." The bike gave a growl louder than Finzi and caught fire. "I bet this thing's faster than spit."

"I do *not* know you!" Cheryl shouted.

"You were never here."

"Don't park it in Pap's driveway."

"OK," I said, "I'll use yours."

Her voice rose an octave. "You're crazy!"

"I'm pumped. I haven't had this much fun in years."

Finzi hadn't left a helmet but I didn't have far to go. "I'll see you at home," I said and raced south on the Trail, itching to open the throttle and feel my whole body snap back in time.

21

I SAW THE LIGHTS in the rearview mirror and knew they flashed for me, so I pulled the bike into a gas station the locals called the Stab 'n' Grab and cut the engine. The officer parked behind me and got out of the patrol car and asked for my license and registration. His nametag said *Pettinato.*

"Hello, Bernie." I gave him my license. "No registration, but you already know that."

The radio on the squad car squawked. He walked to it and called Dispatch. I felt like asking if I could go in and get a beer but didn't want to push my luck. Hopefully Sal hadn't mentioned his ex-wife when he'd reported the theft.

The lights over the pumps cast hard shadows on the pavement. Traffic moved in streaks on Orange Avenue, one of Spanish Point's major north-south arteries—six lanes if you counted the turning lanes, inside a city of a little more than fifty thousand. Until peak season, when visitors swelled the population by a power of ten. If I stayed here, I'd have to learn to deal with the migratory habits of the wealthy. And the weather. The air had thickened, the clouds threatening to burst, the trees trying to outrun the storm. I knew how they felt.

Officer Pettinato returned.

"It's a loaner," I said.

"Uh huh." He handed the license to me. "Det. Delgado would like to see you."

"Do I have a choice?"

"No."

"How come you're not at Spanish Key Beach arresting people for breaking into cars, or those bump-and-rob jobs at the airport?"

He put his hands on his duty belt. I knew that look. It said, "Don't mess." I could feel the starch go out of my shorts, as Pap would say.

"Follow me," he said.

I followed him to police headquarters, where I parked the bike in a side lot next to another cruiser and followed Pettinato upstairs to the detective's office. Pettinato knocked, announced me and left, his boots squeaking on the tile.

The office looked as dark at night as it did during the day. Delgado stood behind his desk and said something into a cell phone. As I walked in, he disconnected and clipped the phone to his belt.

I opened before he could get in a word. "I take it Sal Finzi called."

"He reported that a crazy woman stole his motorcycle."

"It's a loaner."

"He loaned it to you." His tone sounded flat.

"It's collateral, until he pays up. Are you going to arrest me?

"We should."

"What's the charge?"

"How about driving while stupid." He shook his head. "You just can't stay out of trouble."

"You know what that bastard's doing to his ex-wife."

"No," he said, "and I'm sure Officer Finzi doesn't want the entire department to know."

I cocked a finger at him. "Good point."

"Please don't take this the wrong way, but I'm going to suggest that, while she may be your best friend, the officer's legal issues are none of your business."

"Have you seen the way he bullies her?"

Delgado waved in a gesture that took in his small office. "Do I look like I run the Patrol Division?"

"That man is one drink away from exploding."

Delgado held up a hand. "OK, OK, I'll talk to her L.T. Although I don't think Officer Finzi's husband is the only problem here."

"Ex-husband." I clenched my fists and unclenched them and tried to regulate my breathing.

"We interviewed him after your visit. He had trouble focusing."

"Good," I said.

"We could book you for assault and theft."

"Is he pressing charges?"

"No," Delgado said. His mouth thinned and lines appeared on his forehead. "After you told me about his conduct with Officer Finzi, we had a talk."

"And?"

"He'd been drinking after you left and admits he can't remember things clearly."

"Embarrassed he was outwitted by a woman?"

"Yes," he said, "and inclined to settle the score."

"He's all talk."

"He is a very big, very angry man. I would watch my back."

"This wouldn't have happened if he'd paid his child support," I said.

"You were in law enforcement. You know it's up to the courts, not the Lone Ranger."

"The Lone Ranger?"

He nodded.

"And you're my Tonto?"

Delgado shook his head. "You're not scoring any points here."

"Story of my life."

"I know you're upset about your grandfather."

"No shit."

"Work with us," he said. "Or if you can't do that, please stop working against us."

"And if I decline?"

"Would you like a tour of the interrogation rooms?"

"I've seen enough of them." I pictured Walter's boat, how when he turned it into the wind the sails went dead and the boat stalled. I knew how it felt.

"So I'll remind you again to let us handle Darby."

I said nothing.

"Have you heard from him?"

"No." I looked into his eyes and for the first time saw a glimmer of concern. Maybe it was for Pap. Maybe it was my imagination. "I think that worries me more."

He stared at the phone on his desk for several seconds before picking up the receiver. "I'll have someone in Patrol give you a ride home . . . unless you'd like to walk."

"Can I borrow the bike?"

He almost smiled. "Mr. Finzi said he'll pick it up . . . as soon as his vision clears."

"That's one bad-ass ride."

He nodded. "Faster than a hiccup."

A small spark passed between us and I knew why he hadn't popped me. I just didn't know what to do about it.

22

WALTER HAD TO TAKE Louie to the vet for a routine inspection so the next morning I drove the SUV back to One Spanish Tower, the ice-blue office building on the bay. I thought about taking my bike but didn't want my hair to resemble a squirrel's nest when I met with Darby's biggest investor.

Charles Palmer looked less like a financial advisor and attorney-at-law than a startled chipmunk, with puffy cheeks and hair the color of a tarnished pot. He wore a baggy gray suit with a wrinkled blue Oxford and tone-on-tone tie in a look that went out with Regis Philbin. I pegged him on the sour side of fifty.

His son held more promise. From the moment we met at the elevators, Mitchell Palmer radiated good cheer. He looked a shade younger and taller than me, twenty-six, maybe, and close to six feet. Thick muscles corded his neck and he shaved his light brown hair to a stub. He had pale blue eyes that glittered like those of a malamute and ridiculously small ears. His summer-weight light brown suit draped nicely when he crossed his legs, which he did as we sat in his father's corner office with an unobstructed view of the barrier islands.

The decorator had done the walls in rice paper and the floors in oriental carpet. The lacquered furniture looked Asian, the wall hangings Thai, with their bas-relief elephants carved of dark wood. An ultra-high-def TV covered the fourth wall. Palmer had tuned it to the local morning newscast and watched with an open mouth as anchor Leslie Walker, blonde hair grazing the padded shoulders of a red power suit, flashed photos of

Darby and Pap. She'd toned down the cleavage but Palmer the Elder still stared in slack-jawed wonder.

Realizing he had an audience, he hit the mute button on the remote and flicked the channel to Bloomberg and then stared at me with a mixture of curiosity and menace. I could tell he didn't want to talk; he hadn't offered refreshments.

"I told all this to the police a year ago." He shuffled through stacks of file folders and papers on his desk. Except for two leather wingback chairs, the desk filled the room. It could have sunk the Titanic.

In the silence that followed, I felt a twinge above my left breast where Finzi had smacked me and a sting on my knuckles from when I'd scraped the wall. It could have been worse. I could say the same about Delgado. He gave me a bye. I'd have to thank him. Someday.

"I know you were very cooperative with the police," I said, spreading a little balm on whatever wound I'd opened, "but I'd like to hear about your experience myself."

Palmer searched the deck and finally found his quarry, a white coffee mug etched with a green dollar sign and the image of Benjamin Franklin. He slurped, made a face and leaned back in his chair, leather creaking, the mug in both hands, a sick smile lining his lips.

"I only met the man a few times. I don't see how we can be of any help."

My head hurt, and I would have killed for coffee. Maybe had Walter come along I could have dialed back the hostility. Maybe if he'd arrived with that big handshake and cop gravitas Parker would have talked, guy to guy. Maybe I should have brought Louie. He loves chipmunks.

"Mr. Palmer, my grandfather is going to run out of medication any day and that could cause irreparable harm."

I glanced at Mitchell. His face wore the look of sympathy.

"Do you have any idea where Darby could be hiding?"

"Not a clue."

"What about his associates, or the other investors?"

"Look." He leaned forward and set the mug on the desk. "I have a great deal of sympathy for you in this situation, but I have no idea who the investors are, except my clients, and it will be a cold day in hell before I betray them like he betrayed me. And that, by the way, is where Bobby Lee Darby will wind up if I ever get my hands on him."

His face turned a dull red. Mitch left the room and returned with a glass of water.

"Mr. Palmer, my grandfather is missing along with millions of dollars of your investors' money. Don't you feel any obligation to make them whole?"

"Don't get your bowels in twist. Did I say I wouldn't help?"

"I'd like you to look at the list of investors we do have and tell me which ones are most likely to go after Darby. A lot of them seem to be shell corporations." I slid a piece of paper from my back pocket and smoothed it on a knee.

"And if it gets back to my clients that I gave you that information?"

"I will keep whatever you tell me in the strictest confidence."

He chortled. "It's an ethical violation any way you cut it."

"Could you at least identify the corporate officers?"

"I'm sorry, young lady. That's out of the question."

We all rose as if on cue, the leather creaking as Palmer hefted his bulk out of the chair. I thanked him for his time. He apologized for not being more helpful and said Mitch would see me out.

We passed through the outer office with its analysts and admins and down the chocolate corridor lined with abstract art and flower arrangements to the elevator. As I reached to punch the button, Mitch laid his hand on mine.

"I was watching your face in there," he said. "He's really not a bad guy."

"Once you get to know him."

I reached for the button again but he threw a body block an NHL player would envy.

"I'm sorry about your grandfather." His eyes grew large, his soft mouth edging down.

"Thanks." A warm energy washed over me. It felt good. Irrational but good.

"I can help."

"How?" I asked.

"To be honest, I don't know yet."

"Can you help me trace the investors?"

"Can we talk about it over lunch?"

I glanced at my watch. "Why not. Where and when?"

"How 'bout here and now?" He tapped the elevator button and we descended in a pneumatic hush. Half a block later we walked into a coffee shop around the corner called the Purple Pineapple. I'd eaten there once. It had passable food, the ambiance of a chicken shed and a front-row view of traffic. The hostess showed us to a white plastic table with plastic chairs under a wilted royal palm. While waiting for the waitress, we watched the traffic crawl along the Tamiami Trail.

"Ah." I glanced at the highway. "The smell of exhaust in the morning."

"Just another day in paradise."

"And the people keep coming."

"They will," Mitch said, "as long as we keep promoting it."

"You mean real estate agents like me."

He smiled, revealing the whitest teeth this side of Hollywood. The bony ridge of his nose pointed straight down to a wide mouth and strong jaw. Aside from the hair, which he'd buzzed in a military cut, he reminded me of a young James Taylor . . . if Taylor had played basketball and run track.

"Not you," he said. "You're small potatoes."

"Thanks a lot."

He waved his hands, biceps bulging under a tight white shirt, and I wondered how long he spent at the gym. "I didn't mean it that way. You're selling one house at a time. I mean the developers, the tourist promoters, the real estate factories here. . . . They keep telling the northerners this is paradise, the land of opportunity—play golf or hang out at the beach all day and dine outdoors every night. What they don't tell them is that traffic's bad, housing's expensive and flood and hazard insurance will run them more than the mortgage."

I scanned the menu. The chicken salad on a bed of lettuce looked edible. "Or that they'll need to wear long sleeves and hats all year."

He waved a fly from his ears. They were compact with small lobes and a tiny hole in each. "Or they'll have to call a week in advance for reservations at any decent restaurant."

"Like this place?"

He laughed, the sound broad and solid as his chest, and raised his hands. "What can I say? I can walk to it."

"There's a waiting list to get into paradise."

"Yup," he said, "As long as there's winter, they'll keep lining up."

He looked cute in an overgrown way, and I felt a mixture of tension and release. I was debating whether I could trust him when a teen who looked as if someone had worked her over with a three-hole punch took our order. She returned with two glasses of iced tea and, when she left, I started to explain how I'd ended up in his father's office.

"So," he said, "you think the police aren't moving fast enough."

"They're doing what they can, I'll give them that, but I don't know how long Pap can last. He's in a strange place with a strange person, a potentially violent person, and his meds will run out any minute. He'll get more and more confused, so yes, I need to find him."

"And you think dad was involved."

"No." I pushed the drink aside so the waitress could plop down the plates. "I talked to a friend who says your dad's a straight shooter."

"He doesn't want people to know he got taken by a con artist. That's not good if you're in the trust business."

"I need to find out where Darby is hiding, and I think the investors could lead me there—if they want their money or Bobby Lee bad enough."

"So." He bit into the burger. "How's that working out?"

I forked up some salad. "One dead end after another."

"Dad's right. We have to protect the confidentiality of our clients."

I dropped my head over the plate.

"But," he said, "I *can* tell you how it went with Darby."

"Say on."

"He and dad played golf a couple of times. They had an informal agreement that Darby would steer his clients to dad for portfolio management and dad would recommend they invest part of their stash in a basket of alternatives. You know, real estate, private equity, VC funds."

"VC?"

"Venture capital."

"And Darby's bank was one of those alternatives?"

"A ten-bagger."

"You're killing me with the jargon."

He laughed. "It's an investment that goes up ten-fold."

"I remember Darby mentioning it."

We ate. I picked out a grape and popped it into my mouth. He took lunch more seriously, alternating between burger and tea with machine-like precision.

"He would," Mitch said. "He was into all that finding alpha stuff. Buy a private company, take it public and pump up the stock with investors, then sell out and short the security on the way down."

"Is that what he wanted to do with the bank?"

"It's one theory."

"What's the other?" I asked.

"He ran a dark pool."

"That's the second time I've heard that term."

"A dark pool," he said between bites, "a trading platform where clients of the broker interact with each other. The exchange is private and the trades are anonymous until they settle."

"And that means what, exactly?"

"It means you can trade big blocks of stock without moving the market as much. Or, you can trade shares in companies that are privately held."

"Like the bank Darby was supposed to create."

"Like that."

I dabbed the bottom of the iced tea glass with a napkin and sipped. "If your dad knew all this, why did he invest?"

"He didn't find out until Darby made off with the money. That's why he's so touchy. The clients think he should have known better."

"We only see things clearly in hindsight."

"You," he dabbed his mouth with a napkin, "should join the staff."

"I get uncomfortable around authority."

He finished his meal. "So what do you need, to find your grandfather?"

"Well, since I can't get your father to budge on the investors we don't know, I need to interview the one we do."

"And that is?"

"The real estate queen," I said.

"I know her daughter, Melissa. We play racquetball . . . once in a while."

I nodded, a silent acknowledgment of his eligibility. "Can you broker an introduction?"

His smile looked big and warm. "Sure. What do you want to ask her?"

"The same questions I tried to ask your dad."

"So you can find the money?"

"And trace it to my grandfather."

Unclipping a smartphone from his belt, he made a call, laughed and disconnected."

"She's a hoot."

"Who?"

"Casey's daughter. She said a meeting is, quote, 'not impossible.'"

"You're pretty good with the ladies."

"Sometimes," Mitch said. "You want the appointment?"

"Yes. You'll set it up?"

"Melissa said to call her mom's admin." That smile again.

"What's it going to cost me?"

"Dinner and a drink to start."

"I shouldn't, really. I need to focus."

"Your grandfather must mean a lot to you."

I watched his eyes. Everything else seemed to disappear. "You understand."

"I understand you're frustrated and tired."

I seemed trapped by pale blue eyes.

"You like outdoor sports?"

"Love 'em," I said, with a little too much enthusiasm.

"How about kayaking on the bay? I've got all the equipment."

I could feel my stomach flutter. "When?"

"Tomorrow."

"I don't know," I said. "I have to run the paperwork out to Ginny Alexander, you know, Darby's alleged widow. I'm listing her house."

"We can pack a picnic."

I bit a hangnail. "Tempting."

"Have you ever watched the sun go down on the bay?"

"Many times."

"From a kayak? The wind sailing through your hair?"

"You took a buzz saw to yours." Was I always this contrary? Did I not want to be with this man?

"The sun hanging like a yoke above the water?"

I choked on the tea.

"The breeze caressing your bare skin." He ran a finger down my arm and an electric current crackled in my ears and traveled south. I felt surprised the waitress hadn't hear it.

"At first I thought you looked like a brown-haired version of Cameron Diaz."

"Brunette," I said, "and younger."

"Now that we're close, you remind me of Salma Hayek."

"You play racquetball with her, too?"

He laughed. It sounded good, low and easy. He brushed his knuckles along my forearm. The goose bumps on my back started doing the happy dance.

"I know you're worried about your grandfather but you'll think more clearly if you relax."

At that moment I didn't want to think clearly. I didn't want to think at all. But I forced myself above water and took a breath and said, "I'll relax when I track down the investors."

"How's this?" he said. "I'll call Casey Laine if you come out with me."

"OK. Make the call."

And he did.

23

CASEY LAINE HAD THE figure of a Number 2 pencil and a face like a blade. Her hair stood up in black spikes. She had model-quality cheekbones touched with blush and smooth, pale skin that showed faint blue veins at the temples. The bright red lipstick coordinated with jacket and shoes while the eye shadow matched her powder-blue blouse. Thin silver bracelets rattled as she pumped my hand. I pegged her as a mid-fifties gym rat. No wonder Mitch knew her and the daughter.

She'd met me at the door to the suite, in the same glass tower in which the Palmers practiced, and threaded her way around endless rows of desks to her office. Employees formed a pool in the center of the cavernous room. Around the edges, offices with frosted doors lined walls of glass that overlooked the bay, the marina and the downtown. The pecking order seemed clear: senior agents and corporate officers along the outer wall, rank and file in the middle. The furniture looked like real wood, the lighting indirect, the gold-on-brown carpet thick and soft. High-resolution photographs of mansions dominated the interior walls.

Not as stuffy as Palmer's office, I thought, and a heck of a lot livelier than Shaw's.

Laine stopped in front of one of the offices. "Would you like something to drink? Coffee, herbal tea, Jack and Coke?"

"Jack and Coke?"

"The modern version of rum and Coke. My daughter Melissa says that's what young people are drinking these days." She elongated her vowels in a light Southern accent.

"I'd sell mobile homes for a cup of coffee."

Placing a cool hand on mine she said, "Never say that in this town, dear . . . or that you'll negotiate your commission."

She walked soundlessly to a desk the size of Walter's boat, straightened a photograph in a gold frame and sat. A man's Rolex dominated her left wrist, a half dozen silver bangles her right. Rings of black stone and crusted silver covered every finger, including rings like soda-can tabs on each thumb. I doubted she could type . . . or needed to, with a fleet of worker bees slaving outside her door.

I sat to the left in a rocking chair with floral cushions and shook my head. "You were joking about the Jack and Coke."

"Yes," she said. "You seem a bit more refined than that."

"Thank you." I felt like curtsying. I'd worn a white blouse with a single strand of pearls over a gray pencil skirt and black pumps—my presentation outfit, designed to impress. Despite my concern about stereotypes, I felt glad she'd noticed.

"So." She crossed her arms and tilted her head. "What should I call you? CW? Candace?"

"CW's fine."

"I imagine some clients yearn to call you Candy."

"Only the ones with broken legs." I crossed mine and wondered where she was going with this.

"Anything to diminish a successful woman."

I smiled, not expecting to find a feminist at the top of the business community. "You sound as if you know firsthand."

"Names are difficult," she said. "My father wanted to call me Lois."

"Rough," I said.

"Delusional," she said. "As if I'd spend my life looking for Superman."

"Mr. Right's tough enough." On her desk, a gold frame held a trio of photos of a man in his late forties with a deep tan and blazing white teeth. She saw me look. "Your husband?"

"The one and only."

"What do you call him?"

"Like everyone else, I call him Phil, or Philip, when he's done something thoughtless, which isn't often, but when he does, it's usually spectacular. I do not call him Mr. Mayor, if that's what you mean."

"So you kept your birth name."

"And the agency. He had his own appraisal company before he ran for office. Mostly commercial, so there's little overlap, although he occasionally helps us on the residential side."

"How did you get involved in the business?"

"I grew up in West Virginia with nothing. My father and all of my uncles worked in the mines, and I decided I was too much of the genteel southerner to get my hands that dirty, even by proxy. I understand you come from coal country, too."

I felt a tingle along my spine. "How did you know that?"

"Spanish Point isn't as big a town as you'd think."

I wondered what else she knew but decided to let the question pass. "So you moved here to sell real estate?"

"I moved south with Phil when he took a transfer because that's what good wives did in those days. We couldn't believe the difference in prices. My God, you could buy a block of houses in the Atlanta suburbs for the price of a bungalow on Cape Cod. And as the years and recessions went by, we kept moving further south. By that time we had a daughter, Melissa—I saw you looking at her picture earlier."

She pointed to an 8x10 on her desk of a young woman of college age, taken, I assumed, a few years ago.

"And this, as you know, is my husband." The gold-framed photos showed Phil Cunningham dressed in a green sweater while holding a golf club, sporting a white sweater while posing by the inverted blade of a swordfish and swathed in an argyle sweater while waving from the cockpit of a yellow Corvette. In every photo he smiled.

She leaned toward the pictures as if to bestow a kiss. "Say hello to CW, Phil."

I chuckled. Casey Laine certainly didn't fit my image of a corporate drone.

"I keep those photos to remind me that clients, not toys, come first in this business."

"When were they taken?"

"A few years ago, before he ran for city commissioner."

"I thought he was the mayor?"

"We elect five commissioners," she said, "and every April they choose a major and vice mayor among themselves. Democracy in action."

I looked at Melissa's photo again. She had her mother's dark hair and wild eyes.

"Your daughter's very pretty."

"She'll do." Laine chuckled. "You walked past her on the way in. She's working the phones today. I told her she had to learn the business from the ground up."

"So how did you wind up in Spanish Point?"

"Phil and I were on vacation and met a couple who wanted to get out of the business. It was the tail end of a recession and I had cash, so I bought the agency, and a few more. Then I acquired my own real estate and started a property management division. And voila!" Her bangles clanked as she raised her hands to indicate the space around her. "Laine & Co. became the agency of choice for professionals looking for a career in real estate. Stable earnings, a sizeable marketing budget and the in-house expertise to cater to the well-heeled international traveler."

She placed her forearms on the desk, back straight, hands clasped— her let's-close-the-sale position. As she drew a deep breath and smiled, I hoped her polished lips wouldn't crack.

"So what can I do for you, CW McCoy?"

I told her about Bobby Lee Darby's visit and his abduction of Pap and how he had dementia and that I needed to track them down as soon as possible. As I talked her expression changed. She leaned forward and tilted her head to her left, pursing her lips and squinting, as if my description had physically hurt her. When I finished, she leaned back and crossed her arms.

"I knew he was a bastard but I never would have guessed he'd do anything so cruel. Have you gone to the police?"

"Yes."

"Of course you have. I think I saw something on TV."

I summarized the investigation so far.

"But your grandfather is in poor health and Darby is adept at staying hidden."

"Exactly."

"Well, that doesn't surprise me. The FBI couldn't find him and they have far more resources than the Spanish Point Police. Have you tried hiring a private investigator?"

"I'm getting help from a former state police commander."

"Good," she said, and I heard a little heat in her voice. "Then you know about our involvement with Bobby Lee—of course you do, or you wouldn't be here. You're looking to follow his trail."

Through the office window I watched a sailboat motor into the marina and wondered if it was the *Mary Beth*. When I refocused I noticed she was staring at me. "If I can find a pattern in his behavior," I said, "I can find him."

"Well then, we'd better find that pattern. It was Phil who introduced me to Darby. He'd been managing our investments and getting decent returns—that's about the only part of the business I let Phil handle. Then two years ago, when Darby came to me with the idea of starting a local bank for real estate and development professionals, we saw it as a source of acquisition capital. The agency wouldn't need commercial loans at market rates and the family wouldn't lose control of the business by going public. So we pooled our money with that of the other investors and waited for Darby to file the paperwork."

"Only he didn't."

"No." She twisted one of the silver rings. "He didn't. Phil kept saying, 'Give him time, this is a complex transaction.'" She looked at his photos. "Didn't you, Phil?"

"What happened?"

"Just as we were getting anxious about a return on our investment, Bobby Lee disappeared with the money. When the investigators came around, Phil claimed ignorance and poverty. He said we'd lost half of our savings. I said if he ever did anything like that again, I'd divorce him and take the rest." She took a deep breath and put a hand to her throat. "I doubt that will help to locate your grandfather, but at least you know what you're up against."

"What do you know that would help me find them?"

"Just what I've told you."

"You knew the Darbys socially, knew their friends?"

"I've served on a few boards with Ginny Alexander but Bobby Lee was never very civic-minded, unless you count the benefit to save the community theater—what do they call it, the Little Theatre? Aptly named. Wretched place. Inadequate parking, uncomfortable seats and no climate control. But it sits on a valuable piece of property, close to the bay. I've offered to broker a deal with a developer but the actors have this misguided notion that the highest use of the property is for drama." She barked a laugh. "Talk about irony."

I smiled. Laine's honesty stood in pleasant contrast to the Darbys.

She shook her head. "I go on, don't I? Have I given you anything useful?"

"You've given me a perfect description of a con artist."

"That he is."

"What about his business manager. Could he have been in on the scam?"

"Harvey Shaw? We've never met but I understand the FBI cleared him of everything except willful ignorance. I can't believe the man is as stupid as he claims. If he diverted the money, he's covered his tracks very well."

"And Darby's wife?"

"Ginny? You've met her."

"Yes. I worked with her on a fundraiser for special-needs children."

"How does she strike you?"

"Self-absorbed," I said. "More concerned with appearance than debt."

"Or her children."

Casey Laine locked eyes and in the uncomfortable silence I knew I had to ask.

"What did she do?"

"Most of what we know is about the boy, Robbie, although everyone calls him Junior. Phil mentored him when he was still in high school—sort of a Big Brothers/Big Sisters program for what they call at-risk youth. He'd invite Junior to the house, although I wasn't comfortable with that, and they'd practice guitar together—I think Phil was channeling his inner rock star, or living the life by proxy, to be accurate." She took a breath and blew it halfway across the room. "Anyway, some things went missing, small items like jewelry and folding money, as Phil calls it, and I confronted them."

"How did that go?" I asked.

"Not well, although I think Phil was more perturbed than Junior—at me, that is."

"What happened?"

"What happened? Nothing. We never told the parents, or the police, and Phil eventually forgave me for short-circuiting his attempt to reclaim his youth, although I think he might still keep in touch with the boy. He has that missionary zeal about him sometimes . . . bring salvation to the savages."

"Was Darby still around?"

"No," Laine said. "He'd disappeared by then. The son left home and got into minor scrapes with the law, and the daughter. . . . It's a shame the way Ginny neglects her."

"Claire."

"Yes, Claire. She hasn't had an easy life. Her father's under indictment and reportedly dead, although you tell me differently. The bank's ready to foreclose on the house and the courts are selling off their assets, although the investors won't see much of that. You know Ginny is trying to cash in her daughter's trust fund."

My stomach dropped. "No, I didn't."

"I could tell you stories," she said, glancing at her big watch, "but I have another appointment in five minutes." She rose and held open the door to her office. "How are *you* holding up? I can't imagine you're able to track down this man and show houses at the same time."

"Actually, I'm the seller's agent for the Darby house."

"Ginny threw you a bone."

I cocked my head. "I don't understand."

"She feels sorry for all the trouble her husband's caused. Other than that, how's business?"

The question surprised me. I didn't think the owner of a three-billion-a-year agency would care about my career, much less my welfare.

She must have read my face. "It's tough going it alone. You have to do everything yourself and the hours are lousy—never a weekend or holiday to yourself. Have you ever considered joining a larger firm?"

I shook my head.

"It's a good way to plan for the future, and take care of yourself in case you find out after the ceremony that you've married someone like Bobby Lee."

I looked through the glass doors at the grid of desks in open-plan format. When the agents weren't bent over phones and computers they were grabbing jackets too hot for the climate and storming out the door on high heels. Welcome to cubeville.

"No offense, you've built a wonderful business, but isn't it a bit like working in a factory?"

"It is regimented, yes, but agents have the opportunity to specialize. Some don't like paperwork, others thrive on it. We have administrators, clerks, assistants—people who can do the back-office work for you. Our agents speak twenty-three languages. We have specialists in investment properties—foreclosures and short sales."

"Mine is more of a boutique business."

"You wouldn't have to do all of the work yourself."

"I like a challenge," I said.

"Who's your broker?"

"Andrew Wilcox."

Ginny nodded at the phalanx of workers as we moved through the room. "I know Andy. He's a sweet man, semi-retired and living in Naples, if I remember correctly, but not one to take your business to the next level."

"He took me in when no one else would."

"Loyalty. I like it."

She walked me to the elevator and pushed the *down* button.

"We both know it's tough out there," she said. "Even today, some of our clients feel more comfortable dealing with a man, especially some of the international buyers. We girls need to stick together."

"I like to think I'm a little like Chrissie Hynde—the last of the independents."

The elevator doors opened. Casey Laine winked and shook my hand. "Or the last of the pretenders."

24

WE MET AT THE PARK that spread across the southern edge of Largo Key. If I looked to the south I could see the Darby house at the tip of Spanish Key. I decided I'd rather watch my date.

Mitch had worn red Hawaiian board shorts and a white shirt of some synthetic material that hugged every muscle in his chest. He'd brought a boatload of supplies, including a trike that hitched to the back of the kayak so he could wheel it from the car to the launch. Once he dipped the craft in the water, he handed me a thin red life vest and a yellow paddle that matched the kayak and offered me the seat in front. The picnic supper and bottles of water went into oval holes fore and aft that were covered with a rubberized seal and anchored with bungee cords. Pulling the kayak forward, he deftly climbed in the back and started to paddle.

We headed south into Spanish Bay, well outside the boat lane of the waterway. The surface looked smooth, the water so clear I could have read a book on the sandy bottom. We windmilled around the tip of Largo Key and into a cave formed by mangroves and dredging machines. The mangroves closed in tight. They resembled the rhododendron of the North, with waxy leaves and trunks that twisted into a fortress. The further inland we travelled, the darker it got.

"How did these get here?" I asked.

"There's a lake ahead," Mitch said. "Fresh water. The mosquitoes were horrendous. The Army Corps of Engineers dug the channels to flood the lake with salt water and kill the bugs."

A crab skittered as we ducked beneath a branch that skimmed the top of my baseball cap. "It's kinda spooky."

"Not much traffic at dusk."

I caught the paddle on a limb and cursed. "From the bay, you'd never know anyone was in here."

After a few minutes, we glided across the lake, a glowing silver coin in the evening light, and followed a second channel back to the bay. Mitch continued south as we rounded the tip of Largo Key and the park with its long stretch of white sand until we faced the setting sun. The wind rose and we bobbed in the chop.

"Can't go much further," he said. "Too rough for small craft."

He beached the kayak at the tip of the key and helped me out, digging the basket and water from the hold. We spread a blanket and ate and watched the sun burn the horizon to rust. He handed me a bottle of water and I drank deeply, watching the sun, digging toes into the sand, letting the wind cool my skin. As the light faded, he slid an arm around my waist, his body humming, his scent a mixture of salt water and soap. I leaned in.

Nothing moved on the water except the waves. The sun gave up the struggle and disappeared, sizzling into the Gulf like a glowing penny. Even after it set, its light streaked the horizon pink and peach.

"If we can't see," I said as we packed to leave, "how do we make it back?"

"Follow me." With a hand he helped me into the bow and we shoved off, paddling like whirlwinds for the bay side shore. We beached at the landing site just as night fell.

"That was great," I said as we strapped the kayak to the top of his car.

"Feel like a nightcap?"

"I feel like a shower."

"Coming right up."

I followed him north on Largo Key's only through road and slid beneath a towering condo complex that faced the Gulf, emerging to the sound of waves lapping the beach. I banged my flip flops to release the sand and followed him into an elevator to the top floor.

The interior of the condo gleamed in chrome and glass with limestone and marble floors, thick stucco walls and countertops of granite and mica. From the wall of windows in the living room, the view took in a vast, dark, undulating mass of water.

Mitch pointed down the hall. "There's soap, shampoo and towels on the right. How about we meet back here in twenty minutes?" He disappeared into what I assumed was the master bedroom.

I washed my bathing suit in the sink and stuffed it into a plastic bag. Then I turned the water on hot and scrubbed, drying with a towel so thick it didn't absorb the water. I slid into a peach-colored sundress and a pair of sandals and ran a comb through my hair to unsnag the tangles. I took my time, trying not to think about what I knew would happen.

We met at the kitchen island, under a rack of wine glasses. Mitch had changed into jeans and a white shirt with the sleeves rolled to the elbows. When he propped a bare foot on the barstool and reached for two glasses, I felt something brush my insides. And when our hands touched as he gave me the wine, I felt that something move south of the border.

"Cheers," he said.

We touched glasses and slid onto the barstools.

The wine looked as golden as honey and tasted just as smooth. I tried not to guzzle.

"So," Mitch said. "I hear you used to be with the police."

"For a time." I sipped the wine. It tasted cool and dry, the exact opposite of how I felt.

"How was that?"

"Difficult," I said. "I was the youngest detective on a regional police force."

"Were you the only female?"

"No, but we were definitely in the minority."

"The guys harass you?" He refilled our glasses.

I laughed. "Gender didn't matter. Age and experience did."

"Did you get promoted?"

I nodded.

"You must have done something right."

"I was getting there."

"But you're here." He paused. "Something happen?"

I drained the glass and held it out for a refill. "Dispatch asked for all available units to respond to a domestic and I got there first. You can read the rest online."

"I'd rather hear it from you."

My chest felt heavy and I found it hard to breathe. "Three people in the house—man, wife and child. He's holding a gun. The hands of the other two were empty. You always look at the hands first, then the eyes. The father was a fellow officer with a history of drinking and pushing suspects down stairwells. When I entered the home, he was screaming at his wife for cheating on him. The daughter hid behind her. He raised his weapon and I shot first. End of story."

He was quiet. "I take it that wasn't the end."

"No," I said. "Ask any cop. It's never the end."

He topped the glasses. We sipped and said nothing, looked at nothing. He didn't press. He gave me air. It made me feel warm. It was either that or the wine.

Finally he said, "So you quit."

I took in a lungful of air. "I stopped carrying a gun. Refused, actually. They transferred me to public relations. I spent my days fingerprinting toddlers for the department's photo ID program."

"Boring?"

"Sad, when you think of why we did it."

He moved closer. "Why's that?"

"We didn't do it to protect their children. We did it so we could identify the remains."

"I see." He swirled the wine. "So you moved south."

"After I left my marriage. My grandparents moved here a dozen years ago. After my grandmother died, Pap needed help and I needed a place to stay. It seemed like a good idea at the time."

"What happened?"

"Pap was having trouble with his balance and motor control. He'd developed Parkinson's and Alzheimer's but no one knew it—Nana always took care of him. She masked the symptoms better than any drug."

"And you've been taking care of him since."

"The dutiful granddaughter, hauling him to endless tests and doctor's appointments. And they can't do a damned thing except slow it down."

"I'm sorry," he said.

"It's OK." I touched his hand, tracing the veins, watching them swell. He smiled.

"So," I said. "Enough about me. What's your story?"

"You running a background check?"

"Always a smart thing."

He shrugged. "I'm one of maybe a dozen people born and raised in

Spanish Point. Graduated from the University of Florida in finance and came back to join my parents' firm. Dad lets me run a couple of portfolios for new clients and mess with the website."

"You buy and sell stocks?"

He laughed and raised the bottle. I thought about putting a palm over my glass, considering what happened with Sal Finzi after a couple of snorts, but let him fill it to the rim. "No, we manage wealth. The clients tell us how much money they want to earn from the portfolio each year and we tell them how to do it without taking unnecessary risk. We farm the assets out to brokers, hedge funds, mutual-fund companies."

His face looked soft, his teeth shiny and clean, his pale eyes an unearthly blue. When he stroked the inside of my wrist, my heart beat quickened. When he made circles on the inside of my elbow, the pulse beat under my tongue.

"Fascinating," was all I could manage.

"Since you're in real estate, would you like the grand tour?"

"As long as you bring the wine."

Grabbing the bottle, he took my hand and led me through the rooms, from the balcony overlooking the Gulf to the great room with its coffered ceiling and wall-sized TV. The tour ended in the master bedroom.

He set the bottle and glasses on a table by the bed. Over the headboard he'd hung a black-and-white photo of cars racing at Sebring. As I admired the image I felt the warmth of his body behind me.

"Is this where you ask me to look at your etchings?"

Sliding his hands around my waist, he kissed me softly on the back of the neck and started to undo the buttons of the sundress. I felt a shiver climb my spine as the dress and bra slipped to the floor. I returned the favor, taking him down to the smallest pair of underwear I'd ever seen. It showed off muscles like bridge cables.

I snapped the elastic waistband. "You're in pretty good shape."

He turned out the light and we slid into bed, the sheets cool against my back, his kisses light, breath warm, voice a barely audible purr.

"I'm very athletic."

And he was.

25

WE SHOULD HAVE DONE this days ago," I said and poured coffee down my throat in an attempt to revive after a night of gymnastics. Playing the good detective, I honed in on the white bakery bag Walter had picked up in the grocery store. Louie spotted it at the same time and pushed his head between the seats.

"I need food," I said.

"You need sleep. Where'd you go last night?"

"Home," I yawned and stretched. Ever hopeful, Louie licked my hand.

"Whose home?"

"It shows?"

"I haven't seen you this relaxed since . . . never." He sipped coffee. "I'm surprised you have the strength to complain."

"I gotta be me."

"That's the problem right there."

I took a cinnamon raisin bagel and handed the bag to Walter.

"So when do I get to see this guy?" he asked.

"You mean, when do I bring him home to meet dad?"

He chuckled and continued to watch the parking lot. On the car's sound system, Clint Black's "A Good Run of Bad Luck" simmered like stew over a wood fire. I knew how he felt. If we didn't catch a break on the hunt for Pap I was going to hurt someone . . . if I could gather the strength.

Walter scrounged in the bag and dug out a sesame seed bagel. "You heard from Darby?" He broke off a piece for Louie, who wolfed it in one bite.

"No." I broke off a piece of a cinnamon raisin and offered Louie a chunk, dry, no butter or cream cheese. He didn't seem to mind. "You have any words of comfort?"

"No."

We sipped coffee and sat in silence and watched the back of the market. The store had built a cement block monolith with a loading dock and a single metal door and painted everything tan. Not exactly a garden view. Twenty minutes ago Claire had parked her aging silver Toyota Corolla nose in and gone inside. We sat with the windows down, Louie roaming from front to back, his head hanging out the side and his tongue hanging out of his mouth. After last night, I knew how he felt.

I checked my cell phone. No messages. I thought about calling Mitch. Instead I said, "How long does it take to buy groceries for a fugitive?"

"As long as it takes."

"What's he going to eat besides P&J?"

"You have the patience of a gnat."

I slumped in the seat. "I thought that was the attention span of a gnat."

"Same thing in your case."

Robert Darby Jr. worked as a bagger at the grocery store. It sat opposite the bridge to Spanish Key, not more than two miles from his parents' home. Walter, Louie and I had staked it out with the expectation that Claire would supply Darby with groceries. Most people followed the money. We followed the food.

As long as I had the smartphone running, I checked the news—another tourist mugged on Spanish Key, another carjacking near the airport—and wondered why it had taken so long for big-city crime to find its way to paradise. The phone buzzed. I didn't recognize the caller ID but answered anyway.

Darby. No preamble. "You send someone after me?"

"Put my grandfather on the line."

"Big guy, looks like a private eye."

Walter raised his brows. I mouthed *Darby*.

"Listen to me," I said. "I need to talk to Pap, and then I need a list of corporate. . . ."

He disconnected.

"Son of a bitch!"

Louie growled. Walter turned. "What did he want?"

I started to answer when Claire walked around the corner carrying two bags so heavy they stretched the plastic handles. She wore flip flops, baggy jeans and a royal blue T-shirt with a Superman shield on the front. Unlocking the trunk of the Corolla, she dumped the bags, got in the car and headed toward the Tamiami Trail and the bridge to Spanish Key.

"Going home," Walter said.

"Maybe it's the staging area."

We followed. In the bright morning sun, the Darby estate looked even more lush than before, with its dense vegetation and bone-white walls spiraling toward the walkway like the West Indies' version of a buttress. Walter parked the Merc by the wrought-iron gate. Ginny's white Jag and Claire's Toyota sat in the drive, a contrast in wealth and style.

"We have a plan? Walter asked.

I grabbed my camera and the paperwork for the listing and said, "You mind waiting here?"

Walter laughed. "Who are you talking to? Louie or me?"

I patted his knee. "You'll be fine as long as you stay in your car seat."

He scratched Louie beneath the ear. "Women."

"Ginny can't know we're following her daughter."

He shook his head.

"Why don't you check out the grounds?"

"For what?" he asked.

"Buried treasure."

"You know," he said, "it's OK for young women to be seen in public with older men."

"Just a rumor."

I climbed from the car, pushed the button on the whitewashed pillar beside the gate, identified myself and told Ginny Alexander what I wanted. She buzzed me in.

The interior of the house still dazzled. So did Alexander. She wore a red sweater with a plunging neckline, tight jeans and strappy sandals. Greeting me with an air hug, she walked me through the house to the chef's kitchen. With its white ceiling, cabinets, counters and tile floor, the room gleamed like a hospital OR. I could have worn sunglasses.

She stood at the cooking island and, brushing her dark hair aside, fiddled with her right earlobe. Except for a tiny puncture, it looked bare.

Shifting the camera to the other hand I asked, "Did you lose something?"

"Yes, and I'm furious with myself." She held a dark blue cloisonné earring. "They were a gift from my mother. I'll have to ask Claire if she's seen the other one."

"Is she home?" I asked.

Lines formed on her forehead. "What did she do now?"

"Nothing. I just thought I'd say hello."

"Buddies since she crashed your office?"

"She misses her father," I said.

"God knows why." Alexander pocketed the earring, scooped a plastic grocery bag off the counter and tossed it under the sink. "You just missed her. She took the boat. She and her brother are going fishing."

Shit. I didn't see that one coming. Too late to have Walter follow. "Where do they usually go?"

Alexander cocked her head. "I wouldn't have cast you as a fisherman."

"I'm not. My friend is."

"You should invite him over sometime. Is he nearby? I know you said you're from somewhere up north."

"No," I said, "he's right around the corner."

"Good. Maybe he could take the damned boats off my hands. Darby always left the keys in them—I told you that the last time, didn't I. I think he wanted to make a fast getaway. Your friend can take them for a test drive, or whatever you call it."

"He did get away," I said.

"Not far enough, if you ask me."

"And you're not worried about theft in the neighborhood?"

She scowled. "No one else has reported anything."

"And you have no idea who broke in, or what they wanted."

"Not a clue," she said.

"And nothing's missing."

"Just my peace of mind."

"Well," I said, putting the file folder on the countertop, "I hope this will help. I've brought the agreement and disclosure documents. I'll need some basic numbers for the MLS listing—age of the house, square footage, number of bedrooms, full- and half-baths. We can do a walk-through together and discuss the age of the appliances and any upgrades you've made, and then you can sign and date the forms. I'm sure you've been through this before."

"Many times. Sometimes I think my husband was a nomad."

I raised the camera. "I'd like to take some photos, too, inside and out, if you don't mind."

"Anything to unload this elephant before the IRS comes knocking."

As we toured the house, I looked for details I'd missed the first time, such as clues to Darby's location, or where he might hide a few million in cash. I didn't see any. I did see a motive for the attempted burglaries. If Darby had hidden money in the house, was he trying retrieve it? Was someone else? If I could locate his stash, maybe I could trade it for Pap. Against the law but so was kidnapping.

I'd photographed most of the interior when we came full circle to the kitchen. The house loomed large. Built to Miami-Dade hurricane standards, it spread over 7,200 sq. ft. with five bedrooms, four-and-a-half baths and 4,000 sq. ft. of covered and open terrace. I asked Alexander how much she wanted to ask.

"Seven point two million should do it."

"I'll do comps," I said, "but the high-end market is recovering much faster than other segments of the housing industry here. You have a salt-water pool and beach and bay access, so I think we can start there."

We moved into the living room and stood in front of the glass. "What's your time frame for moving?"

"As soon as possible. This house has too many memories."

"I can help you relocate," I said. "What are you looking for?"

"A new husband to start."

She opened a slider in the living room wall and we stepped onto the lanai. I'd walked into hotels less lavishly furnished. Thick posts formed arches to cap a ceiling of inlaid tile as blue as the South Pacific. Paddle fans whirred. Wooden chairs with wheels and sky-blue cushions formed a seating group in front of a fireplace topped with a TV the size of a Jumbotron. An outdoor kitchen nestled into the back wall.

"This is a beautiful view," I said, taking in a panorama that ran from Spanish Bay to the Gulf of Mexico with the white sands of Largo Key in between. As I watched the beach where Mitch and I had picnicked, my stomach jumped like a trampoline and I hoped the seismic upheaval wouldn't show in my voice. "And the furnishings are exquisite."

"Philanthropy doesn't work if you're poor," she said. "A girl needs cash. If Darby *is* alive, the insurance company will want its money back."

"What will you do after you sell the house? Can you stay with anyone? Friends, relatives?"

"Honey," she said, "ever since that bastard stole money from our wealthier citizens, I haven't exactly made anyone's A-list." She stared across the pool at the waters of the Gulf, as still as the noonday air. Then she turned and gave me a crooked smile. "You're not adverse to a little larceny, are you?"

"Larceny?"

"Why don't you help me find the money Darby stole and we'll split it fifty-fifty."

"I don't think I could do that," I stammered.

Her laugh sounded like a bark. "No, you look too honest. That's probably what attracted him to you."

"Pardon?"

"Oh, he likes them young and innocent."

"I'm sorry," I said. "The only thing your former husband and I have in common is my grandfather."

She looked down her nose with cool eyes and a solid mouth. "No, well maybe you're not his type."

"Maybe you'd be more comfortable with another agent."

She waved a bug from her head. "Don't mind me. I'm still reeling from the news that he's back from the dead."

"You don't know where he is then."

"No, and I don't care to know."

"What would you do," I asked, "if you did find him?"

She cackled. "I'd tell him to go back to the ferry and finish the job."

To keep my mind off Darby and Mitch, I photographed the exterior of the house. A quick review of the photos showed flaws I hadn't caught during my first visit. Several roof tiles had cracked, a portion of the mortar had bled through the paint and the lawn needed mowing. By the sides of the house, vegetation ran wild, with branches poking from once neatly trimmed hedges. On the other hand, the pool looked immaculate, from its polished blue rim to the sparkling pebble finish that lined the bottom. Alexander said she couldn't afford maintenance yet the pool looked perfect. She was not one to get her hands wet, and Claire could care less, so who?

"The pool looks lovely," I said. "Is the person who maintains it willing to continue while we sell the house?"

She laughed. "That's Harvey. He likes to swim."

"I think I saw the two of you at the film festival."

She smiled. It came out as more of a grimace. "I hate being alone. Don't you?"

"Sometimes," I said, feeling that Shaw did more maintenance on her than on the property.

"So," Ginny said, taking in the property with a sweep of her hand. "Back to business. How are you going to sell this dump? Do I have to put half of my furniture in storage and sprinkle potpourri around the house like the witches from *Macbeth*?"

"We'll hold an open house for buyers' agents. And we'll bake cookies . . . gingerbread."

"We?"

"I'll come over before the showing if I get enough notice and put the cookies in the oven. You won't have to do a thing." I glanced at her figure. She looked cut, with the kind of muscle definition male weightlifters develop. "Or eat any of them."

"We'll just leave them for Santa with a glass of milk."

Or the burglar, I thought, but didn't have a chance to respond because my phone rang.

26

I T'S AN EMERGENCY!" Mrs. T. yelled. "I don't know what to do! He's in the pool. I don't know how he got in there. He's huge! You have to come, right away!"

For a moment I thought she'd found Bobby Lee Darby and searched my memory to determine whether I'd told her about the man. Although she could have seen the newscast.

"Is it a snake?" I asked.

"No, no."

"Alligator?"

"Yes, yes."

"I'll call Palmetto County Animal Control," I said.

"Oh, please tell them to hurry. I don't want him coming in the house."

"Go inside and close the doors," I said, "and I'll be right there."

Right there would take a while—the house I'd sold Mrs. Taggert sat north and east of the city in a sprawling community called Meadowbrook. It had neither meadows nor brooks, but that hadn't stopped the developer from embellishing.

I could get little else from her, so I hopped in the Merc and told Walter to drive toward University Parkway.

Louie raised his ears. Walter raised his eyebrows. "Who are we chasing now?"

"A gator," I said.

"Only in Florida."

Once we cleared the bridge off the key, we headed for I-75, then turned onto one of the North-South arteries.

"Take a left into Meadowbrook and the next right," I said.

The Merc leaned into a corner like a box spring and drifted down a narrow street lined with oak and palmetto. Mrs. T.'s house sat on the left, a beige adobe with a white roof and borders of hibiscus and bird-of-paradise. Walter parked in the circular drive and started to get out. I put a hand on his arm.

"I'll call if I need reinforcements."

"Yes, mom."

I rang the bell next to a pair of purple doors. None of the paint had slopped onto the stucco wall. Mrs. T. had done a good job.

A woman in her eighties answered the door, her eyes a pair of milky marbles and hair a dandelion gone to seed. She wore a rose-print dress topped with a yoke of doilies as frilly as Queen Anne's lace and a smile that reflected more apology than humor.

"Hello, Mrs. T.," I said. "Are you all right?"

She answered with a flurry of hands and motioned me through the house. "He's in the back." She led me through the lanai into the pool cage. I stopped when I saw the gnarled snout and bulging eyes skimming the surface, a crooked tail fanning the water. It was a gator all right, about five-feet long and in the wrong place.

I put out a hand to stop her from getting too close. "I'd stay back, Mrs. T."

"Oh, I'm staying back. You never know with alligators."

"Animal control should be here soon."

Mrs. T. squeezed my hand. "I don't understand how he got in."

I pointed to a tear in the screen shaped like half a moon. "When did that happen?"

She wrung her hands. "I don't know. He must have come up from the lake."

I watched the creature etch a circle on the surface. "I didn't think alligators liked chlorine. You haven't been feeding it, have you, Mrs. T.?

"They're all God's creatures, you know."

Oh boy.

"What did you feed it?"

She gave an embarrassed smile. "Hot dogs. He likes them best, but lately he's been a little choosy. I know I'm not supposed to but I feed the sandhill cranes too, although I haven't seen them lately."

"That might explain a lot of things."

"I throw it down by the lake," she said. "I never thought he'd come up this far. The cranes and squirrels never bother us, although I do worry about the bobcats."

"You don't feed them, too?"

She grinned. "Just a smidgen."

Oh boy.

"Mrs. T., would you like me to call someone to fix the pool cage?"

"No, no, one of the grandchildren can do that. I can't believe they were coming over to swim this afternoon."

"I'd let your maintenance company clean the pool first. You also might. . . ."

I was going to say "cut back on the feedings" when my phone rang. I excused myself, walked to the opposite end of the pool, beyond the reach of Jaws, glanced at the caller ID and groaned.

"Hello, Jackie, how are you?"

The woman wasted no time. "Kurt and I talked after you left and we've decided to go with another agent."

"We have three months left on our agreement," I said, knowing that I'd let them go rather than fight with reluctant clients.

"You just haven't delivered for us. We feel it's time for a change."

I thought I heard her jaws snap. Or maybe it was the gator.

"I understand," I said. "Please send me a note canceling the agreement. You can mail or email the document."

The phone went dead.

As I rounded the lanai toward Mrs. T., I watched the gator lap the pool and felt sorry for it. The mighty beast could scare the likes of Mrs. T. but it was no match for Jackie.

A truck throttled into her driveway and a man wheeling a metal container like a meat smoker trundled through the side yard and stopped by the pool cage. He stood about six feet tall, with bright red hair and wraparound shades. He introduced himself just as Walter came around the other side of the house. Walter looked at the gator and then at the young man and volunteered to help. I shook my head. Mrs. T. smiled and offered refreshments. We declined.

"Where's Louie?" I asked.

Walter flipped his shades down and smiled. "Parking the car."

The redhead hoisted a long pole with a loop over the water and tried to snare the animal's head. After several false starts, he grabbed the gator and he and Walter wrestled it onto the deck. They coaxed it into the barrel, shut the door with a reassuring snap and the redhead trundled off with his prize.

Clouds smudged the horizon and the wind blew the scent of weeds and water from the lake. Mrs. T. and I stared at the pool. After the excitement, it looked empty, reminding me of Pap's house and everything I needed to do to fill it again. I didn't feel like doing any of it. I felt like going home and pulling the covers over my head and never talking to another human being again.

"I hope they don't hurt Ernie," Mrs. T. said.

"Ernie?"

Walter lifted his sunglasses.

"Yes, I named him after my son."

"The attorney?" I asked.

"Yes. I know he's a wild animal and eats all of the things we think are pretty, but it seemed like the right thing to do at the time."

"Sounds just right," Walter said and headed for the car.

27

THE SHOUTING REACHED ME as soon as I pulled into Pap's driveway . . . the high-pitched voice of a woman followed by the low growl of a man. Something crashed—glass, furniture, I couldn't tell. I thought about the Beretta under the bed, dismissed the idea and ran next door.

The voices grew louder and no amount of pounding brought anyone to the door, so I let myself into the house and came face-to-face with Sal Finzi. He pointed a thick finger at me, shouted, "You stay out of this!" and turned back to Cheryl. He yelled about money and her constant pestering and the interference of the neighbors. In seconds I'd become the bitch next door.

Cheryl stood in the kitchen, back to a counter stocked with a knife rack and a bowl of apples, her face streaked with tears and pain. Her hands were empty. She wore her uniform but not the duty belt, and I sent up a silent *thank you* that she wasn't armed. Finzi loomed in the archway between living room and kitchen, his massive back toward me. His hands were empty, too, although he waved his fists like hammers. I didn't see Tracy and hoped that Cheryl had stowed her at the neighbor's house. I also hoped no one would grab a knife.

The fighting sounded worse than when they were married. He accused her of hiding Tracy from him. She called him a cheat and a liar and a thief. And then it got ugly.

"You think I don't know what's going on?" he yelled. "I've got friends on the force seen you and this guy together after work."

So that's what it was about . . . Officer Charles Stover, the black patrol officer.

"Who I see is none of your goddamned business," Cheryl yelled.

"It's my goddamned business when it involves my kid. There's fifty thousand people in this town and you can't find one of your own?"

From the bowl on the counter Cheryl grabbled an apple and threw it. As it bounced off Finzi's chest, he lunged. He had her by the throat when I grabbed a cast-iron skillet from the stove and smacked the back of his head. He went down on one knee, shook his head, rose slowly and turned. Hate burned in his eyes and for a second I saw the twisted face of Nicholas Church. The big hands came up and he charged and I smacked him in the jaw with the pan. The blow knocked him sideways and he leaned against the dishwasher, shaking the stuffing out of his head.

"That's for stiffing Cheryl." I breathed hard. "And this. . . ." I aimed for his balls but at the last minute shifted to kick him in the stomach. ". . . is for your fucking bike."

Finzi groaned and doubled over, smacking the linoleum with his forehead. I grabbed Cheryl's hand and dragged her to the door. "Get your gear and go to Pap's. Front door's open. Lock it as soon as you're in. I'll call Chip."

"No!" she shrieked.

"OK, Delgado."

I realized I still held the skillet. As Cheryl brushed past, Finzi tried to lever himself off the floor. I stood over him like a batter at home plate. "And this," I said, winding up, "is for Tracy," and knocked him into next week.

My breath came in gasps. Before me floated the face of my father, with his brown pipe and stark blue eyes and mass of curly dirty blond hair. Smoke swirled across his face and the image vanished in a sparkle of light. Grabbing my phone, I punched in the number for Delgado's private line. My hands shook and I had to key the numbers twice. I was still breathing hard when he answered.

"What is it, McCoy?"

"Finzi attacked his wife."

"Is she safe?"

"She's at my house now."

"Are you hurt?"

"No," I said, "just trying to catch my breath."

"Where's the husband?"

"We have him subdued."

"Is he alive?" he asked.

"Yes."

"Tell me what happened," he said.

"He fell down the stairs."

"In a one-story house."

"He's a clumsy man," I said.

"He's an unlucky man. You steal his cycle again?"

"I told you, it was a loaner."

"Uh-huh," he said. "How badly is he hurt?"

"He's not bleeding. Much."

"Does he need an ambulance?"

"I'll ask when he comes around."

He paused so long I thought he'd disconnected. "Need I remind you that at one time you were a sworn officer of the law?"

I took a deep breath. "OK, send one, and Officer Stover. Finzi was asking about him."

"Was he." Another long pause. "Who started it?"

"He did."

"And you finished it," he said.

"I'm a go-big-or-go-home kind of girl."

Delgado sighed. "Remind me not to piss you off."

"Roger that."

28

AFTER GOING A SECOND round with Sal Finzi, I decided that what Cheryl and I needed more than anything was a night out with a couple of long necks and a live country band.

"Let's go to the Roadhouse," I said as we cleared away the supper dishes.

"I can't," Cheryl said. "It's a school night."

"It's almost the weekend and your neighbor can keep Tracy for an extra hour of two."

"I've got work tomorrow."

"We won't be late," I said. "It's not like we pick up guys."

Cheryl sighed with a force that could move curtains. "We never pick up guys."

"You sound disappointed."

"I don't know," she said. "We've had a lot of trouble up there."

The Roadhouse was located in a sketchy part of North Point near the Stab 'n' Grab. A combination bar, dance hall and video arcade, it consumed as much space as an aircraft hangar with about as much charm. The owner, who hunted pigs each winter in the Florida wilds, had decorated the interior in early American neon and concrete, the easier to mop the beer and blood from the nightly fight. The parking lot featured an acre of cars, a mountain of cans and plastic wrap and two operating streetlights. The police had responded to so many drunk and disorderlies that the officers joked about building a substation there.

"You know," Cheryl said as she locked the door, "we're getting a little old for this."

"You love line dancing," I said as we crossed to Pap's so I could change.

"You're just high after bustin' up Sal."

"Maybe." I popped the door, hit the lights and rummaged through the drawers, coming up with a little white tank top that Dierks Bentley would have loved.

I held it up. "What do you think?"

Cheryl shook her head. "You're trouble."

I handed her a helmet and we rolled the bike out of the carport and headed north to University Parkway, the line of demarcation between the gentrified retirees and their poorer cousins to the north. It was early and but we still had to park at the end of the lot and walk a block to the front door. We left the helmets at coat check and passed through the metal detectors and ran into a wall of sound as thick as the Florida night.

The band played some boot-scoot and we danced and worked up a sweat while warding off the boys. After a couple of oldies by the Georges, Strait and Jones, a rocker by Keith Urban and a classic by Lonestar, the lead singer settled into an Alan Jackson number slow enough to gel motor oil and Cheryl and I pushed through the crowd to the bar for a couple of cold ones. I sipped, Cheryl held the bottle against her forehead and we watched the mating ritual unfold.

The band launched into "Achy Breaky Heart."

I glanced at Cheryl. "You all right?"

"Living the good life."

"Tracy?"

She nodded.

"OK," I said. "Maybe we are too old for this."

The bar wrapped around the restrooms and arcade like a kidney pool with about as much liquid. We watched the men pull on their longnecks and the women smoke, breasts forward and shoulders back with a hand resting on a hip. A sudden movement caught my eye and I watched a skinny arm grab another and stop it in midair. I recognized the guy: It was Curly from the ranch east of I-75. Sure enough, his backup band stood behind, all leers for the two women they'd pinned in the notch of the bar. Curly let go and the woman dropped her arm and turned to say something and her face registered: Melissa Cunningham, the daughter of Casey Laine and Mayor Phil Cunningham.

Melissa looked like an early version of her mother, tall and slender with black hair falling past her shoulders and a face bleached of color. She wore skinny jeans and a top that looked like a woman's version of the wife-beater tee. She had spidery lashes, pouty lips thick with gloss and a slight buck to her teeth. The latter must have caused problems when she was a kid, until she developed those enormous boobs and the boys forgot all about dental work. I pegged her at twenty-two or twenty-three. The woman beside her looked barely legal. She had long blond hair and a shovel jaw and no muscle definition in her thighs, of which she showed plenty. She wore a tight white top with rhinestone appliqué, white shorts with cowboy boots and hat and the unmistakable look of fear.

Melissa looked mad. She raised her hand again—she must have tried to hit Curly before—and he batted it away to slide an arm around her waist.

I touched Cheryl's arm but she'd seen the struggle and we both moved toward the men at the same time.

The band had launched into "Friends in Low Places" and the crowd sang along with gusto. I saw Melissa's mouth move and then she and the other woman ducked under the men's arms and hurried toward the exit. The guys followed. So did we.

"You recognize them?" Cheryl asked as we retrieved the helmets.

I told her where I'd seen Melissa and the guys from the ranch.

"I'll have Oz check 'em out tomorrow," she said.

As we approached the bike I heard voices from the other end of the lot. The five stood under one of the functioning streetlights. The men had backed the women against the trunk of a dark blue pickup. I checked their hands, all empty, and Cheryl and I split. I circled to the right and came up on Melissa's side with a clear view of Curly. Cheryl walked up behind the other two, a canister of pepper spray held at her side.

"Melissa," I said.

She turned a startled face drained of color. The other woman had tented her fingers in front of her face and looked ready to cry.

"Back off," Cheryl said in a voice I'd never heard her use.

Moe and Larry spun around.

Curly stared at me. "I knew you were a cop."

"I'm not," I said. "She is. I'd listen to her."

Cheryl pushed past Moe and Larry and stood by the women, canister of pepper spray at the ready.

Curly backed away with his hands in the air and said, "We're just having a little fun, officer." And then he lunged.

As he dove for my knees I spun left and swung the helmet with a crack to the back of his head. His grip faltered and he skidded in the gravel and came up bleeding and charged again. This time I smacked the side of his face with enough force to crush bone. Blood gushed from his nose. He staggered and raised his arms and as I came at him again, Curly ran.

Cheryl raised the pepper spray but the other two disappeared into the dark.

Melissa shook. I slid an arm around her shoulder and told her who we were and asked if she or her friend knew the three men. Both shook their heads.

"You were in the office," Melissa said. Her voice sounded hoarse. "You won't tell mom."

"No," I said, "but word gets around. She'd rather hear it from you."

Cheryl asked Melissa if she wanted to press charges.

Melissa shook her head. "I just want to go home."

Pulling a notepad from her back pocket, Cheryl jotted their names and addresses. The second woman identified herself as Tiffany Jones. Both women looked drained, with a sheen of sweat coating their faces.

"You're not going to arrest me, are you?" Tiffany asked. "I'm underage."

No kidding, I felt like saying but let Cheryl handle it.

"No," she said. "You've had enough excitement for one night."

The trembling had stopped so I let go of Melissa. "Do you want us to follow you home?"

She shook her head

Cheryl handed the women business cards and said if they heard from the three to call her, or 911. They stared at the cards and nodded and got in the pickup truck and left.

"That was close," Cheryl said as we walked toward the bike.

"Too close," I said.

"Good thing we were here."

I climbed on the bike. "Like Butch and Sundance."

She seated the helmet and in a muffled voice said, "More like Laurel and Hardy."

29

I F I FELT RATTLED by the confrontation with the Three Stooges, the feeling intensified when I drove to my office to find Ricky Hunt sitting outside in a new rental, smoking a cigarette, his legs hanging from the open door. As I pulled in he flicked the butt onto the shell-covered parking lot. The car, a light blue compact, bounced as he got out.

Hunt gave me a meaty smile and shook hands with the grip of a professional wrestler and said, "Ready to scout homes?"

I unlocked the door and gestured toward my desk. "Why don't you make yourself comfortable while I do a little research?"

He sat in the same chair as Darby and Claire but with more bulk, the smell of smoke and cologne sloughing off him in waves.

"I'd offer you some coffee but I'm out." I booted the computer.

"Nice place," he said. "Convenient. Right next door to a motel and a diner. Eat, sleep and work. Everything you need in one place."

His belly laugh sounded like a backfiring car. When he smiled, I felt disappointed he didn't have a mammoth cold sore or rotting teeth.

"Too bad you have to do everything yourself."

"It works for me," I said, focusing on the screen. "I see you have a new rental."

"Rental?"

I nodded to the lot in front of the building. "Your car."

"Oh," he chuckled, "my wife has the other one."

"Will she be joining us today?"

"Not a chance. She's shopping at that new mall, spending the down

175

payment . . . or the commission." He laughed and drummed a foot on the thin carpet like a woodpecker beating out a tattoo on an oak.

"I'll just be a minute. I want to check the MLS for any listings that came in overnight."

"I hope you do better than last time."

I glanced up. "Was the last time so bad?"

"Nothing stood out." He spread his hands wide. "There wasn't a unique place in the mix. I'm looking for something distinct, something with history, a story, something people will talk about."

"OK. How would you like to live in the house of Florida's answer to Bernie Madoff?"

He leaned forward in the chair. "You mean the guy who killed himself and came back to life?"

"Lazarus himself."

He smiled. "When?"

"I'll call the owner. Would you excuse me?"

I stepped outside and punched in the number for Ginny Alexander and, after stuffing a finger in my ear so I could hear above the roar of traffic, asked if I could show the house. Yes, but she was upset. Claire had left and she didn't know where she'd gone. The police told her to wait a day and call again.

"It's like trying to get service from Verizon, or hazard insurance in Florida," she said. "Maybe the companies are so rich they don't need the business. I wish I had that problem. I know, I'm rambling again. I'll leave the gate open. The key's under a flowerpot by the front door. Just have the client wipe his feet. I don't want a repeat of that fiasco with the police. They made the Big Dig in Boston look like a kid with a sand pail."

I was beginning to enjoy the drama. "When can we stop by?"

"Give me an hour to put on a face."

She recited the alarm code and disconnected. I called Walter and filled him in on Claire's disappearance and the house tour.

"If the cops find my body washed up on Spanish Key, they should look for Ricky Hunt."

"You want help? Louie and I could keep the car seats warm."

"Thanks for the offer," I said, "but you're liable to confuse Hunt, and he seems baffled enough as it is. Could you keep an eye on Claire's brother in case she goes to ground there? I still don't know what he looks like and I don't need any more surprises today."

He said he would. Then I thought, *where the hell is Mitch and why hasn't he called*, and punched the number for his cell phone. The call went to voicemail. I left a message that I could talk after the house tour then went inside to collect Ricky Hunt and we crunched across the white-shell parking lot to the North Trail Diner.

"So what's the story?" he said as we dropped into a booth with a gold-specked Formica tabletop and torn Naugahyde benches patched with gray duct tape.

"The owner said we can see the house in an hour."

We ordered coffee. The waitress, a middle-aged woman with stiff brown hair and an apron to match, brought it in thick white mugs. I took a sip. The coffee tasted like barroom smoke. Hair of the dog. I drank it anyway.

Ricky Hunt leaned back and rested his elbows on the top of the booth. "Has anyone every told you you're attractive?"

"Not since the sex-change operation," I said and buried myself in the mug.

It took him a few seconds but he finally smiled. "You'd look more attractive if you let your hair down."

"I've worn a ponytail since high school," I said. "I tie it up during take-downs."

"It's kind of tomboyish, if you don't mind me saying. You'd look better with it loose, you know, down around your shoulders."

"Is that how your wife wears her hair? What does she look like, if I might ask?"

He laughed. "She's got more plastic in her than Visa and MasterCard combined."

He hadn't touched his coffee. I scalded my upper lip and kept drinking.

"Mr. Hunt."

"Ricky, sugar, it's Ricky."

"Ricky, then. May I ask you something?"

"You're not going to sue me for sexual harassment, are you?"

"I'd have to take a number," I said.

"Good one." He laughed and pointed a plump finger at me. "Ask away."

"Were you following me the other night?"

He shrugged. "What night?"

"The night it rained."

"This is Florida. You people invented rain."

"Would you mind answering the question?"

"Who wouldn't want to follow a good-looking woman like you?"

"So you *were* following me."

He leaned forward and the smile vanished. "Now, why would you think that?"

I put the mug down and met his eyes. "Woman's intuition?"

"You're putting me on." He checked his watch. It had three dials and diamonds studding the rim at the compass points. "You still want to sell a house, right?"

"Yes."

"We're losing the light. Let's roll."

We walked back to my office, climbed into the SUV and headed south on Tamiami Trail then over the bridge to Spanish Key and along the narrow asphalt that served as the only north-south road on the island. On the way we passed Spanish Key's big dig, with its backhoes and piles of sand and concrete pipe. The crews hadn't made much progress in the past few days. Probably the rain. I watched a crane lower a box culvert into a ditch on the maintenance road but didn't spot Dean Caldwell.

We drove a quarter mile north and, pulling up to the scrolling white walls of the house, found the gate open a crack as Ginny Alexander had promised. I got out, pushed on the wrought iron, slid back into the truck and nudged it through the gap. This time we had the driveway to ourselves. As advertised, the key magically appeared under a flowerpot and I let us into the house, punching in the alarm code and making a mental note to find the owner a less conspicuous place to hide the key. No need to make it easy for burglars.

The house felt deserted and as I shut the front door something pricked the back of my neck. I glanced at Ricky Hunt. Head tilted up, he stood with his hands in his pockets and took in the artwork in the entryway. Harmless . . . for the moment.

We started the tour with the living room and its wall of windows overlooking the pool and moved into one of the spare rooms. I showed him Alexander's Czech glass and Darby's wooden elephants, two collections that ranked right up there with Kurt Stevens and his beer cans. I even showed him the bedrooms this time, and felt pleased when he withheld comment.

"This house has everything the luxury buyer could want," I said. "Waterfront access with a private beach; an unobstructed view of both bay and Gulf—you can see water from all of the major rooms. This isn't a tear-down, either. You're getting a clean, modern, architect-designed home in Bermudian Transitional, not the common Mediterranean Revival you find everywhere else."

"You said there's a den."

"Yes," I said. "A home office. Ms. Alexander and her husband shared the space."

"Let's see it."

The office hadn't changed. Sunlight reflecting from the pool washed the room in a soft glow. Photos crowded the one free wall. Books leaned in random order on the shelves. The desk looked barren.

Hunt looked at the drawers but didn't open them. Walking to the rear wall, he tilted two of the photos of Darby with various actors and then straightened them. Looking for a safe, no doubt. I wondered, not for the first time, if I was helping a burglar case a house.

"I could make this into a recording studio," he said and began rifling through the books.

"Would you like to see the exterior now?" I opened the sliders before he could answer. As we passed through the doors, I waved a hand and went into my Vanna White routine. "The exterior features a covered patio, barbecue area, wet bar and fireplace. The outdoor living room has a view of the Gulf, a salt-water pool with cabana and spa, summer kitchen and both sunny and shaded lounging areas." I gestured toward the southern end of the property. "The landscaping features royal palm, stands of bamboo to separate you from the neighbors and a grotto with a waterfall."

Hunt took it in. "What the hell happened to the lawn?"

"After Mr. Darby disappeared, the Spanish Point Police excavated the yard and beach. They've assured Ms. Alexander that they'll restore the landscaping to its original condition."

"He's back, right?"

"Mr. Darby?"

"Yeah."

"Yes, he's back."

"And you're the one who found him."

"I wouldn't put it quite that way," I said, "but yes, I stumbled on him. Did you have any questions about the house?"

"I hear you're looking for him."

"Most of law enforcement in Southwest Florida is looking for him."

Hands on hips, Hunt stepped back and looked up at the house.

"Pardon me for saying so," I said, "but for an out-of-towner, you seem very curious about a local case."

"I heard about it on TV. Sorry about your grandfather." He turned to stare at the dock.

"Thank you."

"This guy Darby . . . he sounds like a real sleaze."

"Yes, he is."

"I hope you find him."

"Thank you. Ms. Alexander is due back shortly. Is there anything else you'd like to see?"

"Let's talk numbers," he said. "What are the stats?"

"The house has five bedrooms, five full and four half baths, quarters suitable for a house manager and more than 7,000 square feet of living space."

"How much exactly?"

"Seven thousand two-hundred and two."

"How much does she want?"

"The asking price is $7.2 million."

He snorted. "A thousand a square foot. Kinda pricey, don't you think?"

"You're getting an original, architect-design home that's in immaculate condition."

We watched the twin speedboats bob as waves rolled under the dock. I'd forgotten to wear a hat and the sun slowly baked my hair.

Hunt turned and smiled. "How about we talk over lunch, my treat?"

"I'm sorry. I'm meeting a friend. If you care to make an offer, the paperwork's at the office."

"Let me sleep on it.

We walked out the front door. I locked it and put the key under the flowerpot, Hunt watching the whole time. I'd call Alexander as soon as

Hunt left and have her move the key. Then I'd call Mitch again. I hadn't heard from him, Delgado or Darby. I needed to talk to Walter and Claire, and check in with Cheryl. Lately it seemed I had to wait on everyone. Time to switch to offense. I'd drive home, change and, if I had to, go door-to-door with the rental listings to find Pap.

"What did you think of the house?" I asked Ricky Hunt as we drove north on the Trail.

"I might want to go back and give it another look."

I had no doubt he would.

30

I GOT HOME TO find Sal Finzi lying face-down on the living room floor. Someone had smashed in the back of his head. He showed a lot of blood and no pulse. No murder weapon appeared. I sucked in air and thought of my mother and must have unconsciously sniffed for smoke because I found myself scanning the room for flames.

I punched 911 into the cell phone and requested the coroner and Det. Delgado. He wasn't going to believe this. I made sure I didn't touch anything, although my prints would cover every surface. Quickly I walked through the rest of the house. The place looked as if someone had searched in a blinding anger. All of the windows appeared shut and latched. My key had opened the front door, so no sign of forced entry. Why had Finzi ransacked the house, and how had he gotten in? Cheryl had a key. Had he taken it from her, and was she safe?

Finzi's Fat Boy leaned into Cheryl's driveway like a drunk. I ran next door and kissed and hugged Tracy and asked if I could speak with her mother. Tracy said she had homework and turned on the TV in the living room. For once I felt grateful for the noise. I led Cheryl to the dining room table and told her what had happened. Her face grew long and gray with hot red spots on her cheeks. I got her a glass of water.

"He's dead?"

"I'm sorry," I said.

"He's really dead?"

I lowered my voice. "He was struck from behind with a blunt instrument."

"Where?"

"In Pap's living room."

"Oh, God." She stared at me. Tears rimmed her eyes. I shook my head in answer to her silent question.

"I was giving a house tour on Spanish Key. I just got home. His bike's in your driveway. He was here?"

"I heard it but he didn't come in."

"So you didn't give him a key?"

She shook her head no. "He could have grabbed the spare from my purse the other night."

I put a hand on her arm. "It doesn't matter."

She blew her nose and drank the water and recovered her cop voice. "Any signs of a struggle?"

"I can tell you this, right?" I watched her eyes as they grew large.

"You think I did it?"

"Just tell me you were here with Tracy the whole time."

"Of course I was here with Tracy." Her voice shot up an octave. "God, even my best friend thinks I would do something like that?"

"It's OK. Take a breath." I wrapped my arm around her shoulder and gave it a hard squeeze. "Somebody tossed the place. It could have been him or somebody else. Do you have any idea why he was there?"

"Payback, maybe."

That made sense, but not his murder. I told Cheryl I'd called 911 and had to get back. "Is there anything I can do?"

She shook her head slowly and bit her lip. "What am I going to tell Tracy?"

"Nothing for now. I'll let you know the moment they tell me anything, OK? Look at me. Are you OK? I have to leave but I won't if you need me."

She gestured next door. "Go. There'll be hell to pay if you don't. Go."

The city's fire and rescue squad arrived in a red and silver truck the same time I did, followed by someone from the medical examiner's office, a team of techs, the department's photographer and Officers Chip Stover and Bernie Pettinato. I stood on the steps and watched the blue and red strobe lights ricochet from the house fronts and said to myself, "Not again."

No one paid any attention. Then Tony Delgado arrived.

"Tell me what happened," he said as we moved inside.

I did. He asked about the timing and stroked his chin as he listened.

"You didn't invite him in?"

I raised my hands. "I wasn't here."

"And Finzi was next door with Cheryl."

I shook my head. "She says no, but she's home, you can ask her."

"His bike's there, unless you moved it."

I gave him the cop stare. "I didn't touch it."

He surveyed the litter on the floor. "What was he doing here?"

"I have no idea."

Delgado knelt to look at the body. The photographer's strobe light flashed. The medical examiner talked, the techs dusted, the officers searched. Delgado rose and hooked a thumb and Stover and Pettinato went out, probably to canvass the neighborhood.

"No offense, your place is a mess," he said. "Do you think Finzi did this?"

"I can't assume. The guy who clocked him could have done it."

"Darby?" he asked.

"He's been here before."

"Anyone else?"

"If I hadn't been with him," I said, "I'd throw Ricky Hunt into the mix."

"Ricky Hunt?"

I told him about the reluctant client. Fire and rescue bagged the body, hoisted it onto a gurney and wheeled it out.

Delgado ran a hand over his mouth. "You touch him?"

"No."

"You sure."

"Yes," I said.

"Somebody doesn't like you."

"Headline news."

"I'm just stating the facts," he said. "I want you downtown after this for a statement."

"OK."

"You said Cheryl's home?"

"Yes."

"I'll be next door if you think of anything else."

As he turned to leave, his phone rang.

"Delgado."

He listened.

"When?"

I felt incredibly tired, my eyes scratchy, arms limp, leg muscles starting to tremble.

Delgado ended the call. "Harvey Shaw's missing. You know anything about that?"

"No. Should I?"

"I hear you paid him a visit."

"A social call."

"It won't be if they find him like this." He pointed to the blood stain on the living room floor.

I crossed my arms. "I had two shots at Finzi and he lived. I wouldn't need a third."

"Keep it up," he said.

Stover and Pettinato returned empty-handed. Delgado's phone rang again. He listened and then disconnected.

"Bernie," he said, "find out where Officer Finzi was this morning. Chip, you're with us."

Delgado turned to me. "You'll like this. Dispatch just got a call that someone meeting the description of both Darby and Pap were spotted in the parking lot of V-PAC."

I dug the SUV keys out of my front pocket and said, "I'll meet you at there."

"I'm driving," Delgado said and pointed to his unmarked car. "Chip can follow."

"I can handle this," I said.

He slid behind the wheel. "Not without adult supervision."

31

WHAT DID THE CALLER say?" I asked as Delgado's unmarked car crawled through traffic on North Tamiami Trail.

"That two men meeting your description were seen in the parking lot near Baywalk."

"So now it's my description."

The muscle in his jaw hardened. "For a civilian, you are very alert."

I sat as tall in the seat as I could. "Or overly sensitive. Why don't you just say 'you know women' and get it over with."

He almost smiled. I wished he wouldn't. Despite the tough-guy stance, he was starting to look better each time we met, and I didn't need more drama in my life. Yet I kept baiting him. Curious.

As we neared the Vaughn Williams Performing Arts Center, Spanish Point's Baywalk hove into view. The project formed the heart of the city's cultural district. A mile-and-a-half of white fence and pavers, it ran along the intercoastal waterway on a north/south axis between the Ringling Bridge and museum. In addition to my office, it skirted condos, hotels, shops, gelato stands and an amphitheater. The Great Lawn offered space for dogs and yoga and a thirty-foot clock tower overlooked a botanical walk showcasing local flowers.

Settled back from Baywalk between the water and the Tamiami Trail, V-PAC rose like a giant shell embedded in the sand. The grounds included a Coast Guard station, a channel of water bordered by a small public dock and about an acre of parking. We climbed out of the car and walked to the bay but saw nothing except a few sailboats rocking on the green chop and a couple of walkers on the path.

Delgado turned to the condos that overlooked the arts center and the Trail. "You told me your grandfather looked like Tony Bennett."

"That was a private thought," I said. "You shouldn't have shared it with the TV anchor."

"Leslie Walker."

"Marilyn Monroe on steroids."

The edge of his mouth slid up. "I take it you don't like her."

"You saw how she dressed for the film festival. The stilettos were longer than her dress."

"Jealous?"

"Tasteless," I said. "She could have broken her neck."

"Or you could have."

Shading his eyes, Delgado faced the arts center and we started to walk. I set a brisk pace. Halfway across the parking lot I glanced back to see if he could match my stride. He lagged a bit.

I grinned. "You want me to slow down?"

"It's the shoes," he said. "I don't want to break my neck."

Ahead of us the center loomed like a teal-colored seashell and for a moment I imagined Venus rising from the middle. The building's roofline dropped on either side over single-story wings finished in stucco. The grounds featured groupings of palm and saw palmetto with borders of fire-red croton and light-blue plumbago. A pickup truck and trailer sat to the left and we crossed the sidewalk to reach it.

A landscape crew finished packing rotary weed cutters in a white trailer. Three men worked the truck, all dressed in long-sleeved brown shirts, pants and flap caps to keep the sun from burning their neck and ears. From a distance they looked Latino.

"Stay here," Delgado said and crossed the grass. He returned in under two minutes.

"Anything?" I asked.

"Nothing."

"Did they see anyone?"

He started toward the left side of the building. "A couple of roadies loading equipment through the service entrance."

I followed. "Who called it in?"

"A concerned citizen who didn't want to give her name."

"Who did she see?" I asked.

"A tall man with dark hair and a shorter one with gray hair. The tall one could have been Darby without the disguise."

"Anyone with them?"

"A dark-skinned workman." With his notebook he gestured over his shoulder to the rows of condos towering over the Trail. "She probably looked out her window from three hundred yards away and saw someone of Hispanic extraction."

I chuckled. "Thanks to you, those pictures are all over."

"There are a million lawn-care workers in South Florida and to the casual observer they all look like Erik Estrada."

As we rounded the side of the building by the bay I said, "You like Erik Estrada?"

"When I was a kid I wanted to ride motor patrol."

"Pap watches reruns of *CHiPs*."

"You like the bike?"

"I liked the uniforms," I said.

"Tight in the legs."

"I had the biggest crush. . . ."

As we neared the entrance he glanced at me. "On Erik Estrada?"

I felt my face flush. "I did not say that out loud."

"A Latino?" He grinned.

"I was mature for my age."

"You certainly are."

"Just a minute."

Delgado held up a hand as we crossed between a pair of black and gold tour buses to slide through the service entrance. After the afternoon's blazing sun, the interior looked dark, the walls almost black. We headed left of stage, where during a Vince Gill concert I'd seen the resident orchestra store its equipment.

"Who's playing tonight?" Delgado asked as we moved toward the instrument room.

"I don't know. I missed the marquee on the way in."

We emerged in a large room with racks of cases and six people standing around a table set with cans and cups. One man lowered an upright bass, one held a pair of drumsticks and a third drank from a bottle of what looked like soda. Three people stood with their backs to us: a man of medium height with light-colored hair, a taller man with a slick black duck's ass, as Pap would say, and a shorter woman with a headset and a luxurious brown mane that touched her shoulders. The latter two had their heads together in conversation.

As we approached, everyone except the tall man and the woman with the headset turned, curiosity flashing across their faces. The members of the band wore khakis and polo shirts. The older man in the middle wore black slacks, a striped shirt with rolled sleeves and a gold watch. He had wavy gray hair going white and aviator glasses with a yellow tint. He gave us an amused smile.

"Jesus," I said under my breath. "It's Tony Bennett."

The singer spread his hands. "Hey, Kathryn Dawn, look what the cats dragged in."

Wearing the shield on his belt, Delgado didn't have to badge them. After quick introductions he launched into an apologetic explanation of why we were there. As he began, the man and woman in tight conversation turned. I recognized the woman with the headset as the floor manager for the arts center. I recognized the other one, too.

"My God," I said in a dry whisper, "it's k d lang."

Lang looked trim in a black suit, white dress shirt and red ascot, her hair glossy and flat in the style of a thirties crooner. She smiled to reveal pronounced cheekbones and said, "You the Mounties?"

Delgado turned to Tony Bennett and in a deadpan voice said, "Ms. McCoy thought you were her grandfather."

"Who did you think I was," k d lang said, "Princess Leia?"

I must have flushed fifty shades of red.

Tony Bennett chuckled. "Funny that you mention that. . . . Some people say I look like Robert De Niro."

"Much better," I said and added, "That was stupid. Why don't I just say I'm your biggest fan or I have all of your recordings or I loved the duets you did with Ms. lang?" I took a breath. "I'm rambling, aren't I?"

"Well, you did say I look like your grandfather."

Delgado took my elbow but spoke to the group. "Sorry to have bothered you."

I shrugged him off. "As long as we're here. . . . Mr. Bennett."

"Tony, please."

"Tony." I flushed, looked at the other Tony and soldiered on. "So many people can't wait to retire but you didn't. Why not?"

"Retire to what? I am doing what I love best right now. I love entertaining people. I make them feel good and they make me feel wonderful."

"Yes, you do," I said and smiled.

"Thanks, folks." Delgado waved and turned to leave.

"One more question," I said. "Ms. lang, I love 'Constant Craving' but heard you consider yourself a one-hit wonder. Do you ever wish you were back on the pop charts?"

She laughed. "I try to approach music with integrity. It's not worth it to have a successful career as someone else. I'd rather have a minimal career and be myself."

"I know," I said and thought about mine.

Delgado dragged me from the hall. "I know," he mimicked. He chirped the remote and we flopped into his car.

"I am so embarrassed," I said.

"What are you doing, writing a blog?"

"And they were so nice." I buckled the seatbelt.

"Yeah." Delgado started the engine and cranked the air. "Too bad lang is. . . ."

I cut him off. "If you say 'butch' I swear I'll beat you with your service weapon."

"I was going to say it's too bad she's singing the one night I have to work Patrol."

I felt flush. "You're a detective. Detectives don't walk a beat." I heard the echo of a voice from two years ago saying the same thing and realized it was mine.

"We work special events. That's why I was at the film festival."

As he glanced at me, I could feel the heat burn off the top layer of skin.

He grinned. "You *were* jealous."

"Shut up and drive."

32

AFTER MY EXPERIENCE WITH the two Tonys I didn't feel like socializing, but Casey Laine sounded upset, so I agreed to meet her that evening at the Spanish Point Fish Camp.

"That's a bit downscale, isn't it?" she'd said.

"You can walk it from your office."

"Why there?"

"A friend of mind owns it and I like to slip her some trade," I said. "Is the mayor coming?"

"Not if I can help it."

I knew she'd grill me about her daughter and the roadhouse but hadn't decided how much to say. So I called Cheryl and asked her to meet us. In the middle of funeral arrangements for her former husband, she sounded harried but agreed to drop by after her shift.

The phone beeped. I pulled it from my ear and saw a number I didn't recognize.

Cheryl kept talking. "I didn't have time to tell you, what with Sal dying. . . ."

My heart hammered. "Cheryl, I've gotta go."

"Wait!" she said but I'd already punched out.

I put the phone back to my ear. "McCoy.

"I don't have much time." Darby's voice, with more edge this time. "What have you found?"

"A dead body in my house. You know about that?"

"What dead body." He spat the words.

"A security guard named Sal Finzi. He'd broken into my house and someone bashed his head in."

"Why would I do that?"

"You tell me," I said.

"I have enough problems."

"Damned right," I said. "Someone ransacked the place, just like my office."

"I have no idea," he said. "Let's focus, here. What about the money? You find out who took it?"

I gripped the phone so hard I thought the screen would snap and took a deep breath. "Your two biggest investors say they know nothing."

"Who did you talk to?"

"Palmer and Laine," I said.

"That's it?"

"Your business manager says you wanted money the day you disappeared."

"So?"

"Harvey Shaw is missing," I said.

"So."

"You have anything to do with that?"

He grew silent.

"Let me talk to my grandfather."

I heard a double beep and he disconnected. "Damn!" I yelled and thought about throwing the phone into the wall. Instead I climbed on the bike and rode toward the bay. Luckily when you wear a helmet no one can see you cry.

It was early for dinner but the bar at the Fish Camp had filled. I put a haunch on a stool and nodded at Rae and asked for a cup of coffee. She brought a steaming mug and excused herself to wait on a customer at the other end. Today she wore white capris, a leather choker with studs and a black T-shirt so tight it startled the wildlife. I stared at the water and the reflection of a sun as glossy as shellac and shooed Drunk Eddie away to save a stool for Laine.

She appeared a few minutes later wearing a white blouse with a necklace of onyx, black slacks and white pumps that matched her handbag. At least she hadn't worn gloves.

"I didn't think women wore white after Labor Day," I said as she considered flopping her purse on the bar and then, seeing the pool of condensation, slung it over her arm.

"I own half of Spanish Point," she said. "I can wear anything I want." She looked around the bar. "The other half, mind you."

She ordered a Scotch and when it came splashed it past her tonsils.

"Casey Laine, I do believe you are a snob."

"I am, and damned proud of it."

"It's a good act."

She rattled the ice in her glass and Rae refilled it. "It's all an act."

She stared at mansions and condos on the barrier islands. "We sell so much real estate out there, the city should name one of them for me."

"Casey Key?" I asked.

"Something like that."

Since she didn't pass this way often, I did the introductions. "Casey Laine, Rae Donovan."

Laine looked at Rae with more of grimace than a smile and then at my mug. "Would you like a refill? My treat."

I shook my head.

Rae ducked into the kitchen and returned with a plate of what looked like biscuits.

"And what is that," Laine asked in a deadpan voice.

"Specialty of the house," Rae said.

I took a bite and hummed.

Casey Laine sniffed. "I know they look like appetizers but what are they?"

"Deep-fried Pop-Tarts," Rae said.

Laine shuttered. I took another—blueberry today—and sipped coffee.

Rae smiled and leaned on the bar. "How's the mayor?"

"Busy," Laine said, "with his own Marshall Plan for Spanish Point."

"So I've heard." Rae turned to me. "Do you know his honor wants to turn this eyesore into condos for the deserving rich?"

"Only this part of the Quad," Laine said.

"The Fish Camp, swap meet and the Little Theatre," I said.

"This is prime waterfront," Laine said, "the last undeveloped property in the city."

Rae pointed to the two high-rise hotels that bookended her business. "You think we need another one of those?"

"Actually," Laine said, "we do. We're critically short of hotel rooms and that puts a crimp in the tourism industry. They're heading for Tampa and Naples and even Orlando, God forbid. We need to stay in the game."

I thought of a quote from "Star Trek." "The needs of the many outweigh the needs of the few."

Laine twisted a finger through the necklace. "Democracy in action."

That earned a moment of silence broken by the arrival of Cheryl in uniform.

I slid off the stool to give her a seat and made the introductions.

"Well," Laine said, crunching the ice from her glass, "I just stopped by to thank the two of you for helping Melissa. She hasn't told me much about last night but we're both grateful for your intervention. From what I can tell, you saved her life."

"That might be overstating it a bit," I said and wanted to add, and *overly formal* but didn't.

"I don't think so. I owe you, and I always pay my debts."

I said thank you and hoisted the coffee mug in a toast.

She drained her glass and rose to leave. "So who was this jackal who threatened my daughter?"

Cheryl cleared her throat, glanced at me as if to apologize and said, "Robert L. Darby Jr."

33

"And she dropped it like a bomb."

Walter and I sat in the Merc with a panting dog and the windows rolled down. Walter stared at me. I stared at the back of the grocery store. Louie stared at the bag of bagels between the seats.

"Cheryl tried to tell me but Darby called and I signed off too fast and what a monumental screw up."

"Why's that?"

"Why's that?" I said. "Because I had him. I had the kid twice and I didn't know who he was. I should have asked Claire or her mother for a photo, or snapped one with the phone and sent it to Oz."

"What now?"

"They've abandoned the ranch. No Darby, father or son. No drugs, although the pole barn reeked of chemicals.

"Weapons?"

"Just a couple of casings."

"Leads."

"None." I slammed the dash and Louie jumped. "We were that close."

"Maybe we'll get lucky."

"Maybe my ass will fall asleep."

Walter chuckled.

I slid down in the seat and focused on a different crack in the cement-block wall. "So here we are again, engaged in my favorite activity."

"What's that," Walter said. "Complaining?"

"Louie, are you going to let him talk to me that way?"

Louie looked from Walter to me and down at the bag of bagels and decided to reserve comment. Why risk dissing the hands that feed you? He stretched his legs on the armrest and put a head on his paws. I scratched his ear.

Walter sipped coffee. "You waiting for an answer?"

Louie gave me the full force of his big brown eyes and licked my hand.

"Good enough for me."

We'd spent hours surveiling the Darby properties. Claire hadn't shown. Neither had Junior. We checked with Ginny Alexander, the police and Claire's school but she seemed to have vanished like most of the family. I'd flashed photos of both kids at nearby drug stores, gas stations and fast-food places with no luck.

During the stakeouts, Walter teased me about Tony Bennett and Mitch Palmer, in equal measure. I moped and drank a lot of coffee. I'd lost the chance to get an autograph for Pap and Mitch had returned my call so late that I not only missed it but began to wonder what he did in the middle of the night. With other people, that is.

The three of us had parked around the back of the grocery store, in the shade of a giant laurel oak, and every time the wind blew the tree's catkins would coat the windshield with green squiggles and dust. Winter in Florida. On the sound system, Etta James sang a number about how we all needed somebody to love. She got that right. With no bagels forthcoming, Louie circled a blanket on the back seat, lay down and sighed. I knew how he felt.

Walter glanced at me. "What did Delgado say about Finzi?"

"Just what we thought. He died of blunt-force trauma. Tire iron, jack handle, metal-jacket mop."

"They find it?"

"Too portable."

"They know what he was doing there?"

"It's all guesswork," I said. "Delgado's working the revenge theory."

"And you're in the clear?"

"As long as I don't borrow anyone's wheels."

"What about your theory that Darby's involved?"

"Delgado discounts it as paranoia. 'Why reveal himself twice in daylight? What could you have that he'd want, now that he has your grandfather?' Yada, yada, yada."

"What do you think?"

"I think we need more fuel." I grabbed the coffee cups and popped the door just as a skinhead carrying a large box rounded the corner.

Walter looked up as I climbed back into the Merc.

"The kid," I said.

Robert Darby Jr. set the box on the roof of a black Ford Escort and unlocked the trunk. He wore black sneakers, cargo shorts and T-shirt. In the bright light, his banded tattoos looked purple. He stowed the box, closed the trunk and, looking both ways, tossed the keys under the car near the left rear tire. Then he walked away.

"No one does that in the Florida heat," Walter said.

"Not unless you want compost for dinner."

Junior got into what looked like an ancient red Cadillac and drove away.

"Follow him?" I asked.

"Let's wait," Walter said. "See if anyone turns up."

I called in the plates to Oz, who traced the tags in seconds. The Caddie was registered to Robert Darby Jr., the Escort to Ginny Alexander. Nothing new there.

"You want his outstanding parking tickets?"

"I want his ass," I said.

"You up for a drink?"

"Yes, but I can't talk."

"Later," he said and disconnected.

I told Walter about the tags, the invitation and my reluctance to accept.

"You're waiting for Mitch," he said.

"I'm a one-man woman, I guess."

"Sounds like one of your country and western songs."

"I should feel grateful," I said. "At least Oz answers the phone."

About ten minutes later, Claire Darby rode to the back of the market on a bicycle. Chaining the bike to a rack, she retrieved the keys, climbed in the car and drove off.

"Follow the food," I said.

Walter fell in behind the Escort. "Your new motto?"

"I got it from Louie."

Louie raised his ears but not his head. When it came to food, he'd believe it when he smelled it.

Claire Darby took the long way home. We followed her south on Tamiami Trail and across the bridge to Spanish Key and crawled north through traffic on the narrow two-lane. Tourists crammed the road on the right. On the left, yellow backhoes and bulldozers sat by a drainage ditch big enough to house the Washington Metro.

Claire must have had a remote because she swept into the drive and closed the gates before we'd passed the house. We parked on the shoulder and got out just in time to see her pop the trunk and haul the box around the back.

"She's headed for the dock," Walter said.

"She doesn't want mom to know."

The wind blew a wet darkness in from the west. Grabbing one of Pap's green windbreakers from the backseat, I followed Walter along the wall to the beach and watched as Claire climbed into one of boats and clicked the ignition.

"Shit," I said, realizing the obvious, that we couldn't follow in a car. "She's smarter than we thought."

"Your call."

"Let's give her a head start and take the other one."

As Claire cleared the dock and headed into the channel, we ran for the other boat. Just as Alexander had said, the keys sat under the seat cushion. Rounding the bend, Claire turned right to head south on the intercoastal. I rammed the key into the ignition.

"You know how to fly this thing?" Walter asked.

"No," I said and quickly switched places. "But I'm a fast study."

Walter fired up the engine. "Glad you cleared this ahead of time with the owner."

We sped into the channel.

"She doesn't know . . . exactly," I yelled and the boat popped over the waves.

"So we're using it without permission."

"Let's hope Delgado isn't around."

"Might be hard to explain after the motorcycle."

Claire headed due south toward the less-inhabited stretch of Venice. She took no evasive maneuvers and didn't look back.

"Traffic's starting to thin," I yelled to Walter. "Won't she spot us?"

"Maybe," he said and slowed to match her speed as she turned west and skirted the outer tip of one of the spoil islands. It sat at the end of Spanish Key like a giant tortoise, fat and lush, with palm trees and a thick undergrowth of mangrove that overhung the water.

Walter slowed to idle speed. "Even less traffic here."

Claire's boat slipped around the bend. We crept back into the bay and stalled.

That the craft had disappeared so quickly surprised me. "Where'd she go?"

"Follow the wake." He pointed to a bright contrail of water leading straight into the mangroves.

"A cave," I said.

"A channel. Dug by the Corps when they dredged the intercoastal."

A tangle of trees obscured everything except a few gulls on a muddy bank. From beneath the undergrowth jutted the dark gray tip of a wooden dock. Claire's boat bobbed next to it. She killed the motors and climbed onto the pier. On the other side, a second boat gently rocked in the wake. A fishing trawler, it towered above the speedboat, its antenna and GPS dome disappearing in the thicket of mangrove and oak. On the stern of the boat the owner had painted the name *Gulf Breeze X*. Claire hefted the box and stepped aboard.

"Does the name match one of the stolen boats," I asked.

"I does indeed," Walter said.

We had drifted to within fifteen feet of her starboard bow when we heard the scream, a single shriek that scattered the gulls. Walter rounded the stern, leaped onto the dock and tied the boat fast. Drawing his gun, he crouched low, inching forward as I caught up. When we reached the bow of the trawler, he vaulted onboard and took the stairs to the cockpit two at a time.

Claire stood over a pair of legs, hands pressed to her mouth, box and groceries scattered over the deck. A loaf of bread lay across one of the ankles. Walter holstered his weapon and, kneeling by the body, felt the neck for a pulse. The back of the head looked flat, the hair dark with matted blood.

Even though I'd never seen her body, an image of my mother lying on the kitchen floor flashed through my mind. "Is it?" I asked, almost a whisper.

Walter stood. "Yes."

"And he's. . . ."

"Yes."

"When?" I asked.

"Can't tell."

"Best guess," I said.

"Early morning."

"Same as Finzi," I said.

"I'll call it in," Walter opened his cell phone.

I put my arms around Claire and drew her close. "I'm sorry," I said.

Her arms felt cold. She began to shake. I tightened my grip.

"Where's Pap?" I asked, trying to keep the panic out of my voice.

Walter snapped the phone shut and did a quick search of the compartments and sleeping quarters. He came back shaking his head.

"I don't understand," I said.

"Neither do I."

He searched the boat again and I knew he was looking for the weapon. When he came back empty-handed I said, "We're going to wait over there," and guided Claire to the edge of the dock.

We sat on the side of the dock. I put my arm around her shoulders and let her lean in. "Did you see anyone or hear anything?" I asked but she kept her head down, hair covering her eyes. Birds called, insects hummed. We waited until the sharp throttle of motors cut the air. A cruiser with *SPD Marine* on its side pulled up to the dock and a photographer and tech crew jumped out with their cameras and cases and boarded Darby's boat. A second cruiser pulled up with Delgado and someone from the medical examiner's office. The scene looked all too familiar.

Claire felt cold and continued to shake. I asked Walter to find a blanket on Darby's boat but Delgado told us to stand on shore while he questioned Claire. I couldn't decipher the words but his voice sounded soothing, his gestures slow and measured. He talked, made eye contact, took notes. When he finished, he questioned us briefly, but we had little to add.

"We need to take Claire home," I said.

He gave me the hard stare and finally nodded.

I draped my windbreaker over Claire's shoulders and gave her a light hug. "We'll take you home to mom."

She shook her head, her hair making small noises against the nylon of the jacket.

"We have to let her know," I said.

"She won't care."

"We'll stay with you as long as you need us."

Her nose and mascara ran. She put her arms through the windbreaker, wiped her nose on a sleeve and said in a quiet voice, "Can I stay with you?"

"We'll talk about it," I said.

We put her in the second speedboat and climbed in.

Claire sniffled. "How did you find me?"

"We followed you down the intercoastal."

Walter started the motors and headed north.

"Did you follow me last night?"

I looked at Walter. "No. What kind of boat was it?"

"A pretty big one."

"A cabin cruiser?" I said.

She nodded.

"Did you recognize anyone onboard?"

"I couldn't see."

We passed the center of Spanish Key.

It was a longshot but I asked, "Do you know Mr. Shaw?"

"Yeah, he comes around a lot. He takes mom to the opera."

"Does he own a boat?"

"I don't know. I think so."

Walter swung the craft across the tip of the key, slid next to the Darby's dock and cut the motors. As we walked toward the house, I rubbed Claire's back and wondered what we'd say to Ginny Alexander about her late, late husband.

"Was Mr. Shaw's boat big, like your dad's?"

"I never saw it. Mom just talked about how he liked to go deep-sea fishing. You think he knows something?"

As we wound around the pool and entered the house, I thought about sharing my suspicion that Harvey Shaw was not only involved with embezzlement but with her mother. I considered the consequences of taking Claire to Pap's house until we could find Shaw. Instead I said, "He might know a lot."

34

S O HOW'D IT GO last night when you got to Darby's place?" Oz asked as we padded out of the elevator toward the offices of the Intercoastal Advisory Group. He wore black jeans, motorcycle boots and a dark gray hoodie that made him look like a monk.

It was late and I felt exhausted after several rounds with Delgado and Ginny Alexander. But Oz had agreed to lend his digital expertise to our quest to run Harvey Shaw to ground and I needed to remain gracious. I hated to admit it, but when it came to technology, he seemed light years ahead of me, even suggesting that instead of silencing our smartphones during the B&E we remove the batteries to prevent tracking.

"About what you'd expect. Claire folded in on herself and Ginny Alexander declined my offer of help with the funeral arrangements. She seemed more upset that I wound up with her daughter again than the fact that her husband was dead."

Oz donned surgical gloves and handed a pair to me. "For good this time."

"Hard to fake that."

We let ourselves into the office courtesy of his pick set.

"She give you a hard time?" he asked.

"Just the hard eye. Then the cops showed up."

The office felt awkward at night, dark and quiet without the buzzing of admins, fluorescent lights or copy machines.

"At least she gets to keep the insurance money," Oz said.

"She's grateful for the little things."

"But not her daughter," Oz said.

"Not after Claire appeared wearing my jacket and insisted I take her home with me."

"Where is she now?"

"At her house," I said. "Until she runs away again."

We moved past the receptionist's desk into Shaw's office.

"So who killed Darby?" he asked.

"Someone who doesn't want the dead to come back to life." I broke out a tiny flashlight. "I think he and Darby were in it together."

"There's a leap."

The beam played over the sparkling artwork and trophies and came to rest on the desk. It resembled a landfill, with papers and file folders cascading onto the floor.

"The bad guys beat us again," Oz said.

"Same as my place."

"So what are we looking for?"

"Something that shows where Darby or Shaw hid the money—checkbook, ledger, account numbers."

Oz kicked a pile of folders as if paper disgusted him. "They're long gone."

"Maybe," I said. "Maybe they don't know what they're looking for."

He broke out his own flashlight, a black barrel the size of a nightstick, and surveyed the room. "Someone took the electronics."

"There weren't any, at least not in here. Shaw swears he doesn't use a computer."

We started reading folder labels and leafing through paper. The gloves made a tedious job even more difficult. I wondered how nurses and surgeons did anything wearing these.

"What kind of business manager doesn't use a computer?" Oz asked.

"Retro," I said.

"Prehistoric," Oz said.

Sitting on the floor, he started to read. I perched on the edge of the chair and sorted through the folders on the desk. Some listed commercial real estate owned by the company, some held corporate financial records, others account information on investors. I focused on the latter. From the quarterly statements, I gathered that Darby's clients had enough money to buy Saudi Arabia. None of the names impressed, just the amounts . . . a lot to envy but no clues.

I moved to the file cabinets and began to open drawers. It appeared Harvey Shaw had saved every receipt, envelope and instruction manual the company had ever received. He'd even filed yellow legal pads with notes in blue pen. The notes were barely legible, mostly strings of numbers—the handwritten version of a spreadsheet.

Oz worked the cabinets from the other end. "Ledgers," he said, holding up a long red book. He leafed through the pages. "Nothing I haven't seen online."

I shut the drawer with a little more force than necessary and leaned against the cabinets. "I wonder if Darby ever had the money."

Oz sat in the desk chair and spun toward me. "You believe him?"

"Suppose someone tries to reclaim the money from Darby and kills him. The person either grabs the money and flees or continues to search for it. Shaw disappears around the same time, his office is ransacked and so is Darby's house, my office and my home. The intruder kills Sal Finzi. What does that tell us?"

"That Darby stashed the money where no one can find it," Oz said.

I shook my head. "I know it's a lot of supposition but everything points to Shaw."

Oz started spinning circles in the chair.

"Let's work with your assumption that Darby stole the money," I said. "Have you ever seen a million dollars in cash? You can't lug it around in a gym bag, let alone multiples of that. Darby wasn't carrying that much cash when he fled. If he took the money, he either exchanged it for something portable or he wired the funds out of the country."

Oz spun the chair in the other direction.

"You do this when you play video games?"

He stopped. "Carry on."

"OK," I said. "If Darby had the money, why did he come back and claim he's innocent?"

"No idea."

"If he didn't steal the money, everything points to Shaw."

"Or," he said, "Ginny Alexander."

"Or Ricky Hunt."

Oz got up and walked through the reception area and poked his head into several alcoves. "I checked him out," he said, his voice faint, the flashlight beam bobbing like a Ping-Pong ball. "His wife's got all the money. If he kills anyone, it'll be her." He reemerged holding a can of diet soda. "Besides," he said, "he has no motive."

I pointed to the can of soda. "Nothing like leaving a trail of breadcrumbs."

"I wash the cans before I recycle." He began searching the more posh offices along the wall. Darting into one, he sat at the desk and popped open the shell of a notebook computer and hit the power button. From his hoodie he removed his smartphone and a thumb drive.

I leaned over his shoulder, feeling the heat from his head, inhaling a faint scent like cedar that I couldn't identify.

The login screen appeared.

"How are you going to get in?" I asked.

"It's a complicated process of matching psychological profiles with known knowns, as our former defense secretary used to say."

"Translation, please."

"I pulled all of Shaw's business and personal information and cross-referenced it with the most common passwords people use—birthdays, anniversaries, number strings."

"And if you can't crack the system?"

"We'll borrow a few machines and work on them later."

"What if Shaw didn't do online transactions?"

"I agree with you, it's too much cash to physically move."

Except for the login dialog, the computer screen remained blank.

"How long until you can break in?"

"Could take hours," he said. "For most people."

I smiled and inhaled more of the earthy scent. "And for a crack hacker like you?"

He punched up an email on his phone, typed a username and password into the notebook computer and the splash screen appeared. Hands behind his head and boots on the desk, he looked up at me and smiled.

"You must be very pleased with yourself." I felt like a fool, rifling through all of those papers only to have the boy genius crack the computer in seconds. "How'd you do that?"

"I practiced on bras in high school."

I snorted. "Seriously. You're like that girl with the dragon tattoo. I thought you said it would take hours." My head came up when I heard the faint sound of sirens.

Oz ignored it. Leaning forward, he took a long pull on the can. "The FBI scrubbed the computers a year ago. They kept the passwords."

"And?"

Inserting the thumb drive into a port, he sifted through folders until he found one he liked and copied it. "People are creatures of habit."

"So are the police," I said. "You hear sirens?"

"You deactivate the alarm on the way in, right?"

"Shit. I didn't see one."

The sirens grew louder.

Oz yanked the thumb drive from the computer and did a hard shutdown. "We're out of here."

"Take the can," I yelled and jogged to the door.

We ran down the back stairs and through the underground parking deck and nosed the SUV into traffic just as a squad car turned the corner in a flare of lights.

"What'd you get?" I ran a red light, the gloves chirping the steering wheel whenever I turned a corner.

"Corporate investors."

"And?" I sped north.

"No time to read the file."

Taking a hard left onto a side street, I ran the SUV down an alley behind a supermarket and came to a stop by the library.

"What do we look for now?" I asked.

"Bags of money."

"Account numbers would be better," I said.

"And you think Shaw has them."

"Where would a computer-phobic person would hid his records?"

Oz smiled. "His house?"

"You know where he lives?"

He pointed through the windshield. "Condo on Cocoanut, turn right at the corner."

When it comes to street names, Spanish Point likes to celebrate the natural world. The byways derive their names from birds (Osprey Avenue), flowers (Hibiscus Court) and trees (Slash Pine Circle). There's fruit— Lemon, Lime, Orange, Pineapple and Kumquat. And then there's the mother of all of the Point's east-west routes, Fruitville Road, named for an industry bulldozed decades ago to build the American Dream. What the Tamiami Trail doesn't offer, Fruitville does. Tonight it led us without police escort to Cocoanut, although at that hour I wasn't sure if the name was a fruit or a marketing ploy.

"I need coffee," I croaked as we drove past the condo complex and parked on the street.

"I need a massage and a toke," Oz said as we walked half a block to the units. "How 'bout when we get back to my place we trade."

"You tech guys are so romantic." In the dim glow of the streetlights, he looked elfin, with his pointed beard, rounded cheekbones and full lips, a smile simmering at the corners of his mouth. Anxiety and excitement rushed through me, only half of it related to the thrill of burglary.

"I've got a room with black lights and a mirror," he said.

"Every girl's fantasy." I said it in jest but felt the heat pass between us on a low wavelength. Shaking my head as if to wake up, I took the lead into the condo parking lot.

The builder had stacked the units with two floors of living quarters above a narrow garage. The condos fronted on Cocoanut but the garages faced an interior courtyard of pavers. Darkness drenched the building and the lot. We found Shaw's unit and tried the back door. Of course it was locked.

I looked over my shoulder for residents curious about the noise, ears straining for the sound of sirens, stomach jumping at every sound. Oz seemed as calm as a guy lounging in his living room. From the pocket of his jeans he pulled a brown rectangle, pressed a button and the garage door crawled skyward.

"How'd you do that?" I whispered.

"It's like a universal remote for garage doors. Here." He handed the device to me. "You should have one in your line of work."

"My line of work is real estate, not burglary."

"Same difference," he said. He was right. Spanish Point wasn't known for affordable housing.

As we ducked inside the garage, I tapped the button and the door cranked down. We turned our flashlights to the interior. A vintage bronze Jaguar crouched in the middle of the garage. I popped the passenger door. The inside looked clean, except for a single cloisonné earring in the cup holder.

"Ginny Alexander said she lost one of these." I showed it to Oz and slipped it into a pocket.

The rest of the garage looked just as immaculate, a bicycle and a coil of garden hose hanging from pegboard on the wall, fishing rods and a set of golf clubs propped in a corner. Aside from a bucket with a sponge and another with gloves and a trowel, there were no tools.

"I never would have figured Harvey Shaw for a gardener," I said.

"Maybe he's just a big kid who likes to dig in the sand."

"Or Ginny Alexander's back yard."

We searched the bag and the buckets and, finding nothing, walked up the stairs and through the unlocked door to the living quarters. The condo featured an open floor plan with a combination living room and kitchen near the door and bedrooms near the street. Light and traffic sounds filtered through the blinds. I drew them shut, played the flashlight around the room and flicked on a light. The place looked empty and smelled faintly foul, like rotting fruit.

Oz searched the living room. I looked in the kitchen cabinets and the fridge and then the bedroom. No one had slept there recently. The bathroom held the usual supplies—toothbrush, toothpaste, shaver, golf and sailing magazines by the commode. I returned to the bedroom and checked the closet a second time to confirm the existence of two suitcases on the upper shelf. Shaw had left in a hurry.

A small desk sat off the kitchen and I rifled through the drawers, sifting through flyers and unopened bills and finding two tickets to Saturday's performance of Verdi's *Il trovatore* at the opera house.

Oz walked over and pointed the flashlight at my hands. I told him about the suitcases and toiletries and showed him the tickets.

"You find anything?"

"Nope," he said. "No trace of electronics, and I even dug up the potted plants. What's next?"

"I think I'll have another talk with Ginny Alexander."

"How about a drink first?"

I nodded and as we slipped out of Shaw's apartment I stopped to listen for sirens. None yet. Since I knew the way, the drive to Oz's apartment went quickly. We skipped the coffee and wound up standing at the kitchen island in his apartment drinking Mexican beer and shots of tequila. When it came time to use the bathroom, I slipped the battery into the smartphone and watched as several text messages appeared. The first came from Mitch: no news about the investors but did I have plans for the weekend? Not yet, I replied. What I felt like typing was, "Why haven't you called?" But to be fair, I could have called him again, if I hadn't made a second career of B&E. And I was standing in another man's bathroom, feeling guilty and wondering when Oz would make his move.

The second message came from Claire. "Left home. Don't look for me." Troubling. I'd check in with her mother in a few hours.

I swayed back to the kitchen and somehow tumbled into Oz's bed and slept like the dead until 6:40 a.m. when my cell rang, incredibly loud in the dark, still air of the apartment. "Damn," I muttered and thought about letting it go to voicemail. Until I checked the caller ID.

35

WALTER DIDN'T WASTE TIME. "I've got news. Could be bad."

"It couldn't wait a week?" My throat and eyes felt like cardboard and I thought my veins would collapse from the lack of caffeine.

"Dean Caldwell just called. They found a body at the construction site. He stopped the dig after they uncovered an arm."

I shot up in bed and grabbed my forehead. "Who?"

"No ID." He paused. "He says the body's wearing something green."

I tried to swallow. Pap had two favorite golf sweaters, green and yellow, and I had the yellow. I'd also given a shivering Claire my green windbreaker. "How old?"

"They don't know. They stopped the dig and called the police."

"When was this?" I asked.

"Just a few minutes ago."

"Are you there?"

"On my way."

"I'll meet you there."

The moment I slid out of bed, my head felt as if it had hit the floor. I imagined two people with tire irons banging on my skull. In the dim light before dawn, I sensed someone in bed beside me and slowly put a name with the shape. Stumbling into the bathroom to wash and swallow a few pain killers, I watched as Oz propped himself on an elbow, beard pointed toward his privates. Cheryl had gotten it right: I dimly remembered one of those parts as larger than his thumb. The search for my panties yielded nothing but guilt so I gave up and, pulling on last night's slacks, felt a small stab from the earring in the pocket. Another conversation that would have to wait.

Oz managed a groggy smile look that said he was impervious to alcohol and self-doubt.

"I used your toothbrush," I said. "Hope you don't mind."

"Mi casa. . . ." His voice sounded gauzy with post-coital lethargy.

I slipped on the rest of my clothes and stared at him. "Did we have sex last night?"

"Oh, yeah."

"Was it any good?"

"Oh, yeah." He said it slowly, with a smile.

"Then I'm not hallucinating."

He slid his hand over the sheets with a scratching sound. "You want to go again?"

"Coffee," I said in a hoarse voice.

"I can get you an energy drink."

I shuddered. "I need to get to the beach."

"Story of our lives."

"They've found a body."

Eyebrows up, he slid out of bed and started to dress. "Where?"

I gave him all the details I had, which weren't many.

"You don't look in any shape to drive," he said.

"Thanks."

"You want anything before you go?"

"I just don't want this to be Pap."

With traffic mercifully thin at that hour, I raced the SUV over the bridge and up the narrow road. Spotting the construction crew just north of Spanish Key Beach, I skidded to a halt near the maintenance shed and a yellow backhoe imitating a praying mantis. Piles of gray and white sand surrounded a warren of ditches and rows of concrete pipe, their shadows long and sharp in the hour after sunrise. Next to the trench, two workers with hardhats and shovels stood by two other men. I recognized one pair as Walter and Dean. No one looked happy.

The slam of the car door ricocheting through my head, I jogged to the site and peered into the ditch. An elbow and an expanse of what looked like a person's back bulged from the sand. Both were clothed in green. I felt my gut tighten.

"What happened?"

My voice sounded strange and distant and my hands felt clammy and cold. The sun etched the tiny grains of sand into my eyes as if someone had rubbed my face in them. On the road, a few cars drove past the site as if nothing had happened.

"Someone knocked sand into one of the box culverts," Dean Caldwell said. "The men were digging it out to lay pipe." He pointed to a pile of sand next to the trench. The top of the pile looked sheared. "At first I thought it was the damned kids again."

Playing king of the mountain, I thought.

"Then one of the guys says he sees a sleeve and they get in there with shovels and I called 911. And Walt."

Walter stood by the trench, arms crossed, jaw working a piece of gum. He looked relaxed in cargo shorts and a cap embroidered with a sailfish. I knew he wasn't relaxed. "Cops'll be here soon." He glanced at me with a practiced eye. "You OK?"

"I'd feel better if I felt better."

He raised his eyebrows but said nothing and I felt like leaning my head into him and letting the world slip away.

"What am I going to do if it's Pap?"

He put an arm around my shoulder. "Let's wait."

Two cars pulled onto the maintenance road, a cruiser with its lights flashing followed by an unmarked car. Climbing out of the cruiser, Chip and Cheryl pulled up their duty belts and walked toward us. Chip, wearing dark wraparound sunglasses, stared into the hole. Taking Walter's place, Cheryl slid an arm around my other shoulder.

"You OK?" she asked.

I nodded. "Just another day in paradise."

Delgado nodded to us and asked Dean about what he'd seen and whether the workers had touched anything. Dean kept it brief. Motioning to the two workers, Delgado asked them to uncover the body but not to move it. The men lowered themselves into the ditch and started to dig. As they scraped away the sand, a back as broad as a dolphin's emerged. So did a hand with large knuckles and hair matting the fingers. A class ring encircled one of them.

I must have held my breath because it came out in such a rush that

Cheryl squeezed my shoulder.

"It's not Pap," I croaked. "Or Claire."

"It's not Pap," she said and left to help Chip secure the scene with yellow tape.

Delgado lowered himself into the hole and, standing on the edge of the box culvert, bent to examine the body. I leaned in to look at the back of the head. Someone had hammered it, just like Finzi and Darby.

I shuttered. "Shaw?"

Walter nodded.

"Who did it?" I asked.

"No clue. Maybe it's your mystery investor."

My phone buzzed with a text from Mitch. "New info. Meet for a drink?" I thought about replying that I couldn't, that finding the body meant Pap was still missing. Tired of text messages and phone-tag, I walked toward the Gulf and punched in his number. He answered on the third ring.

"Got your message," I said. "What do you have?"

"That's not a great way to start a conversation."

I may have run out of energy but I hadn't exhausted my supply of irritation. "Mitch, I haven't heard from you in days."

"Sorry," he said. "Dad's away and things got busy."

Something long and ropy twisted in the static between the phones and I felt my stomach clench and unclench like a fist. "I thought maybe you forgot."

Another pause, another burst of static and then he said, "Not likely."

My head still hurt, my eyes gritty as old linoleum. I took a deep breath. "Sorry, I'm on edge."

"Where are you?"

I reached the sand and started to pace. "Spanish Key Beach . . . with another body."

"Who?" he asked.

"The betting's on Harvey Shaw."

"Who killed him?"

"We don't know yet," I said. "You have something?"

"You remember there were a number of companies who invested in Darby's operation?"

"I remember. Shell companies fronted by law firms."

"I was going through dad's personal records and came up with a list."

"We already have a list. I tried it on Shaw and your dad."

"Not that list," he said. "The list that Darby used."

A flock of gulls waded toward the Gulf only to run ashore when the waves tumbled in.

"What's it say?"

"That the biggest investor in his operation by dollar amount was USC."

I thought Mitch had hit the sauce harder than I had. "The University of Southern California?"

"Universal Steerage Corp."

"Steerage? I thought that had to do with boats. Who owns it?"

"The owners aren't listed," he said.

"Contact?"

"A law firm in Tampa."

He recited the name. It meant nothing, except another roadblock.

I looked over my shoulder. More people had arrived at the trench, probably the ME. "I'll have to call you back."

I heard him say "You're welcome" just before I rang off.

Hitting the speed dial key for Oz, I said "It's me" and waited.

"What's going on?"

I explained the situation at the beach. "You have a chance to review the files you got from the company computer?"

"I had a late night."

"So did I."

"Can I sext you later?"

"You can set your hair on fire, upper or lower, I don't care." I started walking back to the trench. "I've got the name of Darby's biggest investor."

"Do tell."

I did. "Check the records you pulled from Darby's computer. I'm willing to bet he's got names and numbers."

"I've been through every database we have. Where'd you get it?"

"Inside information."

"Hey, CW. . . ."

"Later," I said and disconnected.

By now uniforms crawled all over the beach—police, techs, the photographer and the ME's people. I walked over to Walter and said,

"Now what?"

Delgado climbed out of the hole and dusted his slacks. "You know who this is?"

"I'd lay odds on Harvey Shaw," I said.

"Funny you mention that. Someone broke into Shaw's office and condo last night. You wouldn't know anything about that, would you?"

A knot formed in my stomach and I shook my head, even though it hurt.

"I'm not going to ask if you found anything, because if you did, I know you'd turn it over to the department." He said it without a trace of a smile. "I will ask if Shaw contacted you before he disappeared."

"No," I said, the knot in my stomach growing hard and hot.

"And I thought we agreed that you would take a breather."

I looked at him closely, at the deep eyes and full lips and freshly shaved cheeks that glowed in the early morning light. My arms weakened and my legs started to shake and in a small voice I said, "I was supposed to look after him."

"We'll find him."

In their bathing suits and visors, the tourists began to file across the street and onto the beach like rows of colorful ants, toting children and coolers and boogie boards, oblivious to murder and all of the other drama in the world.

I gulped air. "You find out who killed Darby?"

Delgado looked across the beach toward the Gulf. "The FBI printed Shaw last time around so the techs were able to ID latents on the boat."

"They were partners," I said. "Those prints could have gotten there anytime."

He peered into the trench. "You have an affinity for the recently departed."

"I'm trying to track a killer."

"So are we," he said, "so why don't we stop playing good cop, bad cop and share what we have?"

I was about to say that trusting law enforcement hadn't worked too well for me when a motorcycle spun onto the access road and Oz's shiny head appeared from beneath a helmet.

36

WHAT'S GOING ON?" Oz said as he joined the crowd at the trench.

"We think it's Shaw," I said. "Someone struck him from behind, like Finzi and Darby."

"With what?" he leaned in for a closer look.

"A heavy object, like a piece of rebar, and then dumped him."

"Might have happened over there," Oz said, pointing to a tree-covered area to the north.

"It would take a strong person to drag the body, or haul him out of the trunk."

Oz pointed to the late Harvey Shaw, now fully exposed. "I don't think she did it."

"Who?" I asked.

"Ginny Alexander."

Almost everyone stared at him—Delgado, Walter, Cheryl. The techs kept working.

"You making house calls now?" Delgado asked.

I saw Oz flush and felt the heat from Delgado, as if he knew Oz and I had hooked up, or worse, that Oz had violated protocol by sharing information. Which Delgado couldn't know, I told myself. Nor could either of them know about Mitch, not even with their omniscient eye-in-the-sky technology. Still, the discomfort buzzed my head like a deerfly.

"Why," I asked Oz, "couldn't Ginny Alexander have murdered Shaw? Because women aren't strong enough to bury a body?" I gave him my best stare.

"Are you going to beat me up to prove it?"

"I might."

Oz chuckled. "Like *Fifty Shades of Grey.*"

"You'll be fifty shades of black and blue if you don't tell me what you found."

He pulled me aside. "You were right about Universal Steerage."

"I was?"

"USC is VC money out of LA," he said. "They invest in start-ups like Darby's bank and take a cut, usually in stock when they take the company public."

"Who are *they?*"

"They are the single biggest investor in Darby's business." His eyes crinkled. "And are you ready for this?"

"More than you'll ever know."

"The biggest investor in the pool is that guy you said was stalking you."

"Ricky Hunt?"

"The man, the myth, the legend," Oz said.

"That explains his interest in Darby's house."

"He's probably out there right now with a shovel and a metal detector."

I looked at Delgado as he talked with the techs and nodded to Walter and Cheryl. They walked over and formed a circle. I asked Oz to run through it again.

"It could be Hunt," Walter said. "He has the body mass."

"Footprints?" I asked.

"Tons," Cheryl said, "but nothing useful."

"The break-ins," I said. "It's Hunt, trying to track down Darby."

"And Shaw and the money," Oz said.

"Ginny Alexander's in danger," I said.

"Unless she killed her husband," Walter said.

I shook my head. "My money's on Hunt," I said.

"Because he gives you the creeps?" Walter asked.

"Good enough reason," Cheryl said. "I should know."

Our heads came around when Cheryl's radio chirped and Dispatch reported a carjacking in progress near University and Orange, just south of the airport. The radio crackled. "Shots fired. All units respond."

Delgado barked into the radio and turned to us. "Finzi, guard the site. Stover, you're with me."

They sped toward the bridge.

"You want to follow?" I asked Walter.

"No," he said. "If we're going to Darby's, we should go now."

"As soon as they're back," Cheryl said, "Delgado's going to search Ginny Alexander's house and car."

"When?" I asked

"They would have served her already," she said, "if this hadn't come up."

I looked at Walter but spoke to Cheryl. "So Delgado thinks she's involved."

"It's not like she's Miss Hospitality," Cheryl said.

37

"WE HAVE A PLAN?" Walter asked as we rolled up beside Virginia Alexander's house.

"Split up and circle."

I pointed through the wrought-iron gate to a couple of cars—a beat-up silver Toyota and a white compact with a zigzag scratch across the driver's-side door.

"Recognize them?" I asked.

"Claire," he said.

"And Ricky Hunt."

"I'll take the front, you cover the back," he said.

"If she moved the key we can't get in." From my pants pocket I dug out the remote I'd gotten from Oz. "You go in the garage. I'll come up from the beach."

He palmed the remote. "Where'd you get this?"

"Oz," I said. "He borrowed it."

"It takes a thief. . . ."

I skirted the white retaining wall as it tapered toward the Gulf. Darby's two speedboats bobbed by the dock. In the distance, gray clouds thickened the horizon and thunder announced the coming storm. The pool lay quiet, the water burbling through the skimmers and pump. Planters with palms dotted the lanai. They would provide some cover. I knelt by the water, listening to it lap against the tile, heat radiating through my pant legs. The wind rose. The sound of a garage door lifting echoing softly through the house. Inching forward on hands and knees, I'd just reached the glass wall when I heard the sharp report of a handgun.

Slamming open the sliders, I ran into the living room and stopped cold.

Walter bent over the floor, clutching his thigh, his gun lying in front of him. Ricky Hunt backed away slowly, pointing what looked like a SIG-Sauer at Alexander and Claire. Chambered at .40 caliber, with seven rounds in the magazine, it could do a lot of damage.

Hunt glanced at me but kept the gun on the women. "Hey, sugar, join the crew."

I edged toward Walter.

"Over there!" Hunt yelled.

"He's hurt," I said and kept my hands away from my body. "I can help."

"I bet you can." His pebble eyes took me in head to foot. "Kick the gun toward me," he said and backed away a step.

I did and knelt by Walter. Blood seeped through his jeans and pooled on the floor. His eyes focused quickly and he gritted his teeth—good signs, given the size of the hole I knew he'd suffered on the other side of his leg.

"We'll get a doctor," I said, ripping off his shirt and using the sleeve to bind the wound.

"Get the gun," he hissed.

"Shut up," Hunt said and pointed the pistol at Alexander. "Where is it, you twat?"

"Where's what?" Her face looked blank, as if she were painting her nails.

Hunt fired over Claire's head, blowing out one of the glass sliders. The girl screamed and ducked behind her mother. *Christ*, I thought, *it's Nicholas Church all over again, and this time I don't even have a weapon.*

Hunt turned to Ginny. "I've got three people I can kill before I get to you, and I'm gonna start with babycakes in ten seconds if you don't cough up the money."

As he swung the gun toward Claire, Ginny Alexander shouted, "No! Don't! We don't have it, I swear. He only gave us the numbers."

"Who?"

"Harv." Her voice wavered and her hands shook, the veins bulging like vines.

"Where are they?

"In the pool."

With the pistol Hunt waved her outside. "You'd better be right."

She stepped around the glass and opened one of the sliding doors. Kicking Walter's gun onto the patio, Hunt motioned all of us to follow. As he bent to pick up the pistol, Ginny inched around the pool toward the dock. "Hey!" he yelled and straightened. "Back here."

Careful not to pull his leg through the shattered glass, I got an arm under Walter and half dragged him onto a planter box.

Alexander shook her head and walked to the deep end of the pool. In water the color of the leaden sky, the chlorinator bobbed like a blue and white buoy. She tapped it with her toe, picked it out of the water and unscrewed the top.

With my hands where Hunt could see them, I got as close as I could before he yelled for me to stop, and then I saw why. Walter's gun lay between us. I could reach it in two steps. He could shoot me in one.

From the mouth of the chlorinator Alexander pulled a plastic bag and withdrew a piece of yellow legal paper lined with handwritten numbers. As water from the chlorinator ran down her legs, she held the paper like a peace offering. Hunt moved to keep his back to the bay, I shifted to keep mine to Walter and the house. Ginny and Claire stood in the middle, with Walter's gun close to the girl's feet. I prayed she wouldn't try to use it.

Hunt never took his eyes from the bag. "Put it down," he told Alexander, "and walk toward Miss Real Estate."

As if she were wrapping a sandwich, Ginny slid the paper into its plastic wrapper and placed it on the tile. Keeping the gun trained on the two women, Hunt bent to pick up the bag and backed away. With his eyes on the pair, his loafer slid on the wet tile and, as he cracked his knee, almost tipped into the pool.

I lunged for Walter's gun and leveled it at Hunt. "Freeze!" I yelled but Hunt ducked to the left and put the two women between us and I couldn't get a clear shot.

"Drop it or I shoot them both!" he yelled.

Blood roared in my ears and my vision narrowed. There was no guarantee that I'd hit him before he shot Ginny or Claire.

"Drop it or they die!"

I tossed the gun into a planter and sat down hard, remembering the day in the marina parking lot after I'd shown him the homes. "So that's why you followed me."

He straightened and had his breathing under control in seconds. "I thought you'd lead me to Darby but his little girl saved me the trouble." He pointed the pistol at Claire.

"You overheard Darby kidnap my grandfather."

"Right time, right place."

"Your good luck."

"Not luck, sugar. You're the kind of agent Darby'd pick: single female not working for a big agency, few resources, needs the business and won't ask a lot of questions. Although you surprised me on that last one."

I felt incredibly tired and rested my head against the planter. "Why go after his family?"

"He stole a lot of money from some very impatient people, and he had to have some help." He sneered at Alexander and edged toward the dock.

"You'll have a hell of a time getting it to them," I said. "It's not as if the feds won't notice."

He laughed. "That your version of 'you'll never get away with it?'"

I shook my head, more at my own blunders than anything he'd said.

"Sugar," he said, "the FBI considers the money missing. The most they'd charge me with is threatening you with a gun, and no one's going to extradite me for that. I'm going to buy my own island and live in a hut with wine, women and weed."

My heart beat so hard I could feel it in my ears. "You killed Darby."

His smile looked more like a grimace. "He was dead when I got there."

"Then who. . . ."

"Shaw," he barked and stared at mother and daughter. Alexander went pale. Claire's face darkened. She looked ready to lunge at Hunt. He'd shoot her and then the rest of us. I needed to reach the gun.

Slowly I rose to my feet. "Because Shaw cooked the books and blamed Darby, who wasn't around to put up a fight."

"That's right."

"And when Darby turned up alive, he posed a threat to Shaw."

"Right again." Keeping the gun trained on Claire, he inched backward.

"So Harvey Shaw killed his partner and you killed Shaw."

He laughed. "No way. I shook him up until he told me who had the money."

"Then who killed. . . ."

He pointed the gun at Alexander. "Why don't you ask Mrs. Darby."

"Mom?" Claire backed away from her mother, and in that one word she conveyed a lifetime of hurt and shame. "You killed Mr. Shaw?"

Ginny looked astonished and, for once, helpless.

"Why?" Claire asked.

Keep him distracted. Keep him on the deck.

"If Shaw had turned himself in and confessed," I said, "the feds would have found the real books." Darby's protests of innocence sounded more plausible, although they wouldn't do him any good now. "Shaw siphoned the money and set up his partner."

Hunt reached the edge of the patio. "He had a little help from his girlfriend."

Diving for the planter, Alexander grabbed the gun and turned as Hunt fired, the bullet slamming her shoulder, the report bouncing off the back of the house. Ginny collapsed in hail of screams and Hunt, firing wildly, ran for the boats. Alexander lay on her side, sucking air and moaning, her arm hanging at an odd angle. Blood began to soak the top of her leotard.

"Claire!" I grabbed the rest of Walter's shirt and shoved it into her shaking hands. "Press this to the wound and keep it there, no matter how much she fights."

The sky lowered, thunder cracked and lightning etched the wall of gray to the north and west.

I palmed my cell phone and dialed 911. "And keep her awake."

When the communications center came on the line, I reported the shootings, gave the county, address and cross streets and disconnected. Vaulting the small wall between patio and beach, I ran after Hunt, ducking under the dock for cover when he started the motors. In a burst of speed, he plowed north into the channel, heading for the marina, where I knew he'd disappear among the mob of tourists.

Jumping into the second boat, I found the keys and shoved off, pushing the throttle as far as it would go, the wind and the twin Mercs screaming in my ears. Hunt raced into heavy traffic, bouncing past channel markers warning boaters to slow to idle speed, his wake tossing the other craft aside. Twice he turned and fired but the chop sent his shots wide. Ahead, small blurs in front of the glass wall of the marina restaurant resolved themselves into people staring at the approaching boats.

As I closed the distance, Hunt veered left to skirt the end of Island Park and then sharp right to avoid a yacht. The boat listed and a propeller breached the water as the craft skimmed along its side. With the tip of the park looming, Hunt yanked the wheel hard left, over-correcting as the hull bounced twice and the craft smacked the shore and went airborne, catching the dolphin fountain and splintering the bottom of the boat into a fiberglass spray. The boat pitched end over end and catapulted two Mercury 450s and Ricky Hunt through the second floor glass windows of the restaurant.

Not good for tourism.

38

FROM THE DECK OF the *Mary Beth*, the voice of Willie Nelson promised nothing but blue skies from now on. His sentiments perfectly described the evening, the fat sun simmering above the horizon, the sky an inverted bowl of tinted glass. I just hoped he was right.

As I stepped aboard, Louie plowed into my legs and whipped them with his tail. I scratched his ear and he moaned and gave me a look that said, 'I'll give you an hour to stop that.'" Walter, dressed in cargo shorts and sailfish cap, unhooked the lines, started the engine and slowly lowered himself on the cockpit bench.

"Why are you even out of the hospital?" I said.

"Nice place to visit but I wouldn't want to stay."

As he guided the boat out of dock, we passed the boarded-up restaurant and the fountain—two of the four dolphins still guarded the park—and cruised through the mooring field.

"So," Walter said as Louie curled on the bench beside us. "How'd Pap like his vacation?"

"I told you where they found him."

"In a convalescent home near Sebring."

"You ever been there?"

"Once," he said. "For the races."

"The town's got a single hotel and a downtown with six shops, three of which are always closed."

"It's a nice place," Walter said. "I ate in a fish house just south of there. They put newsprint on the tables. You could read the comics over lunch."

"Sounds like Pap's rest home."

We slid past glowing beaches surrounded by mangroves, the water a dark brown going to black.

"Who called you?" he asked.

"Delgado. He said he wanted to give me the good news himself."

Walter smiled, showing the gap in his upper front teeth.

"It's not like that," I said.

"So Delgado delivered Pap."

"We went together."

He smiled again.

"Delgado had to question the staff and asked if I wanted to ride along."

"What did they say when you got there . . . the staff?"

"That a man who identified himself as Pap's son delivered him, his meds and his records, all in perfect order."

"They just took his word."

"The staff described Darby as a very nice man," I said. "And he paid cash."

"And Darby got the records. . . ."

"When he burglarized my home and office."

We'd reached the halfway point to the keys when Walter handed me the fingerless gloves and told me to rig the sails—at least that's what I thought he said. Vaulting out of the cockpit, I raised the mainsail and the sail in front of it, the one whose name sounded like an Italian cheese, and secured the lines. Louie looked up as I rejoined them in the cockpit, flopping on his side so I could rub his belly.

"How is your grandfather?" Walter asked.

"You were right, he wasn't hurt. It was a nosebleed. Other than that, he's in good shape."

Walter gave me a look that said, "Really?"

"OK, we're having some issues."

He nudged the helm.

I took a breath. "When we got home, Pap stood in the kitchen and tried to remember where he was, which is what you'd expect, considering what he's gone through. So I scrambled some eggs and we talked and then, out of the blue, he said that sometimes he sees my grandmother standing at the foot of his bed."

"And?"

"And then," I said, "he told me what she says."

"What'd you do?"

"I called the neurologist. He'll see Pap in next week for a med check."

"So you've decided to keep him at home?"

"I couldn't leave him in that place. It's two steps down from a double-wide."

"You have a plan?"

"I don't know." I waved at two people who stood on a sandbar I couldn't see. They appeared to walk on water. I envied them.

"So you'll cook, make sure he takes his meds."

"Of course," I said.

"Can you watch him all the time, with your job?"

I shook my head. I didn't always like it when he made sense.

"What about friends?"

"We watch TV together," I said. "He likes the History Channel."

"Did he meet anyone?"

I laughed. "A former nun."

"Does she think he looks like Tony Bennett?" He grinned without looking at me.

"That was an innocent remark. I think Delgado's almost forgiven me."

"Was your grandfather happy?" Walter asked.

"I guess."

"Why bring him back?"

"To keep him safe."

"You can't watch him twenty-four/seven," Walter said. "Why not let him stay until you figure it out?"

"I don't know," I said. "Sometimes I think I'm more confused than Pap."

"Who's watching him now?"

"Cheryl," I said.

"How's she doing?"

"Now that Sal's dead? She feels relieved and guilty at the same time."

"Tough place."

"I know," I said.

"They wouldn't have charged her."

"No," I said. "That was Ricky Hunt, searching Pap's house for a trail to Darby when Finzi showed up."

"To teach you a lesson." He said it without emotion but it gave me a chill.

"Men don't expect women to steal their ride."

"Or their pride," he said.

We slid past the barrier islands and headed into open water, the wind dying with the sun, bringing with it the scent of seaweed and clams.

"You're up," he said and I climbed out of the cockpit and onto the bow. Walter yelled "Prepare to come about!" and I swung the boom and we sailed past the tip of Spanish Key and into the Gulf of Mexico as the wind faded like a dream. The boat lay dead in the water. I scrambled back to the cockpit and we waited for the sun to flash green and slide beneath water. It looked metallic, as iridescent as the body of a dragonfly.

Walter looked unconcerned with our lack of forward motion. "What about the others?"

"You really want the rundown?"

He nodded and scratched Louie behind the ear.

"OK. Ginny Alexander's still in the hospital, but she's just visiting. After they let her out of med-surg she's headed to trial for the murder of Harvey Shaw."

"Alleged murder."

"So Mirandize me," I said.

"I'd have to frisk you."

"You'd like that."

"I'd bet Delgado would," he said.

"You are so full of it."

"Or your friends Mitch and Oz."

"Now you're getting personal."

He gave a soundless chuckle. "So what does Delgado think?"

"Shaw embezzled the money and framed Darby. When Darby showed up, Shaw had to silence him. Ginny Alexander was having an affair with Shaw and thought she'd get half the loot. When she discovered he was going to bolt, they argued and she killed him."

"Where does Hunt fit?"

"In a coffin, headed back to LA."

"Clumsy," Walter said.

"Me, too," I said. "Hunt thought I'd lead him to Darby and Shaw. Finzi must have caught him searching the house, or the other way around. When none of that worked, Hunt followed Claire to her father. Eventually Hunt traced the money through Shaw to Alexander, and you know the rest."

"And the account numbers?"

"Recovered with his body. The FBI's trying to recover the money now."

He shook his head. "And the kids?"

"Junior was a dead end. He seems to have an alibi for everything."

"And Claire?"

"I hope she doesn't want to live with her brother," I said, "although he's the only friend she's got."

"There's you."

I nodded. "I'll keep checking on her."

"And Darby's house?"

"If the court allows and the attorneys agree, I'll sell it. I could use the money."

"You have a plan?" he asked.

"Better locks on Pap's house."

He chuckled. "What about your job?"

"You mean, am I going to work for that big ass real estate factory and push paper for the rest of my life?" I remembered what k d lang had said about integrity and living life on your own terms. At the same time I reminded myself of the expenses I would assume if I placed Pap in an assisted-living facility.

"I guess it depends on what you want," Walter said, "money or independence."

"Can't a girl have both?" I said.

"We've never talked about that."

"I know," I said.

"How are you doing?"

"Jackie and Kurt Stevens went with another agent," I said.

"Who?"

"Cissy Barton."

Walter laughed.

"I know."

"And she's with Laine & Co."

"How'd you guess," I said.

"What about Tony Delgado?"

"That was random," I said. "What about him?"

"Maybe the detective could use some help with carjacked tourists at the airport."

"No," I said. "I give up. No more cops, no more snooping and no more speedboats."

"How about men?"

I snorted. "Alleged men."

"I hear you're collecting the whole set."

"Hey," I said. "If a guy can play the field. . . ."

He cocked his head. "Is that what this is about?"

"I don't know what it's about." Taking a deep breath, I stared at a place on the horizon where the water blended with air. "You're always telling me to get a life. I haven't dated in years. At least none of them haven't killed anybody."

"Good basis for a relationship."

I shook my head. "Finzi, Darby, Shaw. . . . Three murders in less than a week."

"As a gender, we haven't acquitted ourselves very well."

"You do talk funny for a former cop."

He stood. "Take the helm," he said.

"Why? We aren't moving?"

Walter ducked below decks and returned with a chocolate cupcake perched on a doily resting on a ceramic plate. The cupcake was the kind with a cream center, hard icing and a white squiggle across the top. A single candle sprouted from the center.

"I ran out of room." He handed me the plate and touched a match to the candle. "You'll have to multiply."

"I'll have to remove my sandals."

He put a can of cola and a napkin in my hand.

I took a bite. The cake tasted like childhood, and I knew I'd wear chocolate on my teeth for hours.

"Happy birthday," he said and handed me a thin square wrapped in tissue paper.

I set the plate on the bench and untied the twine and read the title:

"The Ultimate Tony Bennett."

My throat swelled. "The world's gone digital and you're still buying CDs. You probably have a hand crank on your phone."

"I'm slow to change."

"That's a good thing." I dabbed at my eyes.

Louie licked the fingers of my other hand.

Walter sipped from a can of ginger ale. "It's the spray . . . coming off the bow."

I smiled.

"You OK?"

"I will be. Thanks."

I looked at Walter, at the thick cords of muscle in his neck, the deep furrows in his checks, the cross-hatch pattern on his big hands. Even after the death of his wife, he still did the things that brought joy to his life. Not a bad example.

Taking a deep breath I said, "You know what I'd like?"

"Another cupcake?"

"What I came here for . . . peace and quiet." I pecked him on the cheek. "No more drama. From now on, I'm selling real estate and taking care of Pap."

He gave me a cracked smile. "We'll see."

ACKNOWLEDGEMENTS

A big thank you to all of the generous people who helped with the research for this book: from the Sarasota Police Department, Chief Bernadette DiPino, Deputy Chief Pat Robinson and officers Jeff Dunn, Bryant Singley and Kim Stroud; Mike Kessie, chief of the Campus Police Department of New College of Florida and the University of South Florida Sarasota-Manatee campus; and David Lubas, retired lieutenant colonel, Fairfax County Sheriff's Office.

I would also like to thank Captain Tim Solomon and Jan Solomon of Key Sailing in Sarasota; real estate agents Jack and Mary Geldi in Sarasota, Florida, and Diana Cardwell in Saylorsburg, Pennsylvania; Bernice Pettinato for her editorial services; writers Eric Sheridan Wyatt, Helga Harris, Bill Andrews and Noreen Wald; and all of the sharp-eyed readers in the region's numerous writing groups.

ABOUT THE AUTHOR

Jeff Widmer has worked as a dishwasher, surveyor, guitarist, journalist and marketing professional. He is the author of the CW McCoy and the Brinker series of crime novels and several nonfiction books. He has contributed to *Advertising Age*, *US Airways*, *National Geographic World* and other magazines. A native of Pennsylvania, he lives in Sarasota, Florida.

You can connect with Jeff through his author page at Amazon (https://www.amazon.com/author/jeffwidmer), follow him through his website (http://jeffwidmer.com/) or share your comments through Facebook (http://www.facebook.com/jeff.widmer), Twitter (@jrwidmer), LinkedIn (http://www.linkedin.com/in/jeffwidmer) and Pinterest (http://pinterest.com/jrwidmer/).

43521596R00146

Made in the USA
Lexington, KY
02 August 2015